FINDING HIS Treasure

written by
C. L. JACKSON

For Mama,
my greatest treasure

CONTENTS

Prologue 1

Chapter 1   5

Chapter 2   15

Chapter 3   29

Chapter 4   41

Chapter 5   53

Chapter 6   71

Chapter 7   89

Chapter 8   99

Chapter 9   113

Chapter 10   123

Chapter 11   137

Chapter 12   153

Chapter 13   163

Chapter 14   181

Chapter 15   193

Chapter 16   207

Chapter 17   223

Chapter 18   251

Epilogue   257

PROLOGUE

Treasure only remembered two things from her childhood: her mother's tears and the smell of dead flowers.

Her mother, Corinne Jordan, loved only two things: flowers and her husband, Randall Jordan.

Her father, Randall Jordan, only loved himself.

Treasure loved watching her mother put on makeup and dress for a night out with her father. Corinne Jordan sat at her mahogany vanity surrounded by perfumes, make up brushes, powders, eye shadows, and lipsticks. Five-year old Treasure would sit quietly at the edge of the bed as her mother highlighted her beautiful face. Corinne never needed much makeup, and Treasure envied her mother's high cheekbones and bright eyes. Corinne talked to Treasure about taking care of her skin, what colors worked best for her skin tone, how to apply makeup. Her mother's beauty fascinated her, and if she were good, her mother would dab a bit of lipstick on her lips and maybe sweep blush across her cheeks.

"Mama, will I be as pretty as you when I grow up?"

"Of course, you will, sweetheart. And you'll have a handsome husband like your father to boot." Corinne winked at her daughter and smiled.

Randall Jordan worked as an attorney at a prestigious law firm, and her mother as a nurse. Corinne loved telling her daughter the story of how she met Randall in college. Corinne looked starry eyed as she told her daughter of how she left the chemistry lab late one night so tired and preoccupied that she bumped into Randall, sending their books flying. After gathering themselves and separating their books and papers, Randall asked if she wanted to go off campus to grab something to eat. "Normally, I wouldn't have gone, but he had a kindness about his eyes." She would stop and turn to her daughter, "You will always be able to tell a man's heart by his eyes, Treasure."

Treasure's small voice would reply, "Yes, ma'am" as her mother would continue. After a final powdering of her face, Treasure's mother would rise and slip into her chosen dress. Her mother loved getting dressed up, and it showed. Corinne wore a nursing uniform most days and nights, and she wanted to look beautiful every once in a while. And she wanted to look beautiful for Randall most of all.

Corinne's final step, combing her thick jet-black hair, which evinced her mother's Native American ancestry, always fascinated Treasure. Corinne's grandmother had been part-Chickasaw woman with the same luxurious black hair. A picture of Adsila "Blossom" Lee sat on their mantle, her long hair cascading about her shoulders, and Treasure found herself on many an occasion fascinated by the beautiful woman in the black and white photograph wearing lace-up boots and a satin dress. Every time she stared at the black and white photograph Treasure imagined her great-grandmother in full color.

While she worked, Corinne kept her hair pinned in a bun, but on date night, her hair flowed to her shoulders in deep waves. Treasure counted her mother's brush strokes as her mother's hair shone in the light.

But she really loved standing at the top of the stairs as her mother descended. Her father would stand at the bottom, always holding a bouquet of roses, red mostly. Corinne pressed and saved the petals in a box to frame them and present them to Randall on their 25th wedding anniversary. Treasure would look at the love in her father's eyes. Randall always looked in awe of her, as if she were the most beautiful woman in the world. When Corrine reached the bottom of the stairs, Randall Jordan always took his wife's hand and brought it to his lips. They would say their goodbyes to her, leave instructions with her babysitter, and walk off into the night. Treasure imagined her parents at romantic candlelight dinners and fancy balls and that they would always be happy and in love.

"Your father would bring me flowers and recite love poems to me. He wrote me a few too. When you're older, I might let you read some." She laughed and tapped Treasure's nose with her makeup brush. Treasure didn't understand her mother's joke, but she loved hearing the happiness in her mother's laugh and laughing with her.

By the time Treasure turned thirteen, the fairytale had ended. Date nights were far and few between, and her father worked more and more to climb the ranks toward becoming a partner in his firm. Her mother started enjoying a few glasses of wine at night and more during the weekend. When her father came home, her mother was either already in bed, or worse, she was still awake. Treasure's lullabies were accusations and arguments, her mother's cries, and her father's denials and disdain.

By the time she turned fifteen, her father had moved out of the family home. Her parents divorced soon after. Corinne became a shell of herself. She functioned during the week, driven by her anger at Randall. On the weekends, though, Corinne drank too much wine and read and reread the love letters Randall wrote during their courtship and the happy years of their marriage. Corinne made Treasure listen to her read portions of them while she tried to remember every rose petal in the box for a gift that would never be.

For a while, Treasure shared her mother's rage, and though she forgave her father, Treasure vowed never to fall in love.

No man would ever have that much power over her heart and soul.

CHAPTER 1

Riley Taylor placed the beautifully wrapped Christmas gifts for his nieces and nephews in the trunk of his silver Infiniti QX80 and closed the door. A consolation gift for himself, he called it, because what, or more specifically, who he really wanted was completely unavailable. Buying the car gave his mind something to focus on other than the woman he couldn't stop thinking and dreaming about.

His best friend and business partner, Kenzo Dallas, had found love again after his first wife died of cancer. Kenzo had been determined to stay away from women for the rest of his life, and he would have succeeded had Grace not returned to Jackson as a special investigator with the police department. Riley shook his head and smiled. Kenzo swore against dating and marriage for a long five years. Kenzo had to heal and forgive himself for his behavior during his first marriage. No man should be without a woman for that long. Kenzo proved him wrong, and after five years, Kenzo had not only fallen in love but gotten married.

Married! A chill ran up Riley's spine. But he had to admit the idea of settling down had been dancing on the edges of his mind since Kenzo and Grace's wedding three months ago. But marriage! The thought had always given him the hives. Though his parents had a good marriage now, Riley's parents married young and for a while, he stayed with his grandparents until his parents matured a bit. Staying with his grandparents let him see what mature, abiding love looked like. Kenzo's marriage, though, increasingly became a problem for him. While his friend basked in wedded bliss, Riley had to contend with Grace's best friend being the woman he had promised to never see again after their weekend tryst years ago.

Treasure Jordan.

She had invaded his spirit ever since they danced together at Kenzo and Grace's wedding reception. As small as Jackson was, thank God it was large enough to avoid anyone. Yet, as the wedding grew nearer, preparations forced them to see more of each other. Ensuring a stress-free, drama-free wedding became the unspoken rule between them though Treasure seemed to have a permanent scowl on her face every time they were in the same room. Now, he had to see her all the time. When your best friend marries the best friend of a woman who can't stand you, this is what happens, Riley thought to himself.

Riley thought about how beautiful Treasure looked at Kenzo and Grace's wedding. He asked her to dance. Riley shifted in his seat, the memory of holding Treasure in his arms igniting his desire. Riley memorized her scent and her curves beneath his hands. Riley needed Treasure Jordan out of his head. He needed something hard and fast to listen to, but all of the stations were either playing love songs or Christmas music. Damn, he thought. Riley decided to cut the radio off and make some phone calls. After a quick call to his sister, he decided to line up a date for later that evening. He picked Sheila, a twenty-something, who approached him at a bar a few weeks ago. Not his type at all, Sheila would serve her purpose. He needed someone to take the edge off. Knowing he would see Treasure in a few moments already had him on edge. And Sheila seemed willing enough. Riley had been unintentionally celibate since Kenzo and Grace's wedding, which confounded and frustrated him to no end.

~

Whenever the front door opened, Treasure held her breath. She tried to focus on the man in front of her but to no avail. Usually, Treasure relished being the life of the party and wouldn't have minded flirting a little to pass the time. But, tonight, knowing Riley could walk through the door at any moment distracted her. He would arrive soon, and the anticipation heated her. Riley would never miss Kenzo and Grace's first holiday party as a married couple.

Lawrence Dunbar, Jackson's Deputy Mayor, had her cornered in the great room with a rousing discussion of a possible sales tax increase to replace Jackson's water lines. Treasure plastered a smile on her face and nodded, trying to ignore the ill-fitted suit he wore. Bless his heart, she thought. An expensive, untailored suit was a complete no-no. And he didn't cut the sleeve label, Treasure thought. Having reached her limit with Dunbar's self-aggrandizing conversation, she excused herself as politely as she could.

Treasure's body warmed the moment Riley arrived. His scent wafted directly toward her, her eyes fluttering as she inhaled. She temporarily forgot about Dunbar altogether. Riley's natural scent mixed with Versace Eros cologne was unmistakable. Her breath caught in her throat, and her pulse raced. Dunbar's droning couldn't drown out Riley's voice. As much as she tried to focus, Riley's voice cut through the noise like a vacuum. She listened for any indications that he brought someone with him.

Lord, help. Treasure summoned every ounce of strength she had to keep smiling. "Lawrence, excuse me, Grace needs me in the kitchen."

Treasure smiled at him. "Perhaps, we can pick this up later."

Lawrence smirked at her. "Perhaps...over dinner?"

Chile, please. "Perhaps, we can meet after the holidays. I'll call your assistant." By the time "assistant" left her lips, Treasure pivoted toward the kitchen. She needed to remove herself from the temptation of Riley Taylor and sought respite in the kitchen. Many of the women who spoke to her were faithful customers and friends, but she kept walking, her heart beating like a drum in her chest. Wine, she thought to herself. I need wine.

She caught Grace's raised eyebrow. She knows he's here, and here I am running away. Grace wanted her to talk to Riley, but Treasure simply couldn't be around Riley for any length of time before her memories got the best of her. She doesn't miss a thing, Treasure thought. Why did I end up with a best friend who's a damn cop?

Treasure, thankfully, found herself alone in the kitchen. As far as kitchens went, Kenzo and Grace had a beautiful one. Black stainless-steel appliances, a huge walk-in pantry, and a fully stocked liquor and wine cabinet. Though Kenzo had his home professionally decorated before he met Grace, Treasure could see Grace's touches throughout. Treasure looked at a plaque on the wall. The South African proverb stopped her in her tracks. "Love, like rain, does not choose the grass on which it falls."

Treasure pondered the beautiful sentiment. Though she stopped thinking about love a long time ago, she loved experiencing the love between Grace and Kenzo. Unfortunately, Treasure remembered what love looked like when it got ugly. She prayed Kenzo and Grace would stay happily married, because she wished love's misery on no one. Randall and Corinne Jordan gave her a front-row seat to a horror show that she wished on no one, especially a child. She vowed not to put herself through that--ever. Plus, this was lust, not love. Period. You can control yourself, Treasure, she told herself. At least she hoped she could since she didn't believe one word coming out of her mouth.

Treasure poured herself a fresh glass of Malbec and let the wine coat her throat. Closing her eyes, she tried to stabilize her breathing. She would face Riley some time tonight, but she wanted to do it on her own terms. Treasure finished her glass and washed it in the sink. The mundane act of washing the glass in the warm sudsy water gave her a few more moments to still herself. She reached for a paper towel to dry her hands and took a deep breath. You can't hide in here all night, girl, she said to herself. But her weekend tryst with Riley years ago left her reeling in a way she never wanted to experience again. For years, she suppressed her feelings, the hurt, for Riley, but when Grace and Kenzo fell in love, all of those feelings resurfaced. She had to find a way to put him out of her mind again.

Treasure decided to exit the kitchen through the dining room, giving her at least thirty seconds more before coming face to face with Riley Taylor.

Sheer lunacy, but what else could she do?

Treasure double-checked to make sure she cleared the counter, so she didn't see Riley standing there. Treasure looked up one second too late and came face-to-face with Riley. His black Armani suit fit him perfectly, tailored to fit his frame like a glove. Lord, you didn't have to make this man this fine. Treasure's temperature rose as their eyes locked. Her body tingled under Riley's hardened gaze, and Treasure immediately took a step back.

"Treasure," Riley's said huskily. He let his eyes roam over her body. Treasure stunned in a gorgeous red cashmere sweater dress that accentuated every curve she had, and Lord help him, she wore knee-high stiletto boots. He observed her for a few moments, enjoying the view more than he should have. The sight of her aroused him, leading to fantasies of her in his bed.

"Riley," she whispered. The way Riley said her name during their dance at Kenzo and Grace's reception made her knees nearly buckle. He had a way of saying her name that made her want more than she should. And the nearness of him intoxicated her senses. She wished her voice sounded stronger, or at least above a trembling whisper.

"How have you been?" Riley tried to engage in small talk, so he wouldn't imagine Treasure naked. He forced himself to focus on her face, but then there were her lips, full and luscious and demanding to be kissed.

"I'm well. Thank you. The holidays are big business in retail." Treasure realized that she needed to move. Offer him a drink. That would mean she could busy herself, and perhaps, he wouldn't notice her agitation. She flashed a forced smile. "Would you like me to pour you and your date a drink?'"

Treasure's smile never reached her eyes. Riley walked slowly toward her like a big cat hunting prey. "I came alone." He took two steps toward Treasure, like a panther stalking his prey. Images of their dance at the wedding flashed through his mind again. He wondered if she ever thought about that dance and if he could convince her to let him hold her again.

She quickly turned her back to him, but she couldn't help the sense of relief when Riley admitted coming to the party alone. He approached her slowly, and Treasure braced herself for his touch, his nearness. Riley stood directly behind her and whispered in her ear seductively. "Been doing a lot of that lately."

"What?" Treasure's voice trembled.

"Coming alone." Riley and Treasure stared at each other for a few seconds, before he quickly added, "I mean, going to a lot of places by myself lately."

Treasure turned around to hand Riley his drink. "Here you go." As she handed Riley the glass, his fingers lingered on hers. Treasure gasped at the electricity of the touch. Riley's eyes narrowed. He gingerly placed the glass on the counter, never taking his eyes off Treasure. Before she could respond or protest, Riley pulled Treasure to him and slammed his mouth on hers. Treasure surrendered. It had been a long time between kisses, especially one this passionate, and she had to admit that Riley's lips and tongue were lethal. But she and Riley could only do so much in the kitchen. Or at least in this kitchen, she mused. If anyone caught them, she could always blame the alcohol and make a quick exit.

Treasure tasted as sweet as Riley remembered, and he explored every inch of her mouth with his tongue. He slid his hands down the length of her torso, resting them on her hips. Her breasts heaved against his chest. When he finished with her mouth, he kissed her neck. Her pulse raced against his lips. His tongue traced her jugular on a long, deliberate lick. Then, he sucked and bit her neck. Hard. Riley wanted to mark her. He wanted to mark her as his. He placed his hands at her waist, and before she could react, Riley picked her up and placed her on the counter. Riley nestled himself between her legs. The sound of Treasure's gasp in his ear increased his desire for her, and Riley fingered the tops of the black thigh high stockings and garters under her dress. Was she trying to kill him? He pressed his body against hers, his erection, thick and hard against her middle. Intoxicated by her perfume mixed with the natural scent of her arousal, Riley fully prepared to take her on the counter.

His desire pressed against her core, and her nipples strained against her bra. The throbbing need between her legs overwhelmed her senses. Riley's kiss set her entire body on fire. Her dress had risen to the middle of her thighs, and she didn't care. Riley stood between her legs, his hands massaged her breasts and fingered the top of her stockings. More than one night found her with his kiss on her mind, and a few other things if she were honest with herself. But this... Riley started to move against her. The thin material of her panties and the texture of his pants added to the friction and sexual frustration. Treasure realized she was moving against him as well, and her body climbed toward orgasm. The music wouldn't hide her scream, and thankfully, no one had come looking for either one of them. With every ounce of strength, Treasure had to stop this before she made love to this man on her best friend's kitchen counter.

As much as she relished this moment, Treasure's heart simply couldn't take another Riley Taylor-induced disappointment. She summoned her strength and flattened her palms against Riley's chest pushed weakly against him. Her resolve faltered slightly when his racing heartbeat thumped beneath her fingers.

"Riley, stop. Please. We can't do this again." Her weak protestations did little to convince herself or Riley. Riley continued caressing and squeezing her flesh while kissing her neck and ear. Lord, help me, she thought.

"Riley." She called his name again and pushed him back more firmly. When Riley's mind registered Treasure's actions, he stopped and took a step back.

Riley's erection strained against his pants, and he did everything he could to summon some control. Treasure looked well-kissed and her neck was already beginning to show evidence of his assault. He touched her face, and Treasure's eyes fluttered closed. "Treasure, we can't keep doing this. Baby, please." Riley's hoarse whisper sent tingles through her. "When we talked the night of the reception, you said you forgave me but then you disappeared." He paused as she opened her eyes and held her gaze. "Again." He didn't recognize his own voice, but, at that moment, he didn't care. One taste of Treasure would never be enough for him.

Treasure's silence filled the space between them. He was right. She had retreated. They had decided to be cordial in public and explore in private. But she couldn't bring herself to be that vulnerable, least of all with Riley Taylor, Jackson's number one bachelor who never dated the same woman twice. She remembered what it was like to be on the receiving end of his bachelor ways, and though he said he wanted more now, she couldn't lay herself bare like that again. She looked up at Riley who was still searching her face for an answer.

"We can't do this here, Riley." Treasure flattened her palms on his chest to push him back. She slid off the counter.

Riley stepped forward again. "The kiss or the conversation?"

Treasure took a deep breath and smoothed her dress, looking him squarely in the eye. "Both," she said. Riley stepped back and leaned on the opposite counter. His arms hung by his side, heavy without her. Eventually, he put his hands in his pockets to keep him from reaching for her. Riley wiped his hands down his face and forced out a breath. Wearily, he said, "Treasure, we've been doing this dance a little too long. Are you tired yet?"

Treasure stared at the plaque on the wall. "Riley, but I can't do this with you," Treasure whispered. It was true. She couldn't do this with him. She wanted him too much and wanting a man like Riley Taylor would destroy her. Treasure shuddered when it dawned on her that she almost had sex with Riley in her best friend's kitchen with a full party on the other side of the wall. Treasure steadied herself and walked away from Riley without another look.

Riley wiped his hands down his face. Damn, Riley whispered to himself. Her scent was in his hands, her arousal in the air. He was still looking in the direction of her exit as if he expected her to return. After a few moments of looking at an empty doorway, Riley finally left the kitchen to join the party. Riley and Treasure exchanged glances for the rest of the night until he decided he had enough. He said his goodbyes to Kenzo and Grace and eased out of the house without a word to anyone, especially Treasure.

As he was leaving the party, Riley's phone rang, and Sheila's name flashed across his screen. Riley declined the call, got in his car, and drove straight home. Treasure's scent was in his clothes, her flavor on his tongue. He decided not to go back to his downtown condo, and instead, drove to his home in Pocahontas. His sanctuary. No woman had ever been there, and until tonight, Riley had never imagined there ever would be. But Treasure Jordan was changing everything. Riley needed to think--to think about what was happening to him and why Treasure Jordan drove him to distraction. During the long stretch on Highway 49, Riley drove in silence and decided to keep it that way. All he could hear was Treasure's torturous moans in his head and the tempo of her breathing in his ear.

CHAPTER 2

Treasure Jordan walked her last customer to the door and locked it. The young lady had come in frantic and nearly in tears, looking for a dress for an event an hour before closing. The poor thing, Treasure thought, as she shook her head. Luckily, Treasure could devote all of her attention to her since her last customer left an hour before. Treasure soon learned that the Simone was a college student participating in a pageant the following evening. In tears, Simone told her about the fabulous dress she ordered online, only to find that the dress was for a doll, not a person. When Simone pulled the dress from her purse, Treasure bit her tongue to keep from laughing out loud.

Treasure owned Treasure's Boutique, a high-end designer boutique in Jackson's Fondren District, offering designer clothes straight off the runways of New York and Paris. When she opened Treasure's five years ago, no one thought the boutique would survive. She chose the clothes in her boutique carefully for her clientele, and when big events happened in Jackson, Treasure wrote every dress down. None of her clients showed up at the same event wearing the same dress. Not only was it a horror for the women, but it was professional suicide. She fostered relationships with women in Jackson, learned their styles and body types, and most importantly, learned their friends and their enemies. She scheduled private consultations for those who wanted to maintain their privacy and maintained a list of all the Divine Nine members and events. Cross referencing her inventory with her clientele saved her business on several occasions.

After depositing Simone on one of the black velvet couches outside the dressing rooms, Treasure brought her a bottle of water and some tissues. Treasure could tell Simone was a tall and shapely 14. Finding a flattering dress stressed out every woman, but more so when you weren't model thin. Treasure prided herself on her range of sizes, and particularly her larger sizes. Part of Treasure's appeal lay in highlighting the beauty of all women. Frankly, she found it to be good business sense. Designers ignored most of the women in the world because they didn't fit a sample size 4 dress. Treasure selected a beautiful gold lame gown, toga style dress that perfectly complemented Simone's mocha skin and shoes to match. When Simone emerged from the dressing room, she had tears in her eyes. Simone looked like the goddess Nefertiti in the dress

"There's no crying in my store!" Treasure said, handing Simone a tissue and dabbing the corners of her own eyes. "You look gorgeous." Simone stood in front of the mirror as Treasure made a few adjustments.

Treasure placed a crystal choker around Simone's next as she gave final instructions. "Make sure you take some flats or slippers backstage tomorrow night. All shoes hurt after a while."

"Yes, ma'am." Simone continued to marvel at herself as Treasure stood beside her.

"Step out of those shoes, my dear. I'll bag them and the jewelry while you take the dress off." Helping Simone made Treasure happier than she had been in a while. While she donated dresses and her styling services for charity and community organizations, Simone gave her a rare one-on-one opportunity. Rarely did Treasure have a client who made her remember why she opened her store so many years ago.

Simone didn't look at the price tag until she entered the dressing room taking it off. Her stomach dropped at the $1500 price tag. She wondered how much the shoes cost. The shoes had to be at least $400. Her shoulders sank as she returned the dress to the velvet hanger. She shouldn't have come in here. The dress alone cost as much as she paid in tuition for a semester after financial aid.

"Ma'am?" Simone trembling voice called out to Treasure.

"What's wrong, dear?" Treasure hid her smile as she approached the dressing room.

"Ms. Jordan, I can't afford this dress, or the shoes. I'm sorry I wasted your time." Simone readjusted her purse on her shoulder and handed Treasure the dress.

Treasure raised an eyebrow at her. "I see. Well, I suppose that you'll have to come back and work it off then." Treasure turned to walk back to the register ending the conversation.

"Ma'am?"

"You can work the cost of the dress off by working weekends and some evenings. I need some help with the inventory, and I need a temp." Simone's shocked face amused Treasure. "Didn't you say you were an accounting major?"

Simone, shocked, could only respond, "Yes, ma'am."

"Well, since the pageant is Friday night, come in by 9:30 Saturday morning. We open at 10."

"Yes, ma'am."

"Great." Treasure placed the dress in her signature dress bag and the shoes in a shopping bag. She handed both to a speechless and grateful Simone and walked her to the door.

"And Simone, I am an alumna of the College. I'll find you if you don't show on Saturday. Good night."

Simone nodded as Treasure ushered her out of the door. Simone placed the bags on the back seat and slid into the driver's seat of her old Honda Civic, and thought about the luxury vehicles that usually graced her parking lot. She wondered if her usual clientele could fully appreciate a young woman like Simone.

Treasure stood at the door making sure Simone safely entered her car and exited the parking lot before pushing the button on the automatic shades for the front windows. She turned around and headed to the back to finish reconciling the day's receipts. Treasure rounded the counter when a heavy knock at the front door startled her.

Normally, Treasure would ignore the knock. She didn't have a private consultation and the day had been a long one. But Treasure thought it might be Simone, so she decided to answer it. One more sale never hurt anyone.

She wished she hadn't.

~

Riley finished having dinner at Isham's, a new restaurant in Fondren, with a couple of investors for his latest project, when his phone rang. When Kenzo's name flashed across his screen, Riley sighed. Kenzo, his best friend and business partner, trusted him, but Riley had long accepted that Kenzo would always be a nuisance at the beginning, middle, and ending of any deal.

"'Wassup, Ken?" Riley said, knowing exactly what his partner wanted.

"Well? How did the meeting go?" Kenzo used his business tone. Most cowered at that tone. But Kenzo's anxiety lived in that tone, so Riley paid it no mind. Being a good partner meant knowing each other's quirks, particularly the irritating ones.

"Beautifully. They have a few concerns about location and specs, but they love the project." As Riley walked to his car, he glanced in the direction of Treasure's store. The lights were still on. He checked his watch. It was nearly 8:30 p.m. Her store closed at 7:00 p.m. Despite Fondren's artsy, liberal community, she shouldn't be in there alone.

Riley barely paid attention to Kenzo's prattling of ideas and asking questions. "Yo, man, look, I need to handle something. I'll debrief you tomorrow. Cool?"

"Alright. I'll be in at eight."

Laughing, Riley said, "Duly noted, boss" and pressed "End" on his screen. He slid onto his leather seat and pressed the Start button. As he listened to the hum of the engine, he thought about their kiss at the Christmas party. Thinking about their kiss sent his libido in overdrive. As he drove over to the parking lot in front of her store, his slight irritation became raging anger. Treasure knew damn well not to work alone in the store this late at night. He surveyed the parking lot. Every darkened storefront made her lights seem brighter. Damn, this woman, he thought. As he drove into the parking lot, he spied a young girl in her twenties leave with a couple of bags. Treasure's smile transfixed him on the spot. She threw her head back and laughed, further irritating him. Treasure was smiling at someone else other than him, and he didn't like being bothered by that fact. Her smiles were rare, at least with him around, and Riley wanted her to smile, free and easy, more than anything, at him.

Riley waited until Treasure closed the door and her young customer had driven out of the parking lot. Now, the empty parking lot save Treasure's champagne colored Lexus RX 350L reminded him of a horror movie. He shook his head and his hands gripped his steering wheel. He should be on his way home, not sitting here worried about a woman who clearly wanted nothing to do with him.

Riley shook his head. Treasure wanted him as much as he wanted her. He couldn't figure out why she acted skittish around him. It didn't make sense. They had a wonderful weekend a few years ago, and they brokered an agreement not to see each other again. Riley never violated that agreement, because Treasure said that they needed to enjoy their time together with no strings. All he could do was send her flowers, a first for him, and try to forget Treasure and the best sex of his life. They didn't reconnect until Kenzo and Grace started dating, and their reunion didn't go well at all. The memory of the scene they caused at the reception for the Noelle Project still stung. For months, every time he and Treasure were in the same room for any length of time, she made an excuse and left, or she said nothing. She was only cordial during the wedding preparations for Kenzo and Grace. Being Best Man and Maid of Honor forced them to interact, but at the wedding, he tried to break down the wall she built around herself. Every time he thought they could explore something more, Treasure would retreat. Riley took a deep breath and knocked on the glass door.

Treasure blinked. Riley Taylor at her door? She frowned. "Riley, what are you doing here?" Treasure couldn't handle Riley Taylor right now, not with him looking and smelling sexy as hell. What was it about Riley Taylor in a suit that could turn her on so much? His cologne mixed with his own scent overwhelmed her. His chiseled jawline was tight, and the crinkle in his brow made his anger crystal clear.

Riley's right eyebrow raised. "Are you going to let me in, Treasure?" The question hung between them for a few seconds, as Treasure tried to determine if she was ready to play the game with Riley tonight. *Whatever you do, do not kiss him again,* Treasure said to herself, as she opened the door wider so that Riley could pass her to come in. She locked the door again and hesitated a moment before turning around to face him.

Riley waited. When Treasure finally faced him, Riley couldn't believe that he was standing in her store like a lovesick fool. But he was here now, and she was going to listen to him.

"First, you shouldn't be here at night alone. Jackson is too dangerous, and Fondren, despite what some folks think, is still Jackson." Riley needed the anger to calm his nerves. Anger was easier to start with--and safer. As long as he was angry, his focus wasn't on her mouth, or the way her breasts lifted as she crossed her arms, or the defiant pout of her mouth.

Treasure was silent. She crossed herself to protect her body from responding to his presence. Riley's presence took all the oxygen in the room. While Riley ranted and raved about her safety, Treasure wondered how he had the nerve to come in here and tell her what to do, she had to admit Grace often said the same. She decided to stop him before he went any further.

She held up her hand to stop his rant. "Riley! Treasure's Boutique has been here, in this location, for years, without a problem. And as a matter of fact, I was about to leave." She turned to walk toward the counter, but then she remembered. She turned to face him again.

"Is there a second?"

"What?" Riley was still fuming. She was always here late, always putting herself in harm's way. He rode past here every night before going home despite being out of his way. Riley parked in her car was still there and waited for her to leave. He never told Kenzo, because it was crazy and a little stalkerish. Not seeing her car in the parking lot on some days frustrated him too, because he wouldn't get a fleeting glimpse of her that day.

Treasure took a deep breath. Mad Riley's adrenaline spiked his scent and cologne. Jesus. "When you started fussing at me, you said, "'First.' I asked was there a 'second.'"

Riley almost looked stunned, but quickly caught himself and regained his composure. His shoulders dropped, and he looked directly at her. "Yes, Treasure, there's a second." He slowly walked toward the counter like a panther hunting prey. His deep brown eyes were nearly black and seemed to look straight through her. Riley's voice dropped an octave to a husky murmur.

"I've been trying to figure out why you keep avoiding me, why we keep playing their game between us. He ran his hand down his face, as he said, "And why for the love of God, do I keep trying? I should be..." He took a deep breath. He started again, "When we talked at the reception, I thought we'd figured things out, and then again at the party..." Riley's voice trailed off. His anger grew by the second. Treasure had to be the most infuriating woman in creation. But he never laid eyes on a more beautiful woman than Treasure, and once he held her in his arms, no other woman could fill them.

"Riley, I can't..." She moved behind the counter, creating space between them. Treasure needed a barrier between them, and she also needed something to lean on. She couldn't falter. She buried her feelings for Riley for five years. To deal with Riley and those feelings had the potential to make her as distraught as her mama. Who needed crazy love like that?

"Can't what, Treasure?" Riley asked calmly. "All I asked you to do was try?" Riley didn't care that he was making a fool of himself, or about the pleading in his voice. This was now or never. Riley Taylor never chased a woman in his life, and he damn sure didn't beg. He refused to keep chasing a woman who didn't want to be captured.

Treasure decided to put both of them out of their misery, but she wanted to be completely honest with him. This had gone on long enough, and it needed to end. "Let's talk in my office."

"Lead the way," Riley said. He wanted to hold out hope that she had changed her mind, but he could see the tension in her body. When they entered her office, Treasure sat behind her desk. Riley recognized the power play and immediately realized he was being dumped before they were ever a couple. He almost laughed out loud, but the sadness in her eyes stopped him cold. He sat in one of the leather chairs at the desk and waited for her to speak.

What possessed me to bring him back here? The room was too small, and Riley's presence was overpowering. She closed her eyes for a second and took a deep breath. When she opened them again, Riley was still there--waiting and looking at her for answers. Treasure decided to be completely honest. Perhaps, her honesty would scare him off, or at least agree that a relationship would never work.

"Riley, when we spent that weekend together, I was the one who said that Monday morning would be the end of it. But by Monday morning, I wanted more. And I found myself hoping that you would want it to, but when I received the flowers, I realized I was another weekend tryst for you. And I didn't like being another Riley Taylor conquest." Though she was trying to look him in the eye, she couldn't do it long. Riley's jaw tightened, and his eyebrow raised in confusion. He decided against interrupting her. Riley wanted Treasure to say whatever she needed to say once and for all.

"And it scared me." Treasure's voice was so low that he almost missed it.

Riley leaned forward in his chair. "What scared you? "Me?" Fearless came to mind when he thought about her, not fearful. He remembered her passion and sense of adventure most. She was a quick wit, sarcastic, and a spitfire. He didn't understand this timid version of Treasure, and he definitely didn't like it.

Even with the desk between them, Riley was too close to her. His eyes were piercing, and she let out a sarcastic laugh at how innocently he could ask the question. "Not you, Riley. But the idea of you. I could really fall hard for you, and let's face it, what we shared was all either one of us, especially you, wanted at the time." Treasure took a breath before adding, "And after seeing what can happen when a woman lets a man consume her very being, I vowed a long time ago never to let that happen to me. Monday morning, I almost broke my rule. The fact that I would risk my heart after only three days scared the hell out of me." Treasure shook her head, and whispered to herself, "Three days."

Riley realized whatever happened in her past affected her future. With him. He had an idea but asked anyway. "What woman?" he asked.

It took Treasure a moment for his question to register. She looked at him blankly. "What?"

Riley repeated himself. "What woman? Who was the woman who let a man, to use your word, 'consume' her life."?

Treasure looked away from him for a moment. "My mother." She told Riley the short version--her parents' divorce nearly ruined her mother. Treasure tried not to think of her parents' divorce, because as long ago as it had been, her mother was still in love with her father. Her father had moved on, which hurt her mother deeply. Treasure had to watch her mother pine for a man who might have been worthy at one time but not anymore. The tears fell before she could catch them.

Riley quietly came to her side of the desk and took her hand, leading her to the love seat. To his surprise, she came willingly. He wanted to pull her to him, to kiss her tears away. A sense of protectiveness came over him. He pulled out a handkerchief and wiped the tears from her face. When he finished, she took it from his hand and inspected it. The handkerchief seemed to pull her out of her sadness for a moment, and she went into designer mode.

"I haven't seen a handkerchief since I was child. The monogram design is lovely. But..."

"But, why do I have it?" He chuckled. "My grandfather, Marcellus, always carried a handkerchief. He and my grandmother Lynn raised me." Riley rubbed the raised thread of the monogram. "My parents were young and really ill-prepared for marriage or to be parents, so he scooped me up and took me home with him. I have a few of his handkerchiefs at home, but I ordered this one. I guess having one keeps him with me, I suppose. Having one always reminds me of what kind of man I'm supposed to be, because of the man he was."

Treasure touched his arm. "I wish I could have met him. And your grandmother?"

"She was amazing too. Her name was Lynn, but everyone called her "Mama." Marcellus, though, always called her "Miss Priss." Riley laughed. "He always joked Lynn Taylor was the prissiest thing he ever saw...and the prettiest." Riley smiled at the memory. "When it came to her, the old man was mushy as hell. They both loved me, spoiled me, made sacrifices, and sent me to school." He fingered the handkerchief again and looked at the floor. "I had the best of both worlds. I had one set of parents, a grown set and one set who grew up with me. But old Marcellus and I had some good times." Riley's voice trailed off for a second. Treasure sat and waited.

Riley shrugged and took Treasure's hand, rubbing the back of it. He rarely talked about his grandfather to anyone but family. That old man had given him more than anyone in life. When his parents eventually married and had more children, Riley stayed with his grandparents. He loved his parents, but by then, Riley was old enough to make his wishes clear. When Marcellus died a few years after Riley graduated from college, a part of him had died too. His grandmother's death shortly thereafter surprised no one. Marcellus and Lynn's marriage lasted over sixty years, and his grandmother's heart broke a little more every day she had to live without Marcellus. She told him she met Marcellus in her dreams, and one day, she would stay there with him. Though she smiled and laughed when she said it, Riley believed her when no one else did. Riley found her smiling, one of Marcellus's handkerchiefs in her hands.

Treasure looked up at him. "Riley," she said softly, touching his arm with her free hand. The contact brought him out of his memories, and he turned to her. He put his memories of Marcellus, Mama Lynn, and his childhood in the back of his mind.

"Look, Treasure, I'm not your father, and you're not your mother. But

I do think we have this undeniable attraction to each other. But for some reason, we keep playing this game with each other. God help me, I can't figure out why. But you set the terms. I just want a chance. I need a chance. Let me prove I'm not as bad as you think I am." Riley tried to determine if she were listening. He added, "Do you think I would be here, if I didn't really want to be?"

Treasure remained silent and bit her bottom lip, looking down at her hands.

Riley winced like he was in pain. He tipped her head up to look at him. "Baby, you can't worry your lip like that. Not this close to me. I'm trying to be a gentleman, here, but you're really trying me."

Treasure laughed, and the sound warmed him to the bone. Riley pretended to be hurt and grabbed his chest over his heart. "You got jokes, huh?" She laughed a bit harder.

Stifling another laugh, Treasure covered her mouth. "I'm sorry, Riley." Truth was, laughing felt good. And truer still, frowning and scowling at him all the time exhausted her.

Riley became serious again and held Treasure's hand a little tighter. "May I take you to dinner tomorrow night?"

Treasure looked away, unsure of what to do.

Treasure pulled away from Riley and stood up, trying to put some distance between them. "After all I told you, Riley, why would you still want to try this?" As much as Riley had haunted her dreams over the last few years, and now she worried she wouldn't be able to handle it if her fantasy came true, or if it turned into a nightmare.

Riley stood up and approached Treasure, coming face to face. He tilted her head up forcing Treasure to face him. "I wanted you from the moment you walked into the restaurant." He moved a curl out of her face. "You wore the sexiest green dress. I still remember it. It threw me completely off guard. I don't understand, and I can't begin to explain, why I acted like a jerk at dinner, but I'm sorry." He gazed into her eyes for a moment before continuing. "But you and I have a connection I've never experienced with anyone else, and I'd rather explore it now, rather than look back one day and wish we had." Riley had never been so honest with any woman, and he surprised himself. "If it doesn't work, it doesn't work. But hey, at least we tried." Something about Treasure made him want to be honest with her. He wanted to kiss her but decided against it. Riley continued, "Tell you what, we'll take this slow. You control the pace. Scout's honor." He held his hand up with his three-finger salute.

"You were a boy scout?" Treasure raised her eyebrow at him with a shy smile.

Riley chest swelled with pride at putting a simple, beautiful smile on Treasure's face. He reached out and touched the side of her face. "Eagle, baby, Eagle."

CHAPTER 3

Riley looked at his watch for the fifth time in as many minutes. Unable to focus, the marketing report he should be reading might as well be reading him. Kenzo noticed how distracted Riley seemed, and Riley swore he caught Kenzo smirking at him. He never should have told him about his date with Treasure.

Riley stretched and let out a yawn. Sleep eluded him all night. Treasure's scent was in his spirit and not kissing her had left him tortured all night. Riley replayed their conversation in her office in his head. He would have to be careful with her. She was deeply wounded from her past, or at least, what happened between her parents. Riley didn't make matters any better with his asinine behavior and playboy reputation. His agenda never included "paragon of virtue." And that fateful weekend four years ago, he acted like a jerk at dinner, got her into bed, sent flowers, and never spoke to her again. Riley shook his head. How could I have been so stupid?

He threw his pen onto his desk in frustration. It was three o'clock in the afternoon. Riley walked over to the window. He could see most of Capitol Street, and their suite of offices on the top floor of the Standard Life Building meant at least some progress in Mississippi had been made. He thought of the stories his elders told him of the Movement, of shopping on Capitol Street, "going to town" his great-grandmother called it. They could shop, but they couldn't try on the clothes. His great-grandmother said her mother stopped shopping on Capitol Street when her friend and NAACP leader, Medgar Evers, called for a boycott. And now, here he was, looking down on all of it...from the top. Riley always took pride in his work, and he was really proud of being part of Jackson's downtown revitalization. Work still needed to be done, but he and Kenzo were getting there one project at a time.

His pride led to embarrassment as his thoughts returned to his insulting behavior on his date with Treasure four years ago. He threw his hands up. You idiot, he told himself. He was completely out of line that night, and in his arrogance, insulted her business because he didn't deem it as important as his own. He threw his head back in frustration. After all the stories his grandmother told him, laughing with sad eyes, he should have known better. Tonight, he would have a real opportunity to redeem himself, and it may be his last chance to convince Treasure the boy she met years ago was not the man before her today.

Riley's thoughts veered to how that first night ended and the weekend began. Treasure had been the most passionate lover he ever had but one he couldn't control. Most women wanted to please him, which only enthralled him for a moment. They demanded nothing from him. But not Treasure. She demanded as much as she gave. A shudder went through Riley's body at the memory, but tonight would be different. He reminded himself he didn't want to go there yet. After last night, he wanted Treasure to see him differently as a man. Riley realized he wanted to see himself differently as well, as a man worthy of a woman like Treasure.

Riley grabbed his suit jacket and keys. He might as well go home. He thought about getting a workout in to relieve some tension. After giving his assistant, Della, instructions for his meetings the next day, Riley headed for the elevator. He called his trainer, Deondre, to see if he had an opening.

Getting in the ring for a few rounds would be what he needed to clear his mind.

Riley prayed he could follow his own rules tonight.

~

Treasure stood in her walk-in closet surrounded by clothes and realized she had nothing to wear. Everything was either too revealing, not revealing enough, or plain. At 7:15, Treasure had showered and applied her makeup, but she still needed to decide what to wear. Usually, Treasure would call Grace, but she wanted to keep this night to herself for a while. She and Riley's entanglement was already awkward for Grace, and she was sure, Kenzo. It would be messier now, especially if things didn't work out. But there would be no date if she didn't find something to wear. Treasure laughed at herself. *Alright, Treasure, you do this for a living? What would you tell a client?* Treasure blew an errant curl out of her face and reached for her long black dress covered in roses. Fun and flirty, the dress hugged her curves but had a sweetheart neckline that showed only a hint of cleavage. She slipped on a pair of black Louboutin stiletto sandals, and at 7:45, did one final twirl in the mirror as she spritzed on her perfume and headed downstairs. At precisely 8:00, the doorbell rang.

Treasure took a deep breath and whispered to herself, "Well, Lord, here we go."

Riley's knees almost buckled when Treasure opened the door. She was a vision, and he doubted very seriously if he was going to be able to restrain himself at any point. He swallowed hard and managed to say, "You look beautiful, Treasure."

"Thank you, Riley. I'm ready." Treasure smiled at him. Riley looked dangerously delicious standing at her door, looking more like a supermodel than a real estate developer. Riley paired a black blazer and cream cashmere pullover with black True Religion jeans. She looked him up and down. "Lord, you don't play fair, she thought. You look handsome as well," she responded, fighting the urge to outright swoon at the sight of him.

Riley stepped back so she could lock the door. When she turned around, Riley's mouth watered at the rose highlighting her shapely behind. He threw his head back, Lord, come on. He righted himself before she turned back around and held out his hand to lead her to his car, a black Jaguar XJ.

"Nice car."

"Thanks. I bought Star when Kenzo and I closed our first big deal." He opened her door, and she slid onto the leather seat. When Riley entered the car, Treasure had only one question.

"Star? You named your car?"

"Yep. My mom always wanted a Jag when I was growing up. I bought it for her. So, technically, the Jag belongs to her, but she lets me keep it at my house." Riley did an exaggerated wink at the word "lets" and Treasure let out a hearty laugh. "But when I need to take her somewhere, I drive the Jag. She's happy with that."

"How sweet of you," she said, laughing.

"What a beautiful sound," Riley countered.

"What sound?" Treasure asked.

"You. Laughing. I like to hear you laughing and having a good time."

Treasure let out a small sigh. She didn't want to like him, but he was making it hard. She preferred thinking of him as Jackson's resident playboy, not this man who could make her lose herself. They drove in silence for most of the ride to the restaurant, listening to the radio rather than talking. Treasure kept her hands in her lap, and nearly laughed out loud when she realized that she was holding her hands like a prim and proper southern lady to keep her from having not-so-prim-and-proper thoughts.

Riley decided to take Treasure to a new restaurant in the Eastover section of Jackson. The owner, Leon, was a high school classmate, who'd retired from a career in the military after twenty years. His restaurant, Voyages, served some dishes he picked up during his stays abroad but with a southern flair. Leon had made the booths private and by reservation. Riley was able to reserve a curtained booth to give them some privacy to talk but not so private to give him any salacious ideas. Riley quickly surveyed the crowded restaurant's main dining area. Good, Riley thought. But then, Jacksonians were fickle, at times. Crowded in the first six months was good, but to hold patronage, one had to be on the pulse of their needs. Jackson would celebrate and close you in the first year without blinking an eye. Riley couldn't help, though, but be proud of his friend and hoped he would be able to introduce Treasure to him.

As the hostess led them to their private booth, neither Riley nor Treasure spoke. Treasure acknowledged a few people along the way, as did he, to the table. Whatever anonymity either one of them wanted didn't last long. Riley realized that their first date was much more public than he realized. The thought creased his brow, but he softened when he and Treasure entered one of the last booths. It was still in the main dining area, but unless you were looking for them, no one would know they were there.

Treasure smiled at the hostess, who left their menus and silverware on the table and took their drink orders. The menus were leather-bound folios with choice selections of the day inserted. Smart move, Riley thought. He also noted that Treasure asked for a glass of water in addition to her wine. To break the awkward silence between them, she said, "Voyages has been on my list for a while." She paused before adding, "I guess you come here often?" Her eyes held a question Riley didn't mind answering.

"I do. Business dinners and private parties, mostly. My friend, Leon, owns the place, but this is my first time in one of the private booths." Riley looked directly at Treasure, both understanding the meaning behind his statement, and he noted the relief as her features softened.

"Well, what do you recommend?" Treasure didn't understand why knowing that Riley had never brought one of his dates here pleased her. But it did.

Riley continued, "Leon didn't want an extensive menu, but he changes it frequently enough that you could have choice favorites but always explore new tastes." He reviewed the menu. "I recommend anything with risotto. Leon makes the best in the city."

Treasure nodded. "It is. You definitely have to have variety in your selections and price points." She paused, remembering their last conversation about business. Her voice lowered. "But you don't want to talk about business." She looked around the restaurant to avoid his gaze. Treasure worked hard and faced so much negativity in the early years of her business. The memory of Riley's disdain still stung especially when folks, family included, all told her she was wasting her time. Treasure was proud of her decision and work. Styling Simone last night was proof of that. She straightened her back against the booth, placing what little space she could between them.

Riley took a deep breath. "Treasure, let me apologize again for disrespecting your work and your business. Chalk it up to feeling myself a bit too much in those days. Believe me, I've kicked myself several times over it. Please, continue."

The contrition in his eyes moved her, and this time, for some reason, she believed him. "I have customers who willingly pay designer gown prices, sometimes as high as $5000. But I have some clients who can't afford half of that amount, but they deserve to look good too." She told him about Simone's initial panic, and as they were laughing about the moment Simone pulled the dress out of her purse, the server approached the table.

Riley motioned for Treasure to order first and he followed. Treasure ordered the shrimp scampi risotto while Riley opted for barbecue shrimp grilled in a banana leaf pouch.

When the waiter took their menus and walked away, Treasure remarked, "I'm surprised that you didn't order a steak," Treasure teased.

"Well, I do love a good steak, especially a filet, but tonight, I wanted to try something new." He paused, thinking about what "something new" meant for him. Tonight's dinner with Treasure was definitely new for Riley, and he was surprisingly pleased about it. He stared at Treasure's hands as she held her wine glass. Delicately yet comfortably. The small hurricane candle on the table flickered and highlighted Treasure's face, making it glow. Riley leaned forward and touched her hand, catching Treasure off-guard. Riley whispered, in a voice he didn't recognize, "Thank you."

Treasure blinked. "Thank me? For what?"

Riley made circles on the back of Treasure's hand. "For tonight. For agreeing to dinner. Thank you."

Treasure nodded at him. She shifted in her seat. Riley was saying and doing all the right things, but she wondered if she were another conquest. But she remembered that he said that she would determine the pace, and she told herself to take things slow and easy. She rushed into things fast last time, and by Monday morning, she was a mess of emotions. Treasure couldn't afford to let that happen again.

As they made small talk about Jackson politics, business philosophies, and celebrity shenanigans, both Riley and Treasure were becoming more at ease. By the time dinner arrived, Treasure and Riley were laughing at his and Kenzo's infamous rescue mission of Grace the previous year. Grace was conducting an investigation on a sex trafficking ring, and Kenzo got a feeling that Grace needed him and grabbed Riley and another friend, Marcus, to assist. Treasure had been angry about being left out of the happenings at the time, but by the time the words "guns," "kidnappers," and "murder" popped up, she appreciated the bliss of ignorance. Riley's account was so animated that Treasure had tears in her eyes from laughing.

Between bites, Riley told her, "So, here we are, three black men, with a damn arsenal, on the Coast, in a casino. And Kenzo, goes bursting through the stairwell door with a damn duffle bag of guns and ammo. I'm like, 'Dude!' I swear the brother was going to get us all killed, or worse, put in jail. We were in Ocean's Fourteen, I swear." He shook his head in mock disgust.

Treasure covered her mouth to keep from laughing too loudly. She was glad that Riley had the curtain drawn, or their laughter would have disturbed the entire restaurant. Treasure realized that she enjoyed laughing with Riley rather than running away from him or scowling at him as she always did. The thought was sobering, and her face must have reflected it, because Riley asked her immediately if something was wrong.

"Treasure," Riley said, with concern in his eyes, "are you okay? You looked a million miles away for a moment."

Treasure looked at him blankly for a moment before saying, "No, no, I'm fine. I'm sorry."

"No need to be sorry," Riley said. Riley had promised to take this slow, let Treasure determine the pace, but he was feeling a sense of protectiveness that he never had with a woman. "Do you want to tell me what put a frown line across your beautiful face?"

Treasure blushed, and Riley loved knowing that his compliment had that effect on her.

Treasure decided that there was no reason to lie to Riley. "I was thinking how much I was enjoying laughing with you."

Riley's eyebrow lifted. "And that upset you?"

"I'm not upset," Treasure said. She folded and refolded her napkin to avoid looking at him.

Riley reached across the table and lifted her chin. "Tell me."

Treasure gazed into Riley's gorgeous eyes and took a deep breath. "I'm scared to enjoy tonight." She paused, "And you."

Neither said anything for a while, and the lull in the conversation filled with various tensions. When the bill arrived, Riley gave the waitress two hundred dollars, stood, and extended his hand to Treasure. As Treasure placed her hand in his, a jolt of electricity with through her body. His hand was soft where it should be and hard where it should be. She imagined those soft fingertips and calluses against her skin. Treasure looked up at Riley, his eyes darkened with desire.

When she stood, Riley pulled her flush with his body. He summoned every ounce of control he had not to kiss Treasure right there in the restaurant. His desire for her was clear and present, and for a second, Treasure thought about stepping back, worried that someone would see them. But Riley's eyes held her captive.

"Riley," she whispered. Treasure placed her hands flat on Riley's chest to gently push herself away. She could barely breathe. His scent was in her nostrils. Her skin still held the memory of his touch after all these years. "Let's go."

Riley smiled down at her and winked. "As you wish, sweetheart."

~

Treasure thought he was taking her home, but Riley had other ideas. The ride had been relatively quiet, except for the occasional small talk. Riley glanced over at Treasure, who was looking out of the window. As if she sensed his staring, she looked over at him and flashed him the most beautiful, shy smile. Riley returned hers with a smile of his own.

"What?" she asked in a whisper.

Caught, Riley grinned at her and took her left hand in his. "I hope you like part two of our date." And he sincerely did. This part took a bit of doing on his part, but he managed to pull it off. This was all new to him. His dates normally didn't require this much effort. He didn't realize how much fun he was having wanting to please a woman outside of the bedroom.

"Part two? Riley, what do you have up your sleeve?" Treasure couldn't help but smile at him, because he was grinning like a kid at Christmas. But she was still nervous. Too much time spent with him was dangerous, and both of them were pretending not to think about the pleasures of the fateful weekend. Slow. Take this slow, Treasure, she thought to herself. Riley gave her hand a squeeze, and as she looked at her small hand in his large one, Treasure had a shiver run up her spine, remembering how strong those hands were. Riley asked if she were cold. Treasure wanted to melt into the floorboards but managed to say she was fine.

Riley shifted in his seat and gripped the steering wheel. Her perfume was driving him crazy, especially in the confines of his car. He drove down Pascagoula Street and turned into the parking lot of the art museum. The director owed Riley a favor, so he arranged to bring Treasure there after dinner for dessert. Riley stole a glance at Treasure. Her brow furrowed, giving her the most beautiful frown.

"Ready for part two?" Riley asked, as he unbuckled his seat beat. For the first time since he was a teenager, he really cared whether she would like him and what he had planned. He promised her that they would take things slow, and he understood after learning more about her parents. Put that with their brief dalliance a few years ago and his reputation and he fully understood Treasure's hesitation.

"I suppose so," Treasure said. The art museum, huh? Who was Riley Taylor? When Riley opened her car door and extended her hand, part of her didn't want to take it. Her body responded to his touch against her will every time. Treasure looked up at him as she slid her hand in his, and her entire body flooded with warmth. Riley's eyes connected with hers. She was sure her heart stopped. His eyes looked deep enough to swim in, and when he smiled at her, her knees almost buckled. *Girl, this one is going to make you lose yourself,* she said to herself. Treasure corrected herself. *No, Treas, you're already lost. Just don't surrender yet.*

When he opened the car door, Riley couldn't help but appreciate how Treasure's dress revealed her shapely legs and God help him, a healthy bit of thigh. Treasure's diminutive hand fit perfectly in his. He stared at their hands for a few seconds before looking at her. The way she looked at him as she rose from the car only increased his desire for her. A keen sense of awareness and electricity passed between them, the desire in her eyes a mirror of his own. Riley fought the urge to do more, but she remained guarded around him. Every time it seemed as though she was relaxing a little, Treasure would catch herself and the wall would creep up between them. Riley mentally reminded himself of his promise. He was a man of his word. But that didn't mean that he couldn't help her make the decision sooner rather than later.

Treasure was simply the most beautiful woman in the world, and he fought the urge to do more than hold her hand. Riley took in a deep breath and reminded himself of his promise yet again.

Riley enjoyed having Treasure's hand in his and never let it go for the rest of the night.

CHAPTER 4

Treasure was busy helping Sarah Bridgewater find a dress to her daughter's wedding when the phone rang. Simone answered it, and she could tell by the poor girl's voice that something was wrong. Treasure tried to split her hearing between Mrs. Bridgewater's complaints about her husband's complaints about wedding costs and Simone's growing agitation with the caller on the phone.

Rolling her eyes and angrily sifting through the racks, Mrs. Bridgewater exclaimed, "To hear him tell it, he was living on Skid Row somewhere. His only daughter is getting married and he's acting like we're looking for a prom dress!" Sarah Walker and Matthew Bridgewater met and fell in love at Ole Miss. As beautiful and kindhearted as she was, Sarah Walker was a poor white girl from Greenwood, Mississippi, in the Mississippi Delta. Conversely, Matthew Bridgewater's family were an old white family with old money much of it made through land grabs and sharecropping from Reconstruction to Jim Crow. Rumor was that the Bridgewaters questioned the purity of Sarah's bloodline, and most black folk in Jackson with ties to the Mississippi Delta, believed, and some verified, the rumors of Sarah's grandmother passing and marrying a white man. But Matthew threatened to leave Mississippi with Sarah and never return, which made them begrudgingly relent to a grand wedding at their plantation. Whether Sarah's grandmother was black was a question for whispered conversations in safe spaces.

Though Sarah Walker married extremely well when she married into the Bridgewater family, she never forgot how the old Bridgewaters treated her as a young bride and how they treated poor people, black and white. So, when she was able, she put that old Bridgewater wealth to good use, becoming one of Mississippi's go-to philanthropists. The Bridgewaters supported causes that were clearly for the betterment of poor people and people of color. One year, they even hosted the local NAACP annual fundraiser at the Country Club of Jackson. When Treasure dressed her for the event in a lovely black Bolin gown, she and Sarah Bridgewater laughed in hushed whispers about how the founders of the Country Club were rolling in their graves. In a conspiratorial tone, Sarah Bridgewater said, "Let them dance in there for all I care." Now, it was time for their only daughter, Shelby Christine, to marry, and Sarah Bridgewater was sparing no expense, including financing a trip to Paris, with Treasure in tow, if necessary, to find the perfect dress.

Treasure shook her head and smiled. "He dotes on Shelby. He'll probably have First Baptist remodeled to match her colors."

Mrs. Bridgewater laughed. "You're probably right."

Simone worked the front counter while she assisted Mrs. Bridgewater. The phone rang, and Treasure closed her eyes when Simone said, "But she's with a private client, Mrs. Jordan." She excused herself from Mrs. Bridgewater, still combing through dresses. Lord, Mama, what is it now? And then it hit her like a bolt of lightning. It was her parents' wedding anniversary. This was always a hard day for her mother, which meant it was hard for Treasure as well. Treasure motioned for Simone to give her the phone and listened to her mother's tirade for a full minute before saying a word. The slurred cadence of her speech meant only one thing. She glanced at Simone, who began straightening the racks on the other side of the store.

Corrine was so drunk that she thought she was still talking to Simone when Treasure picked up the phone. "Little girl, I want to speak to my daughter, and if..."

Treasure stopped her. "I'm here, Mama. What's wrong?" Treasure tried to hide the irritation in her voice.

"What's wrong?" her mother screamed. "What's wrong? Your damn daddy is what's wrong. I asked him to come and check on something in the attic, and he told me to call a handy man. A freaking handy man. How dare he?" Treasure held the phone. She learned early to ride the rant out. When her mother took a breath, Treasure capitalized on it.

"Mama, I have an important client right now. Would you like me to come by when I finish with Mrs. Bridgewater?" She hated to have to tell her who, but name-dropping would speed things up. If Corinne Jordan understood anything, she understood what social status and wealth meant in Jackson. And the Bridgewaters were both.

"Well, fine, then. Go deal with Mrs. Bridgewater and come home then. I've got half a mind to go to your father's office and curse his damn clothes off of him." Treasure rolled her eyes. Her mother talked more than she ever acted. By the time she arrived at the house, her mother would be passed out drunk on the sofa.

~

Treasure's mother never disappointed her. As she expected, Treasure found her mother passed out in the living room, surrounded by dead flowers and love letters from her father. She started to wake her and make her go to bed, but Treasure simply didn't have the energy. She walked around the house, stopping in front of the mantle on the fireplace. Dust had settled on the photographs. Her great-grandmother's face stared at her, and Treasure wondered what those eyes had seen from her perch on the mantle in the last thirty years. *What does she think about her granddaughter passed out on the couch over a man? Well, Mama Blossom, everyone didn't find a good man like you did,* she whispered to the photograph.

Treasure turned and realized that the entire house needed a good cleaning. Treasure listened to her mother's light snoring and occasional murmurs for her father. After nearly twenty years, Corinne Jordan still loved Randall from a place Treasure couldn't understand. Treasure stared at her mother. She was still a very beautiful woman, and in her sleep, she looked peaceful and serene. Only Treasure was privy to the painful ranting of a woman's whose heart never healed. *Damn, Daddy,* she thought. Shaking her head to clear her thoughts, Treasure decided that it was best to clean what she could while her mother was sleeping.

As she moved throughout the house, Treasure thought of Riley. She was always thinking of Riley these days. Since their first official date, Riley had kept his promise to let her set the pace. She appreciated that more than Riley would ever realize. During the couple of weeks of dating, Riley remained a perfect gentleman every time and in every way. Treasure could fall madly in love with Riley, but the woman passed out drunk on the sofa was the primary reason she would be sure about who and what she wanted.

But a couple of nights ago, she almost forgot that her heart was off-limits. He took her on a midnight picnic at the planetarium. Treasure smiled. Only Riley could weave himself into forbidden places. She smiled broadly at the memory of the two of them under the stars. Riley looked delicious in a pair of dark-blue Rock Revival jeans and a white linen shirt that complemented his skin tone, and Treasure's thoughts ventured down a risqué wayward path. But the way he would look back at her with such desire in his eyes made her blush and her core contract. Treasure's temperature rose as she thought about it.

Riley's excitement was infectious as he pulled into the parking lot of the Jackson Planetarium. The city completed some major renovations to the planetarium making it the largest in the South. Riley's huge grin tickled her. He truly looked like a kid at Christmas, and she was sure that if she wore flats instead of heels, he would have had them running to the auditorium. When they arrived, she realized that they were alone in the theater. As he led her to their seats, she stopped short. "Riley? There's no show tonight? How?"

He turned to her and grinned. "I always have a trick or two up my sleeve. They usually don't have a show on Tuesday, but I know people who know people." Riley flashed that killer smile of his and her body betrayed her. Try as she might to resist, her body's memory of Riley was stronger than her countenance. He led her to the center of the auditorium, and as they were getting settled, he asked if she wanted a something to eat. While he pulled popcorn and drinks from a basket in the seat, Treasure looked around. She let out a little sigh. Riley was making it hard to resist him, but Treasure had to be strong.

Riley returned with drinks and a picnic basket. Taking a blanket from the basket and spreading it out, he said, "I hope you have an appetite. I thought we'd have a midnight picnic under the stars." Riley nervously looked at Treasure, hoping that she would appreciate the idea. When Treasure's eyes lit up, Riley exhaled.

Treasure couldn't remember the last time she was on a picnic. "Oh, Riley, this is lovely." She grinned up at him. "But midnight?" She pretended to look at her watch.

He shrugged his shoulders with a grin. "Yeah, but somewhere in the world it is. In here, it can be whatever time we want it to be." Riley's eyes softened. As he held out his hand to help Treasure sit on the blanket, he added, "We can always be whatever we want to be, sweetheart." Riley kissed the back of her hand, Treasure thought she was going to melt right there. No man had ever been as kind or thoughtful as Riley had been these last few weeks. Treasure wondered when he was going to tire of her, when he was going to change and hurt her again. But she couldn't worry about that now. She was having too much fun.

When Treasure smiled at him, Riley thought his heart would burst. Seeing her smile because of something he did pleased him Hell, Riley couldn't remember ever being this happy. Soon, the light show transported them into a world of twinkling stars, moons, and planets, but all Riley could focus on was the warmth of Treasure's hand on his arm when something surprised her or delighted her and how she would occasionally glance in his direction and smile at him.

When the light show ended and as they were gathering their things, Riley pulled her into a kiss that shook her to her core. The stars were still being projected on the domed screen, and it was such a perfect moment. Riley commanded her mouth, nibbling on each lip before his tongue entered her mouth. His hands scorched the bare skin on her arms and through her blouse. Treasure nearly fell limp in his arms. Her nipples tingled as his hardness pressed against her. Her core throbbed with desire. Only Riley had the power to make her flesh this weak. Where did the man learn how to kiss like this, she thought, as his tongue teased the inside of her mouth. Treasure moaned when Riley tore his mouth away from hers and started kissing her neck. His hands were massaging her breasts through her shirt. Treasure was completely aroused, and from a distant place in her mind, she let go. She let her hands explore him, and when she rubbed the length of his hardness through his pants, he groaned, arousing her more. Was she moving, or was he? She needed relief, but if she let it go on much longer, she was going to lose all resolve and let him take her on the damn floor.

Things had gone too far and not far enough. Riley couldn't stop himself. He was holding her too tightly against him. Riley's erection throbbed for her. He almost lost all control when she touched him.

"We need to go, sweetheart" Riley whispered against her skin. He placed a kiss on her forehead and rested his forehead on hers. Riley slowly caressed her arms and took her hands in his, weaving their fingers together. Treasure shuddered. Still holding her hands, Riley stepped back and took a look at Treasure. Riley had never seen a more stunning woman. Her lips, swollen from their kiss, and her flushed cheeks made her glow more brightly than any star seen that night. Against his better judgement, Riley leaned down to kiss her again when the attendant opened the door.

"Saved by the bell, I guess," he said. "We really need to go now." Riley and Treasure accepted that they were dangerously close to losing control. Treasure's lips stung at the loss of contact, and she was sure Riley could hear her heart was thumping in her chest. Riley planted a quick kiss on her forehead and with her hand in his led her out of the auditorium.

"Randall, you promised me. You promised me."

Her mother's mumbling interrupted Treasure's thoughts of Riley. She let out a deep breath as she looked at her mother and shook her head. Treasure gave up trying to convince her mother to find peace within herself. Her mother simply refused to accept the divorce as final. Before, she thought her mother's love bordered on the obsessive, but after she went through her own lovesick trial with Riley, she understood. The only difference was that Treasure did date some. She couldn't wait on Riley to change his mind. He changed it on his own. Yes, that was the difference, she thought. Treasure refused to spend years waiting on Riley like her mother waited on her father. Her mother never dated, and since she refused to be seen out alone, she rarely attended any of Jackson's social events. There was never a chance for her to meet anyone.

This house had become her mother's coffin, where her memories lay in effigy to her youth and her failed marriage. Treasure didn't want to admit it, but her mother had become comfortable in her grief and pain. The thought stopped her cold. Treasure realized how close she was to becoming like her mother. She took a seat in the big club chair that had once been her father's and looked at her mother, who still referred to it as her father's chair. Everything was still the same--the furniture and the feelings.

Riley didn't intend to hurt her all those years ago, but he did. The rejection was too familiar, and though the arrangement had been her idea, somehow, Treasure found it easier to blame him. For a long time, she convinced herself that Riley was another Randall Jordan, like most men. And maybe he was, but she deserved the chance to find that out for herself rather than living in her mother's painful memories, or one day, she might be the one passed out on the sofa. She prayed that Riley was the man he said he was or was presenting to her.

Despite his well-earned playboy reputation, Riley had definitely been a gentleman with her. He was true to his word, allowing her to set the pace, which was making it really hard not to fall for him again. Treasure was already in too deep, but she had to keep it light with Riley. He didn't push her, and she asked for nothing, required nothing. Riley seemed interested in her. He pursued her. He called her. Riley was the consummate player, and she couldn't help but wonder when he would be ready to move to the next conquest, leaving her to nurse another heartbreak. This time, she prepared herself. This time, Treasure would enjoy the time she had with him until it was over.

She moved quietly through the house, washing and putting up clothes, gathering the trash and taking it outside, and wiping down the tables and countertops. Her phone rang, and Treasure couldn't believe how happy she was to see Riley's face pop up on her screen.

Treasure slid her finger across the screen. "Hi, Riley."

"Hello Beautiful," Riley said, his voice deep and sexy. "I was wondering if you wanted to meet for dinner tonight?"

Treasure smiled but hesitated. "I'd love to, Riley, but I'm at my mother's." Her voice dropped a bit, as she added, "And I can't leave her right now, not today."

The anguish in her voice concerned him. "Is everything okay? Need anything?" Riley's gesture warmed her insides, but she knew Corinne would not be able to take Riley's presence right now. "No. But thank you. I'll call you later."

Riley tried not to hide his disappointment. And when she declined, he realized that he missed her and had been missing her all day. "Cool. Have a good time with your mother and call me later. And don't worry about the time. I'll be up."

Treasure's voice trembled as she simply responded, "Okay." She was on the verge of tears. Would she end up drunk on the couch pining for a man who didn't want her? Riley had been patient and kind. But her father had too.

~

Riley stood under the shower head and let the water flow over him like a waterfall. His entire body was sore and tense. His trainer, Deondre, had been brutally efficient today. On the days when he and Deondre had a boxing workout, Riley delivered a few good licks, at least, before Deondre put him on his back. But today, he couldn't focus on anything. His mind was on Treasure. His mind was always on Treasure. He wanted her more than he had wanted anyone in his life, and his promise to let her set the pace was wearing him out and down. Damn me and my big mouth, he thought to himself. The water had begun to cool, but Riley stood there. Cold showers had become a routine these days. Keeping his word was killing him. Every time he was near her, his desire for her was clear. And though Treasure fought her desire for him, he believed in his heart that she wanted him as much as he wanted her.

Riley thought about their time together. She laughed more now, and he loved making her laugh. She had a deep, sexy laugh that was infectious.

But her smile was what brought him to his knees. Treasure's entire face lit up when she smiled. Her deep brown eyes would dance at him as her lips slowly parted into a sweet grin. Riley was getting aroused at the thought of seeing her smile, and he imagined her smile looking up at him as he made love to her. But he couldn't allow himself to go there yet. Living on the memory of their weekend a few years ago and the near misses in the last few weeks drove him mad. A chill when up his spine. He shuddered, thinking about the passion she held inside her delectable body.

Neither one of them had brought up the topic of exclusivity, and Riley was completely cool with that. In his mind, Treasure already belonged to him. She didn't believe that he could ever be faithful to one woman. And until recently, he thought the same thing.

But Treasure changed everything. She was everything.

Riley realized that the conversation would be coming sooner than later, because sexual energy filled every kiss and every moment they spent together. So much so that Riley started to question his sanity. As much as he wanted to make love to Treasure, she deserved more than to be approached like a horny teenager. If he could forget the silkiness of her skin on his fingertips, or the honeysuckle of her scent, he could handle the wait. But he couldn't, and every day was becoming harder and harder. Literally. Holding her, kissing her, hearing her laugh, seeing her smile sent his libido into overdrive. Jesus, what the hell was I thinking, He braced his hands against the tiled wall. No woman had ever consumed his thoughts like Treasure did, Riley thought as he reached for his towel on the shelf and dried himself roughly.

Riley's phone rang, and he wrapped a towel around his waist. He thought it might be Treasure changing her mind about meeting him tonight, but he couldn't hide his disappointment when his sister's name flashed across his screen. "Yeah, sis, what's up?"

"Well, hello to you too, Riley," she said. "Emma said that you promised her a sleepover this weekend. I'm calling to confirm."

Riley threw his head back. Kids didn't forget anything, and especially little girls. "Damn, Diahann, I forgot I told her that. I'll pick her up Friday night." He laughed. "Emma is definitely your mini-me. She was half asleep when she asked, so I was sure she wouldn't remember."

"I told you, Riley, a lady doesn't forget anything. Especially promises. You'd do well to remember that. So, what's this I hear about you and Treasure all over Jackson?"

Riley rolled his eyes. "Nothing. We're learning each other. Hanging out."

Diahann laughed. "Riley Taylor. Who do you think you're talking to, or did you forget that you told me about that steamy weekend tryst years ago? You went against my advice to call her then, so I hope you don't mess up and not follow my advice this time."

"Which is?" Riley said on an exasperated breath.

"Admit that you are in love with her."

Riley said nothing in his defense, but his sister seized this rare opportunity, taking his silence as assent. "And this time, be honest with yourself and her. Listen, I'll talk to you later. Bath and bedtime around here. Bye, Riley." Diahann didn't give him a chance to respond as she ended the call, but Riley was still processing that Diahann thought he was in love with Treasure.

Riley dropped his head into his hands. His sister was right. He was in love with Treasure Jordan.

Damn. Now all he had to do was convince Treasure of that. Well, it shouldn't be too hard, he thought. It only took her a year to go out with me. This should take only a damn lifetime.

CHAPTER 5

Seth Newall gripped the bottom of his glass tightly to control his anger and frustration. Anyone looking at the prominent Jackson businessman would have thought he was having the time of his life at the Black Men United annual fundraiser. This year, the fundraiser was downtown at the remodeled portion of the train station. Union Station gave plenty of space for intimate conversation as well as room for a full band and dance floor. Newall chaired the purchase and development of the building for the City of Jackson in 2003, and it was perfectly situated at an intersection of Capitol and Mill Street and across from the King Edward Hotel. Pockets of strong commercial and residential development downtown began to revitalize the area, but downtown Jackson's glory days were still more history than future.

As Chairman, he was responsible for courting new donors and schmoozing existing donors all night. He caught sight of his wife, Gail, who was still beautiful in her late 50s. Her hair was turning a gorgeous silver that complemented her mocha-colored skin and her red satin gown perfectly, and she could still work a room. As she spoke to the Mayor and his wife, Gail looked up at him and smiled. Seth winked back at her and raised his glass. He needed the Mayor to support his development plan in

West Jackson, so any good will she could garner would go a long way at his next meeting. He married wisely, not for love. Their match was a business deal--plain and simple. But Seth had to admit a fond affection, even love, for the woman who bore and raised three wonderful sons for him. He provided Gail a life of luxury and status, and she gave him a consummate hostess and mother for his children.

But the two people laughing and talking on the other side of the room had his full attention.

Jackson's secrets were openly kept. Though Seth played around, he never disrespected his wife in public. But Treasure Jordan was making that commitment difficult. Outside, he was the picture of cool, but inside, his blood was boiling. He decided a long time ago that he wanted Treasure in his bed and maybe as a second wife. Seth smiled to himself. Yes, he thought, Treasure Jordan would easily step into Gail's shoes. She might wear them better.

The only problem was that Treasure rebuffed every advance, every overture. She laughed at him like he was some lecherous old man. Once, she asked if Gail would be joining them for dinner when he invited her out one night. Treasure bordered on downright nasty the last time he approached her, so he backed off. And here she was...grinning and cozied up to Riley Taylor.

Seth hated Riley and that partner of his, Kenzo Dallas. Those upstarts were upsetting the balance of power in Jackson. That revitalization project in Harrington Heights was cutting into his business dealings in the city. Seth excused himself from the conversation with Gregory Funches, the owner of one of the largest construction companies in the state and moved stealthily toward the happy couple.

Riley spied Seth Newall coming but didn't take his eyes off Treasure. She was talking about her plans to attend New York's Fashion Week later that year, and the excitement in her voice captivated him. "Do you need a chaperone in New York?" he asked, tracing her exposed collarbone with his finger. Riley's featherlight touch against her skin sent a shiver down her spine. Riley's eyes darkened with desire as he leaned down to kiss her.

Every laugh from Riley and Treasure made it clear that they were having a good time, so much so that they never acknowledged Seth's presence. . Seth cleared his throat as Riley's lips touched Treasure's. Riley and Treasure opened their eyes at the same time. She stepped back a bit to acknowledge Seth's intrusion, but she could have sworn she heard Riley curse.

Treasure couldn't have known that there was no love between Riley, Kenzo, and Seth since Kenzo tried to partner with him on one of their early real estate deals near downtown Jackson. At first, Riley and Kenzo appreciated the mentorship, but Riley always bristled at the way Seth talked to them. Kenzo took it in stride as paying their dues until they got wind that Seth was making a side deal for the land. He and Kenzo pulled their company out of the deal, taking their financing with them and killing the entire project. Since then, Seth Newall stayed away from them and vice versa, but that night, Seth was trying to make a point to him.

Gathering herself, Treasure mustered as much southern charm as she could, "Hello, Mr. Newall, how are you? Everything looks absolutely lovely. And Gail is stunning as always."

Seth inwardly cringed but maintained his composure. She always brought up Gail's name like he needed to be reminded that he had a wife. "I'm well, Ms. Jordan. I was wondering if I could speak to you about speaking to our mentoring program at Black Men United." Seth touched Treasure's arm. Riley growled. Treasure slid away from Seth's touch and closer to Riley. There was always something sinister in her dealings with Seth. She didn't like him, and she could tell that Riley didn't care for him either.

"I'd love to speak to the boys, Mr. Newall."

"Oh, no, not the boys. Well, not yet. We're trying a new program for young ladies as a joint venture with Black Women United." Seth refused to acknowledge Riley's presence. Seth's irritation grew as Riley glared at him. Treasure stepped closer to Riley who put his arm around her waist possessively. This young buck needed to recognize who he was messing with, but Seth didn't have a problem giving Riley an education.

"I should contact Gail, then?" Treasure needed to end this conversation before Riley started growling again.

"I'll tell her to contact you soon. Thanks, Ms. Jordan. As usual, you have been most accommodating." Seth emphasized the "Ms." and "accommodating" while looking in Riley's direction while grabbing Treasure's hand. Treasure could tell Riley was fuming. His jawbone jumped. Treasure pulled her hand back quickly. Seth Newall made her flesh crawl.

Riley was the first to speak once Seth was out of earshot. "I can't stand him. What the hell was that about?" Surely Seth didn't think his Treasure was that type of woman. He didn't realize that Treasure would misinterpret the question.

Treasure took in a breath. She turned sharply toward Riley and, "If you're thinking what I think you're thinking, then..." Her beautiful brown eyes were big, and her nostrils flared at him.

Riley took her hand and brought it to his lips, placing a kiss on the inside of her wrist. "Treasure, I'm not thinking anything, and definitely not what you think I'm thinking. Take a walk with me." He didn't wait for an answer but took her hand and led her outside. Riley had a feeling Seth's prying eyes were still on them. As he and Treasure headed to the patio, Seth Newall confirmed Riley's suspicions, sneering in their direction with a smug smile on his face.

~

Seth's words clearly upset Treasure, but it didn't matter to him if she were mad at him or Riley. Treasure Jordan would be his in the end anyway.

He motioned for one of the young servers to bring him another glass of champagne. It was time to give the toast and begin the evening's program. Seth downed the champagne in one swallow, winked at his wife, and made his way to the podium. He walked to the podium, assured and confident that he created a wrinkle for Riley's plans for the evening. And if it didn't, he had other options for Riley and that partner of his. Treasure would be another matter. He had a different approach for her. Treasure would be his, and Riley Taylor would be history.

After the program and the party resumed, Seth smiled his way to the kitchen. He gestured to one of the waiters passing out champagne. Seth had given some boys from the youth center an opportunity to serve and make a few dollars, but the young man following him now was special.

This kitchen was so busy with bakers and servers that no one paid attention to the two men maneuvering through the maze of the kitchen staff. It all looked normal, and no one would question Seth Newall at his own event.

When Seth found a private office, he entered and motioned for his companion to close the door. The young man locked the door behind him. He learned the hard way how an unlocked door during a private meeting could prove hazardous.

"Ernest, how is the Fondren project?" Seth's voice dropped to a low roar as he looked at Ernest hard.

Ernest, or E-Money, as his boys called him, studied the man before him carefully. To folks in Jackson, though, he was Seth Newall, businessman. E-Money only called him "Zeus" or "Z" depending on the situation. This was clearly a Zeus moment. "Alright. My boys handling the folks there. Little shit right now, a few broken windows, car jacks, but no casualties. Just like you said, boss."

Seth nodded his head. Ernest always followed orders to the letter, like his father had before him. "I need this to go smoothly, but we need to pick it up a bit. I want that retail area cleared by the first of the year."

Ernest rolled his shoulders and pulled at his shirt collar. These serving gigs in monkey suits were uncomfortable as hell. "No problem, Zeus. I got you." Ernest turned to leave.

"Wait. I have something else." Seth paused for a moment, looking down at his shoes. When he looked up, Ernest could tell that Seth made whatever decision he needed to make. "Include the girl in the next round."

Ernest's hand stopped on the doorknob. Treasure Jordan had been off-limits for years. The orders had been clear: Hands off. Ernest turned around. "You sure, Zeus?"

Seth reflected a moment and picked imaginary lint from his jacket cuff. He was sure. "Make sure you put your best people on the job. Better yet, you handle it yourself."

"Alright, Z. I'm out. " E-Money didn't turn around or wait for a response. Seth was breaking the first and only rule. Don't make this personal. Shit went left when you make it personal. And this was going to go left, but he always followed Zeus's orders.

~

Treasure was livid. If Riley Taylor thought she was going to be the bounty in some tug of war between him and Seth Newall, he could go straight to hell. And if Seth Newall ever tried to approach her again, she would speak directly to Gail. She respected Gail as a friend and loyal customer, but neither she, nor Gail, deserved this level of blatant disrespect.

"Beautiful night, isn't it?" Riley said, looking up at the clear Mississippi night sky. When Treasure didn't respond, he looked at her. "Treasure."

"Yes," she shot back, her tone angry and clipped. Treasure couldn't believe that he was talking to her about the damn weather. She was willing him to turn and face her. How dare he... Riley signed, interrupting her thoughts.

Riley took a weary breath and turned to face her. Looking directly at Treasure, he asked, "Is there something you want to ask me?" Riley asked, his brow raised.

"Ask you? Like what?" Treasure hissed. Riley was confusing her. "I don't need to ask you anything, Riley Taylor."

Riley smiled, "My full name. Oh, I must be in trouble." He chuckled. Her nostrils were flaring, and her face flushed. She clearly was not in the mood to laugh. "Well, for starters, you could ask me why I'm not thinking what you clearly think I am thinking about you and Seth Newall."

Treasure steeled herself and took a breath. His smile and his honesty were unexpected. Damn him. Nothing about Riley was ever what she expected. A couple walked into the building. She recognized the dress she was wearing as one of hers and nodded at the couple. She turned toward Riley, but she couldn't look at him. Softly, she said, as if to no one in particular, "Okay. Why?"

Riley ran the back of his hand against her cheek and tilted her head up. Treasure's eyes fluttered closed. She didn't want to look at him. She couldn't. "Treasure, look at me," Riley said. Treasure slowly opened her eyes, tears threatening to fall. Riley touched the corner of her eyes with his thumbs and wiped the tears away. "I'm not thinking what you think I'm thinking for one reason and one reason only. Being Seth Newall's side piece, or anyone's side piece, isn't who you are." He kissed her sweetly on her lips, almost chastely. With a chuckle, he added, "And even if he tried it, which he clearly has, you would have set him straight, which you have. Plus, he was putting on a show for me, not you."

Tears stung Treasure's eyes. Knowing that Riley didn't even question it, that she didn't have to explain herself to him, meant the world to her. She hated that Seth Newall put a damper on her evening with Riley and that she allowed it. Seth Newall had made overtures before. She always laughed them off. Tonight, though, was different. Propositioning her in front of Riley mattered more than the other times. What Riley thought of her meant more than it did before. But Riley said he didn't believe what Seth was trying to insinuate, and that was both endearing and frightening as hell.

Riley kissed her forehead and said, "C'mon, let's go back inside."

Treasure pulled at his hand as he turned toward the entrance. "No, Riley, I'm ready to leave now." Treasure's voice trembled, and she was on the verge of tears again.

Riley pulled her close to him and tilted her chin upward. "Sure?" Treasure's tears nearly stopped his heart. All Riley wanted to do was make love to the woman standing before him. Her tears had ignited a protective spirit within him. But as much as he wanted to make love to Treasure, Riley didn't want it to be because one of them was angry at Seth Newall. The second, first time he made love to Treasure Jordan, he wanted them only motivated by their need and want for each other, not a blowhard like Seth Newall.

"Yes, I'm sure." She nodded. The plea in her voice matched the one is her heart. Treasure realized that she was ready for all of Riley Taylor, and she could only pray that he was ready for all of her. "Take me home."

"Baby," he said softly, as he pulled her close, his desire pressed against her. "If you want me to take you home, I will. But I think we should go back inside. Seth Newall doesn't run a damn thing between us." He kissed her and then added, "You promised me a dance, and I do plan to hold you it. Then, I promise, I'll take you home."

Riley's warm breath against her skin heightened her desire. She inhaled his scent. The Versace Eros mixed with his manly scent always smelled so good. Treasure leaned into Riley's chest. He stood hard and firm against her, and Treasure had no doubt that he was right. Lord, she prayed, if you can make my will as strong as his chest, I would be most grateful.

He held up his hand in a scout's salute and winked at her. Treasure had to giggle a bit at Riley's boy scout salute. Riley smiled at her, and exhaled. "That's my girl. Let's go." He raised her hand to his lips and kissed it. As much as Treasure didn't want to go, she trusted Riley. He was probably right anyway. Treasure shivered as Riley placed his hand on the small of her back as they walked back into the building.

Thankfully, Seth Newall was nowhere to be found.

The band was in full swing, so they easily merged into the throngs of people on the dance floor. Riley wanted Treasure to forget about Seth Newall and twirled her around, catching her off-guard and making her laugh. Riley exhaled. Treasure's deep throaty laugh eased the tension between them. After a few up-tempo songs, the band switched to a slow song. Riley held Treasure close and tight. Dexter Allen was singing Lenny Williams' "'Cause I Love You," and Riley's heart constricted in his chest. His heart pounded, and for a few seconds, Riley didn't move. Treasure realized that something was wrong and looked up at him. Her eyes held a question that Riley answered the only way he could.

Riley cradled Treasure's neck and kissed her in the middle of the dance floor. He poured everything he could into his kiss, his desire, his love, his need. Treasure surrendered, glad the crowd of lovers around them cocooned them. Her body heated as Riley pulled her tightly against him. Riley's hands travelled to her waist, and the heat from his hand in the small of her back was scorching her skin through the flimsy fabric of her dress. Riley couldn't hide his desire for her any longer, and Treasure's heartbeat thumped in her chest as Riley held her tightly against him. The throbbing at her core and Riley's tongue exploring her mouth was driving her insane. They weren't dancing anymore. They were making love fully clothed.

Against her body's wishes, Treasure ended the kiss. She and Riley stared at each other, both of them breathing hard. Treasure's full breasts heaved with every ragged breath. Riley had never been so hard in his life, and if he didn't take his woman out of there, the entire party would get one helluva show right there in the middle of the dance floor. And he didn't care who would see it, not even Seth Newall.

Without another word, Riley led Treasure out of Union Station. Treasure could barely breathe. Her need for Riley was all consuming, and Riley's firm grip on her hand told her that he was right there with her. The silence between them was only broken by the faint sounds of the band still jamming behind them. Riley opened Treasure's car door. She slid onto the leather seats and pressed her legs together and waited. She would go wherever Riley took her at this point. As Riley rounded the car, he thought for a moment that he and Treasure should go to his condo or the King Edward. He wanted Treasure that badly, but as soon as he thought it, he decided against it. He wanted Treasure at home and in his bed.

~

Riley's downtown condo would have definitely been closer, but he wanted to take Treasure to his real home in Pocahontas. Riley inherited the twenty acres and ranch style home from his grandfather along with a couple of horses. Almost automatically, he turned on the Robert Smith Parkway to Lynch. Riley navigated Jackson's notorious potholes like a professional driver. But Lynch was closer to I-220, which meant he would have Treasure home with him faster than had he taken I-55.

Neither he nor Treasure had said a word on the drive home. Treasure had never been to Riley's home in Pocahontas but was sure Riley would take her there the moment he walked her out of the party. Tonight would change everything between them.

Riley gripped the wheel so tightly that his hands were nearly cramping, but he had to do something to keep from reaching over and touching her.

He forced himself to look straight ahead. But that didn't stop him from inhaling her scent of arousal mixed with her perfume. Riley finally stole a quick glance at Treasure. Her hands were in her lap, and the deep slit in her dress showed a hint of skin. Riley winced at the sight of her flesh. When the vision of her thighs, open to him, flashed across his mind, Riley had to shift in his seat to ease the pressure from his erection. Riley never wanted a woman as badly as he wanted Treasure, and he almost regretted his decision to drive to his main home.

Riley decided not to pull into the garage but drove to the circular drive at the front of the house. The tension between them was nearly steaming up the windows. Riley and Treasure were both breathing hard and trying not to show it. Riley's hands shook nervously. Tonight, would be different than any night before with any other woman. Making love to Treasure would change everything.

Man, control yourself, or this will be over before it gets started, he told himself.

The throbbing between Treasure's legs was becoming unbearable, and Riley nearly sprinted around his car to open her door, and Treasure exited the car a bundle of nerves and need. A surge of electricity and warmth radiated through her as soon as their hands touched. As soon as their eyes met, Riley's eyes darkened with desire. Treasure took a sharp inhale as she rose from the car, her hand in his, her gown falling away to reveal a healthy thigh.

With the click of the front door lock, Riley pulled her to him and kissed her passionately. As he explored her mouth with his tongue, Riley walked her further into the house. Riley pressed Treasure against the wall, consuming her with his kiss. Treasure responded, her moans sending vibrations through him. Treasure's core contracted with need. Riley needed Treasure's skin against his.

He swept her up into his arms and headed upstairs so quickly that

Treasure gasped. The sound was like a sweet serenade in his ear, and his desire rushed through him when he thought about the sounds she would make when he made love to her.

Treasure rested her head on Riley's shoulder and nuzzled his neck, inhaling his scent. His manly scent and the faintest trace of his cologne was permanently embedded in her senses. Before she realized it, Treasure turned her head and licked Riley's neck before she began nibbling and sucking on the same spot. She smiled against his skin when Riley froze.

Riley closed his eyes and steadied himself. Treasure's tongue and lips against his skin was sending his desire for her into overdrive.

"Baby, if you don't want me to take you right here on the stairs, stop now." Riley summoned enough strength to keep climbing the staircase. But Treasure didn't stop and moved her delectable mouth to his ear. Treasure nibbled on his earlobe, and her tongue darted in his ear as she caressed his neck. The sensations overwhelmed him.

"Jesus, woman? You. Are. Killing. Me." said Riley in a forced whisper. He steadied himself for moment. He really wanted to make good on that threat, but he wanted to make love to Treasure in his bed, where he desperately planned to keep her.

As soon as they crossed the threshold of his bedroom, Riley put her down and swung her around to face him. He needed to see her first. The scent of her arousal was in nostrils and now he wanted her on his tongue. Riley grabbed her waist and pulled her to his body and tightly as he could and kissed her more passionately than he had any other woman. Riley's hardness pressed against her. Riley's tongue was doing vicious things to her mouth; he was consuming her with every lick. Every suck. Every nibble. His hands caressed her body, and her dress was irritating her heated skin.

Dear Lord, she thought. Riley broke the kiss so he could remove her dress, and he didn't think it was possible for a woman to look sexy and innocent at the same time. Riley's mouth went dry. Treasure was a vision before him, wearing a pale pink lace bra and matching boy shorts. Treasure's caramel skin, the curve of her breasts, against the pale pink lace, was a sight to behold.

Riley's eyes roamed Treasure's body, engraving the image in his mind. His wolfish gaze scared her. She worried whether she was enough for him since she resembled nothing like the women Riley usually dated. She instinctively crossed her arms over herself.

"Riley?" Treasure looked at Riley. He was staring at her so intensely. Had he changed his mind? Did he not want to do this? Suddenly embarrassed and exposed, Treasure lowered her head. Was she sexy enough for him? Had he changed his mind? He was still mostly dressed, which made it worse. Treasure forced herself to look away from Riley's piercing stare.

Riley realized what Treasure was thinking and reached for her. He uncrossed her arms and grabbed her chin. He cupped her face in his hands and placed the sweetest kiss on her forehead. "You are so beautiful, Treasure. I needed a moment to look at you." Riley continued to kiss her softly, missing no part of her face. With every kiss, he whispered, "My. Treasure," his breath hot against her skin. Her legs weakened. Her name on his lips was a new sound, and she closed her eyes to enjoy the melody of it in her soul.

He made a trail of kisses to her belly button. His tongue darted in the small dip of her flesh as his hands rested in the curve of her waist. Treasure steadied herself by gripping the taut muscles of Riley's broad shoulders as he knelt before her. Riley eased Treasure's panties down and inhaled her scent. He placed featherlight kisses at her mons, torturing them both. Treasure's legs opened slightly, allowing him full access to her womanhood. Riley's mouth clamped on Treasure's core, and he lapped up her juices like a man dying of thirst. Treasure's grip on Riley's shoulders tightened, and she couldn't tell her moans from Riley's. Right before she exploded, Riley rose, and Treasure whimpered.

Riley needed to be inside of her. Dangerously close to making love to her on the floor, he kissed her passionately. Treasure tasted herself on his lips. It was the most erotic thing she ever experienced. Riley moved them toward his bed never taking his mouth from hers. When the back of her legs hit the edge of the bed, Treasure's clawed at his shirt, pulling it from his pants. Riley still had on too many clothes, and she was nearly naked. She splayed her fingers across the hard muscles of his back to bring him closer. The heat from Riley's hands, his lips, his tongue, and his fingers teasing her, loving her created a fire within her only Riley could extinguish.

Somehow, they fumbled onto the bed. Treasure's arousal perfumed the air. Her scent traveled through him. Riley shuddered. No other woman invaded his spirit like Treasure had. She was his, and tonight, he would make her believe it.

As Treasure positioned herself on the bed, Riley undressed himself. Treasure gasped at the sight of him. She dreamed of every inch of his caramel-colored skin and muscles for the last five years. She counted his abs from memory like some folks count sheep. And now, they were here again, but this time would be different. It had to be.

Riley undressed slowly, watching Treasure watch him. And he didn't mind giving a good show. When he eased out of his boxer briefs, his manhood sprang free. As Riley sheathed himself with a condom, he held Treasure's gaze as he climbed into bed and eased his body over hers. Riley opened the front clasp on Treasure's bra and shook his head. Her breasts were perfect. He latched onto a hardened nipple and sucked hard while massaging the other. Treasure moaned as her back arched in response. Her throbbing between her legs almost became painful. Riley was purposely torturing her, his large hands touching every place, blazing a trail of fire against her skin, but the one place she needed relief, he was avoiding. Riley moved from one breast to the other, and then began inching downward. He kissed, nibbled, and sucked her body, leaving no inch of skin untouched. Treasure alternated between pleasure-filled moans and hisses and calling Riley's name.

When he nestled himself between her legs, he blew against her core, and Treasure thought she would orgasm right then. Riley closed his eyes and inhaled her scent. When he opened them, Treasure was looking at him with tears in her eyes. He lifted her right leg and nibbled the inside of her thigh.

"Riley, please." She was writhing and whimpering now. "Stop teasing me." Riley grinned against her skin. She was right. And he would rectify that now.

"Whatever my treasure wants," Riley whispered before teasing the sensitive ball of nerves at the top of her core. He held her tightly against his mouth as he brought her to orgasm. Treasure screamed and bucked her body against him as the orgasm slammed into her body. With closed eyes, she grabbed the sheets and balled her fists, as Riley brought her to orgasm again. Every nerve in her body came alive. She memorized the texture of Riley's tongue and his fingerprints on her skin.

Riley savored her taste, but he needed to be inside her. As he kissed and nipped his way up the length of her body, Riley realized that everything he wanted was right here. He kissed her as deeply as he could, as he thrust himself inside her. Treasure's gasps turned into a guttural moan of pleasure. Riley moved inside her, lifting himself slightly, so he could see the pleasure on her face. Treasure opened her eyes and found Riley's looking down at her. His eyes filled with pure desire and strength. She lifted her head and latched on to his nipple, lapping and sucking it in time with his thrusts inside her. She couldn't differentiate her moans from his.

Her music was driving him insane, and with every thrust, she welcomed him inside her. Between her moans of pleasure and the way she gripped his shaft, Riley could barely focus. Her heartbeat and his manhood throbbed in unison. Riley surrendered himself completely to Treasure, finally accepting the truth. Only Treasure had the power to make him into a man.

Riley sweetly whispered, "Treasure, my treasure" in her ear with each thrust. Treasure's entire body liquefied. Riley could tell her orgasm was building, but he wanted her to explode around him. "Come for me, baby," he said. It was all Treasure needed to send her flying over the edge. Treasure exploded around his shaft and Riley slammed his mouth on hers, swallowing her screams. Her orgasm triggered his, and soon as his orgasm ripped through his body, Riley threw his head back and let out a primal yell. His orgasm lasted longer than he could thought possible. With every shudder that racked through his body, Riley knew Treasure would be the last woman he would ever love like this for the rest of his life.

Riley looked down at Treasure as their breathing normalized and kissed her forehead. The sheen of sweat on her face made her glisten and when she smiled at him, he thought his heart would explode.

"That was fun," she said. "Umm...when can we do it again?" Her smile grew into an outright grin, and Riley couldn't help but laugh himself. Riley was still embedded in her warmth and his body instantly responded. Riley kissed her again, nipping at her bottom lip. "How about now?" He shifted his hip forward. Treasure moaned and Riley's semi-hardened state turned into a full- blown erection. His desire surged knowing she wanted more of him, of them together, He kissed her again and thrust forward.

"Is this what you want?" Riley asked, huskily, in her ear. His warm breath against her ear sent a shiver through her body, and Treasure's mouth went dry. She couldn't answer him. Treasure could only gasp as Riley filled her completely. As he thrust inside her again, Treasure's back arched. She didn't think it was possible for him to go any deeper inside her. She began moving in perfect time with him, the friction of his skin against hers ignited every nerve ending in her body. Riley dropped his head, his breath hot against her neck. She wrapped her arms around him and let her hands travel the length of his back. She memorized every muscle and sinew of his back.

Treasure's skin was on fire. Every stroke of him inside her drove her to orgasm. Riley nibbled and sucked her neck and earlobe between every thrust of his shaft. Her entire body belonged to Riley. This wasn't making love. This, Treasure thought, was a worshiping.

And she didn't mind it one bit.

CHAPTER 6

Ernest "E-Money" Walker yawned and looked at his watch and shifted in his seat. Treasure's Boutique had been busy all day, so he waited. Zeus's instructions had been clear though E-Money didn't understand why Zeus was so concerned about this woman or her little shop. How did she go from off limits to a target overnight? Ernest shook his head, watching a few of Treasure's customers leave the store and walk to their cars. They were laughing and talking, not paying a bit of attention. Easy pickings for a purse grab. Or a car jack. One was driving a 2020 Lexus 350 and the other was standing near a big body Benz. Ernest had been partial to Benz's since he was a kid. Zeus's Benz was his first luxury car ride, so Ernest always went for those first. He could tell that the women were carrying real LVs and Gucci's. He wouldn't even bother with the contents--credit cards were trouble. And federal. Cash and goods were cleaner and safer.

He stretched as he repositioned himself in the car. E-Money surveyed the storefronts in the area. More people needed to clear the area before he could make his move on Treasure. The first contact had to be clean. Zeus taught him that lesson during his early stick-up days for candy and a red Faygo. Just before closing time always proved to be the best time.

Distracted owners and clerks were less vigilant with who was coming in the door.

As he sat there, Ernest started thinking about his assignment and Zeus. Ernest didn't have to understand why Zeus was breaking his own rules by making this personal, but the man had been like a father to him since he was twelve years old. He would follow Zeus until the end. But something was off with the man and it had to do with this woman.

So, whatever this woman did to lose favor, Ernest determined not to do that.

When his mama overdosed on heroin and had a massive heart attack at 29, E-Money became a scavenger in the streets. Living with his father's people wasn't an option since E-Money had never met his father or his people. His father had been killed in prison while serving life for murder. His mama had been pregnant with E-Money when his father went to Parchman, or the Farm, as most folks called it. His mama always said he looked like his father. High, she would hold him and say it nice and sweet. But when she was sober or even near sober, she could be downright evil about it.

By the time he turned eight, he stole candy from gas stations, and by twelve, E-Money thought he owned the streets. He soon learned how wrong he was. With his father in jail and his mother dead, authorities placed Ernest in the foster care system. He ran away from every foster home until they put him in one that didn't care about whether he ever came home as long as his check arrived on time. He and his foster brothers would rob little old ladies coming out of grocery stores, their classmates for their lunch money, and if they were lucky, candy from the Stop and Go during the afternoon rush.

One day, E-Money lifted some candy from a store on Northside Drive and had almost made it out of the store before Zeus grabbed him by his collar, whipped him good, and put him to work in the store. He couldn't explain it, but that whipping felt good. Even with his fists balled up and his face puffed up, Ernest realized that no one had cared enough to whip him in a long time. From that day, Ernest followed Zeus around like a puppy. Zeus would send him on small errands, put a few dollars in his pocket. For the first time, he mattered to someone.

Ernest imagined Zeus was his daddy and not some convict he'd never met. He even stood a little taller when someone said he looked like Zeus, or better when they asked if that was his daddy. He might as well have been. Zeus had been more of a father than his own. After a while, Zeus told him to bring his foster brothers along. Zeus talked to them about life and the world. He gave them jobs, put money in their pockets, and the knowledge to survive the streets. When E-Money aged out of the system, Zeus set him up in an apartment building with his foster brothers on the Westside. Zeus outlined everything to E-Money, including his life as strait-laced businessman, Seth Newall. Zeus trusted him with his most guarded secret. That trust meant everything to E-Money.

~

Treasure stretched and rolled her shoulders. Prom and cotillion season were colliding, and while Treasure was ecstatic about the business, keeping who was wearing what to what and with what was exhausting. The girls and the mothers. Lord, maybe I should have been a tailor. Men are so much easier to dress. They wear what you tell them to wear, she thought to herself. She smiled, thinking about the one man who would care. Riley. Damn, that brother can hang a suit. A chill went up her spine. She shook her head. She needed to focus. Treasure and Riley planned to meet for dinner, she needed to prepare her daily deposit first. She was glad most of her clients paid by check or charge, so she never had much money in the store.

Treasure looked toward her door. She should have locked it when Dr. Paige and her girls left, but it was still light outside even if just barely. She finished the deposit and locked it in the safe. It had been a good day, she thought. She closed her eyes and said a prayer of thanks.

Owning a small business in Jackson or anywhere in the world for that matter was a huge financial proposition and risk. And to be a black woman at that! Everyone thought she was crazy. She always laughed about the fact her parents agreed on one thing since the divorce--not to open a retail store. After fielding offers from at least five Fortune 500 companies when she graduated with her master's from Wharton, she decided she wanted something of her own. And she wanted to be a success in Jackson. Treasure amassed a consistent and growing clientele in a few years. She always thanked God at the end of the day, deposit or no deposit.

Treasure's eyes were still closed in prayer when the door chime ring. When she opened her eyes, Ernest had closed the door. He stared menacingly at her for a moment before moving through the racks and displays. She opened her mouth to ask him to leave, but technically, startling her was his only offense.

"Good evening, may I help you? Treasure tried to stay as upbeat as she would with any other customer, but he was making her nervous even though he looked vaguely familiar. His face looked familiar but couldn't place where she would have met or seen him. The suit he was wearing didn't fit properly, and Treasure couldn't help herself but wonder who this man was. He looked like he was in his mid-twenties, but more than anything, he was out of place. The suit. The non-responsiveness. Treasure stopped short as he looked menacingly in her direction.

E-Money looked at Treasure. Zeus lost his damn mind for good reason. She was absolutely beautiful, and he could sense that she was afraid of him but trying not to show it. Interesting. Beautiful and smart. She should be afraid, E-Money thought. He said nothing but continued to walk the store.

When he didn't respond right away, Treasure wondered if the man didn't hear her. No, he heard me, Treasure thought. Her senses were on high alert. She thought about dialing Riley's number, but quickly dismissed the idea. Silently, she scolded herself for her fear. She rounded the counter and approached him. "Sir, we're technically closed for the night, but if you tell me what you're looking for, I can help you." She held her breath.

E-Money realized that she was going to make this easier. When she was within reach, he spun around fast. Treasure jumped back. "Ms. Jordan, you have a nice place here."

"Thank you," she responded. "Are you looking for something for your mother, wife, or girlfriend?"

E-Money shook his head slowly. "No, Ms. Jordan, though I can see why your place is successful. If I had any one of those, I'm sure they would love what you have here." He looked around the store in feigned contemplation. "Yes, I'm sure they would."

Treasure's head tilted in confusion. "Well, what can I do for you? I'm closed." Treasure chastised herself for not locking the door, for not calling Riley immediately at closing. She took a breath, and slowly backed away from him.

E-Money sneered "Ms. Jordan, Jackson's crime problem is getting worse, and I would hate for a beautiful woman like yourself to lose everything because they made the wrong decision."

"A wrong decision." Treasure repeated his words. The sinister finality in the phrase horrified her.

"Yes. This area has been experiencing a spike in crime, and a woman such as yourself should protect her investment." Ernest searched Treasure's face for fear but found none. He could tell that her earlier apprehensions were giving way to anger. Good, he thought. He loved it when the fools tried to bristle, because they usually came crawling when they had nothing left. He resumed walking around the store, touching the dresses, and sifting through the racks.

Treasure's hands were shaking, but her anger sat on top of her fear. "Who do you think you are? You need to leave. Now. Don't make me call the police."

E-Money took four long strides, and Treasure found herself face to face with the man. Treasure refused to move or shrink. He was so close that she could smell his cheap cologne.

"Ms. Jordan, consider this a friendly call. No need. We will have plenty of time to," he paused and looked at her hard, "discuss business. Have a good evening." With that, E-Money turned and walked to the door. As soon as he left, Treasure ran to the door and locked it, pulling down all the shades. She made a mental note to check with her security company and the other businesses first thing in the morning.

Treasure retrieved her purse from her office. Panic set in. Would the man be waiting in the parking lot? She peeked out the window. Her car was the only one in the lot. Everyone else had sense enough to go home at a decent hour, she mumbled to herself.

Treasure called Riley. He answered the call immediately, and when he asked her about her day, she hesitated. She decided not to tell him about her strange encounter at the store over the phone. At least, she wouldn't tell him yet. She needed to handle it by herself. She had been a businesswoman for a long time, and no man, including Riley Taylor, was going to handle her business. It was the same reason she hesitated to tell Grace. Treasure hoped she could handle this before she had to involve them.

~

Riley checked his bedroom clock. 5:45 p.m. He was picking up Treasure at 8:00 p.m. for dinner. They ate dinner together most nights out, but tonight, Riley, wanted to eat at home in peace and quiet. They usually spent a quarter of their time out, speaking to random people. Both of them understood that Jackson was too small, and even smaller for businesses like theirs, so they had to be accessible. But Riley didn't want to be accessible tonight at least not to the whole world.

He had plenty of time to dress and marinate the steaks. Riley smiled. He was glad Treasure was a woman who still appreciated a good steak. Most of the women Riley dated pretended to be vegetarian, or in the least, on whatever diet was the rage at the time. He caught a few sneaking a piece of meat or a piece of dessert. Riley shook his head. But not Treasure. She loved a good meal. Treasure just loved life period, which is what he loved most about her. As he dressed, Riley's eyes landed on the picture of his grandfather that he kept on his dresser. His granddaddy always told him, "Son, find you a woman who can enjoy herself with you and without you. A woman who has a life of her own is far less trouble than a woman whose only pastime is you." He never understood the old man's logic until now. Riley didn't do clingy, pouting women. He ended things the moment a woman staked a claim or acted entitled to his time. Marcellus, as usual, was right. Treasure was her own woman with a full life outside of him, which suited him fine.

Riley just wanted to be a part of it.

~

Treasure was still shaking when she arrived home whether it was from anger or fear, she couldn't tell. A few years ago, Treasure purchased a small home in Fondren close to the boutique. She could walk to work most days if the weather was nice, but the real draw was the artsy community. Every home either had brightly painted exteriors or doors that made coming home, on her roughest days, a little brighter. When she drove by the art museum with the Barack Obama sculpture outside, Treasure always smiled.

When they first put it up, she and some of her neighbors guessed about how long it would take for someone to tear it down, set it on fire, or worse. But no one had bothered it after a decade. Obama's face had become as much a part of the community fabric of Fondren as Brent's Drugs and Piggly Wiggly were.

Treasure's house had been originally painted a shade of pale pink with a white door, making it look like a dollhouse. She decided to keep the pink, but she wanted a brightly colored door like everyone else. She painted the front door a vibrant, deep shade of emerald green. Inside, Treasure selected jewel tones for each room. Taking her time to decorate, she enjoyed the process of finding the right piece for the right place. Her cousin, Sheri, was an interior designer in Houston, Texas, and when she visited, they would consult on the next piece and practically live in design and antique stores. Treasure was almost done decorating after six years. A few more touches and she would be satisfied.

From the outside, the house looked deceptively small, but inside it had three bedrooms, two of which were upstairs. Her bedroom was her sanctuary. Treasure decided to knock down the wall between the rooms to make one huge bedroom for herself. She created a large walk-in closet and have enough room for the antique four-poster king-sized bed she inherited from her great-grandmother, Blossom. The bed had been carved by her husband, Mack, as a wedding gift. Treasure always smiled when she thought about the love that went into carving the headstone. Legend has it that her great-grandfather, Mack Lee met Blossom at a church picnic and decided she would be his wife and began carving their marriage bed. He courted her for six months before they kissed for the first time, and he never left her side after that fateful moment.

Treasure always wanted that kind of love. The love Mack and Blossom had. The love her parents had once. The love she hoped she had with Riley.

Treasure undressed to take a quick shower. Riley would be picking her up soon, and she wasn't ready for their date, physically or emotionally. She thought about cancelling but doing so would set off alarm bells with Riley. Plus, she realized, she wanted to see him. Riley would calm her, make her laugh, and tempt her senses in a way that no one could. Treasure stepped between her double shower heads and let the water sooth her muscles. She thought about the young man and his threats. Too young to be a kingpin, he was clearly well-versed in intimidation but worked for someone else. Treasure closed her eyes. His face still too familiar. Treasure didn't forget faces. Names, maybe. But never faces. Treasure took a deep breath as she reached for her jasmine-scented body wash. She tried her best to scrub the stench of fear and rage from her skin. She didn't want to think about her encounter anymore tonight, but she decided to call Grace and her security company in the morning.

Treasure was getting angrier by the minute. No one was going to ruin the business she built through hard work and sacrifice. Treasure vigorously grabbed her robe and sat at her vanity. She purchased the vanity from an estate sale, because it reminded her of her mother's vanity and the happier times of her childhood. Treasure took a long hard look at herself. As she applied her makeup, her cell phone rang with her mother's ringtone, a screaming banshee. Treasure let the call go to voicemail. She needed all of her strength to survive this evening without telling Riley or calling Grace. She definitely didn't need her mother upset. Sorry, Mama, I'll call you tomorrow, she whispered as she applied her mascara.

She walked into her closet and pulled out a white jersey knit wrap dress. Treasure loved that the dress hugged her curves in all the right places and complemented her caramel skin tone perfectly. Riley loved surprising her, so she had to be ready for anything. Treasure realized that she didn't care either. She appreciated that Riley preferred supporting local restaurants in the area, fancy or "eclectic," which was their phrase for "hole in the wall."

Treasure reached for her floral print Ted Baker shoes from her closet shelf. The purple and green in the shoes gave her a pop of color. As she stepped into them, the young man's face popped into her head again. Treasure closed her eyes and took a deep breath. Treasure shook her head. She didn't want to think about that anymore. Riley would be at her door exactly at 8:00 p.m. Riley was never late. She didn't even check her watch anymore, because Riley was always on time down to the minute.

She was walking toward her bedroom door when her doorbell rang. Treasure smiled. He's early, she thought. The clock on her nightstand read 7:30. Treasure was still smiling as she descended the stairs, knowing Riley was on the other side of the door.

Treasure called out, "Coming!" when she was halfway down the staircase. She ran her hands down the sides of her dress, smoothing out the fabric. Just as she reached the bottom step, her front window shattered.

~

Riley eased his Jaguar around the corner onto Treasure's street a few moments before eight. In the distance, flashing blue lights lined the street, but he thought nothing of it. Police lights were always flashing in Jackson. Crime was up in certain areas of the city, but Fondren always seemed well patrolled. But he didn't want to think about whatever was happening at someone else's house. His mind was on Treasure. After a long day, her smile was the only thing he wanted to see tonight.

Until he was two houses from hers, Riley realized the flashing lights were at her house.

What the hell? Riley sped up and whipped the car into Treasure's driveway. Riley cut the engine and exited the car in one swift motion. Officers were outside taking fingerprints along the door and the window, and some were interviewing neighbors who had come outside. He quickly brushed past the officer who tried to stop him from going inside.

"Sir! Sir! You can't go inside the house," the young officer said to Riley back. Riley paid him no mind. Riley's heart was beating fast, and the five seconds it took him reach the door seemed like an eternity.

"Treasure!" Riley called into the house. As soon as he entered, Treasure ran toward him. She was visibly upset but in one piece, and Riley had never been so relieved in his life. She rushed into his arms, and after a moment, Riley pulled back a bit to see her face. He traced her cheek with his thumb and whispered, "Are you okay? What happened?" Defeat clouded her beautiful eyes.

Treasure couldn't say a word. She had been as strong as she could stand for as long as she could stand until Riley arrived. With Riley, she could be scared. Approaching her at her business was one thing, but this was her home.

Treasure trembled in his arms. Riley held her for a moment while surveying the scene. "Baby, what happened?" Riley was still holding a silent Treasure when Cedric Tims approached the pair. Riley immediately recognized him as one of the golfers he occasionally player with at Grove Park.

Detective Tims answered before Treasure could find the house. "Hey Riley, I'm the lead on the case, but right now, it looks like it's probably some kids throwing rocks in houses. Vandals hit several houses tonight. Some other houses down the street reported similar incidents."

Riley took a moment to look around the room. Shards of glass littered the floor at the window and doorway. The Crime Scene Unit was packing up and taking a few samples. "Kids?" Riley's eyebrow raised. "Kids didn't do this, Cedric. This isn't a pebble. Someone threw a damn boulder in her window." Riley's frustration was palatable, but he was trying not to raise his voice.

Cedric took his pen from behind his ear and flipped through his notes. "Riley, trust me, we're going to make this a priority. Let's see what forensics says in the morning." The last thing Cedric needed was for Riley

Taylor to ingratiate himself in this investigation, especially considering his relationship with Grace Harrington Dallas. "I'll call you when we have something."

Treasure turned toward the officer. "Detective Tims, thank you. Please thank the officers for me." She didn't want to face the mess of her living room, but she would need to deal with it sooner rather than later. Glass was still everywhere, and the window still needed boarding. "Do you have the number for the service that you mentioned?"

Cedric clicked his pen. "Already done. They should be here shortly. They're pretty fast, so as soon as they arrive, give them your homeowner's policy information, and they'll bill them directly."

"Treasure!" Riley, Treasure, and every officer on the scene, turned at the sound of Grace Harrington Dallas's voice.

Cedric took a deep breath. Well, here comes the cavalry, he thought, as Grace and Kenzo walked through the door. Dealing with victims was hard enough, but this one was going to be much harder with Grace Dallas looking over his shoulder.

"I'm okay, Grace. Decided to do a little redecorating." Riley held her hand and it was like an anchor, but he reluctantly let go when Grace grabbed her for a hug.

"I'll say," Grace laughed. Grace nodded at Detective Tims. "Detective." Grace had considered him for her task force on sex trafficking last year, but Robbery Homicide needed him more. Between the trafficking and the homicide rate, Grace questioned how Jackson was still standing.

"Ma'am." Cedric eased out of the now crowded room. It was going to be a long night, and he wanted to be prepared tomorrow. Undoubtedly, Grace would pull the report even if she was going to allow him to lead the investigation.

The clean-up crew arrived, and Riley gave them instructions while she and Grace sat at the table. Kenzo had disappeared into the kitchen and made coffee.

Treasure spoke first. "How did you hear this fast?" This was all happening so fast. Her head was spinning. "Police scanner, or did someone call?"

Grace took her coffee mug from Kenzo and took a sip. "Girl, you forgot who I am. Hell yes, I got a call. Just tell me what happened." Riley and Kenzo emerged from the kitchen each with a mug. Riley handed Treasure a cup of her favorite herbal tea.

Treasure took a deep breath. She might as well tell the story once. Grace's eyes narrowed, and Treasure could see the wheels turning in her head. As prim and proper as Grace was, she fiercely protected the people and causes she loved. Sandwiched between Riley on her left and Grace at her right, Treasure prepared herself for the coming interrogation. Kenzo placed his hand on Grace's back. It was comfort and support all at once but as natural as anything in the world between the two of them.

When Riley placed his hand on hers, she looked up at him. His hand warmed her. Her body always responded to his touch no matter how slight. Treasure recounted the day's events so fast that she barely took a breath. She didn't look at Riley's face; she couldn't. Instead, she focused on his thumb rubbing the back of her hand as he held it. The worry in his touch saddened her and racked her with guilt. Treasure told them everything, including the encounter with the thug who came into her boutique. She prepared herself for all of them to explode, but only Riley spoke. And when he did, Treasure's heart constricted from the pain in his voice.

"Why didn't you call me?" Riley's voice was low and filled with hurt. He didn't even try to hide it. Someone had threatened his woman, and she didn't think to call him.

Treasure faced Riley. "I've been in business a long time, Riley, and I planned to tell you tonight at dinner. It just seemed like a harmless threat. Even when others had problems, I never did." Grace probably wanted to ask the same thing. She looked at her friend, "And I planned to call you too, Grace, but I didn't think someone would throw a rock through my window too."

Grace touched her arm. "Did you tell Detective Tims about this mystery man coming into the boutique today?"

"I did." Treasure let out a weary breath. Riley remained silent, but his tension rolled through him to her. His jaw twitched.

"Ma'am?" One of the cleaning crew cleared his throat. "We've got you all cleaned up. We've boarded the window until you replace it in a couple of days. Hardwood floors made clean up easy. Glass sticks in carpet something awful." He handed her a clipboard.

Treasure had almost forgotten that they were there. She rose from the table to sign the release forms and provide her homeowner's information. Riley stood up when she did. When she completed the paperwork, she turned to her friends. "Listen, I'll be fine." Treasure was about to send everyone home, including Riley. She needed time also to process the day.

Grace stopped her, putting her hand up. "Either you're crazy or you think we are. Now, I can arrange for protection, or you can come home with us. But you're not staying here alone."

Treasure pleaded, "But, I'll..."

Riley cut her off and completed her sentence. "...be coming home with me." Treasure opened her mouth to object, but she decided against it. Quietly and firmly, Riley said, "Treasure, I need you to go pack a bag, so we can go home." Treasure nodded and went upstairs to pack.

Grace looked between Treasure and Riley and then at Kenzo. Grace braced herself for Treasure's comeback to Riley telling her what to do and what was that "go home." But when Treasure didn't say a word, Grace looked at her husband. Well, damn, would you look at that? Kenzo shrugged at his wife. He understood Riley. It was sheer hell knowing that someone was out there trying to harm your woman and you can't do anything about it.

Treasure ascended the stairs, her steps labored and weary. When she was out of earshot, Riley without even looking at Kenzo, said. "Ken, call Marcus."

"He's already on it, man. I texted him ten minutes ago." Marcus was a private investigator and computer whiz who was also a close friend. If anyone could find a connection between Treasure's mysterious visitor and this vandalism, Marcus could. And if he couldn't, only one other person could. But damn, if his wife would care for that option at all.

Treasure placed her dress on the hanger and returned it to her closet. She grabbed a pair of jeans and a t-shirt and changed into them. Still stunned from everything that happened, Treasure walked slowly into her en suite and packed her essentials in a small duffle bag. She grabbed a blue t-shirt dress, a few more tops, and another pair of jeans and stuffed them into the bag. Treasure's hands were shaking. She sat down at the vanity for a moment and took a few cleaning breaths. First, someone threatens her, and then, her house is vandalized. She wanted to believe that the two incidents were unrelated, but hopeful thinking wouldn't fix the problem. She experienced a lot of things in business, but this was new territory for her. No one was going to scare her though. No one.

~

Neither Treasure nor Riley said a word on the way to Riley's house. Home. Riley looked at Treasure out of the corner of his eye. He didn't realize how much he liked the sound of "home" until it came out of his mouth. Since the first night they'd made love, Riley and Treasure spent most of their time together on the weekends at his main house in Pocahontas. His house was becoming a home with her in it. Treasure gave it life, and now, his life with her was being threatened by someone or something he couldn't name.

Treasure closed her eyes and focused on the hum of the car's engine. The peaceful silence soothed her. No radio. No idle conversation. She let the silence lull her to sleep.

Treasure stirred as Riley pulled into his driveway. Her face turned slightly, and a ray of moonlight highlighted her sleeping face. Riley thought about his sister's words. "Admit that you are in love with her." He was in love with Treasure, and he could finally admit that he had been since that fateful weekend long ago. He pulled into the garage, waking Treasure in the process. Groggily, she said, "I'm so sorry, Riley," she said, "I didn't mean to fall asleep."

Riley, amused, said, "Shh, no need to apologize." Riley exited the car and came around to open Treasure's car door. Riley grabbed her bag out of the back seat and led her into the house. "Baby, go on and have a seat," Riley urged. Treasure silently went through the kitchen to the living room and sat on the sofa. She curled her legs beneath her and stared into space.

"Just give me a few minutes. I have dinner ready in a moment." Riley thought that if she were hungry, if he could feed her, then she would be okay.

Treasure said nothing. Riley didn't say anything further as he moved about the kitchen, and she listened with disinterest the sizzling of the steaks and the clanging of pots. Soon, the aroma of whatever Riley was cooking wafted toward her, and her stomach growled. As much as they ate out, Riley was an excellent cook, and clearly, her body was hungry even if she didn't want to exert the effort.

Riley plated the steaks and risotto and brought them to the kitchen table. This was not how he planned the night to go, but Riley wanted to make the best of it. "Ready to eat."

Treasure rose from the sofa. "I guess I am. Everything smells good." Treasure and Riley sat down to eat, but the silence between them was awkward. Except for a few niceties, the taps of their silverware against their plates was the only sound in the room. When both of them had finished, Riley picked up their plates and placed them in the sink. He held out his hand for Treasure and led her up the stairs to his bedroom.

Treasure changed into a nightshirt and climbed into bed. She was asleep as soon as her head hit the pillow. Riley leaned on the door frame at the threshold of the room, watching her sleep. He didn't understand the overwhelming sense of protectiveness washing over him. Until tonight, Riley never experience such helplessness and powerlessness. His job was to protect the woman he loved. Riley soon slipped downstairs to call Marcus.

He hoped Marcus had some answers and soon, because Riley would make their escapade on the Coast seem like a party.

CHAPTER 7

Treasure felt warm, especially her face. She blinked slowly and followed the beams of sunlight into the room. Her eyes landed on Riley, sitting in a chair a few feet from the bed.

"Riley?" Treasure asked, blinking to focus.

Riley had been watching Treasure sleep most of the night. After he spoke to Marcus, who was still investigating the matter, Riley fixed himself a drink and tried to process how he was feeling. Was he angry that someone was trying to intimidate Treasure and or hurt because he had to find out with everyone else? As she slept, Riley listened to her breathing, her light snoring. The only solace he took was that she could sleep after all that happened.

"Riley, why are you way over there?" Treasure sat up and reached out her hand. Something was wrong? Riley was staring at her, his jaw set so hard, it was nearly stone.

Riley rose from his chair and slowly walked to the bed. "Good morning, Treasure." His tone was flat and sounded tired.

Treasure's brow crinkled. Her name didn't sound right in his mouth. Her action, or inaction, upset him last night, but it was strange waking up in Riley's bed without him in it. "Why didn't you wake me? How long have you been up?"

Tension ripped through his body in waves. Riley didn't answer her questions, but asked her in response, "You needed to sleep. Ready for breakfast?" He moved to push a curl out of her face but dropped his hand by his side. He couldn't touch her right now.

Treasure nodded. She was starving, but she couldn't focus on that. Riley had never looked so weary, and knowing she had something to do with that strained look on his face pained her. She threw the covers back and began to swing her legs over the side of the bed.

Riley stepped back and motioned toward his bathroom. "I brought your bag upstairs. Take a shower and get dressed. I'll have breakfast ready."

Treasure weakly responded, "Okay" and she moved silently across the room.

Riley stood there for a moment before heading downstairs. He and Treasure would talk then, but Riley needed a few more moments alone. Treasure took a quick shower and threw on the t-shirt dress as she thought about what all she needed to do today. It was still early, before the shop opened, so she had plenty of time to eat and make a few phone calls.

Treasure smelled bacon as she descended the stairs. Riley was placing two plates of bacon, eggs, and grits on the table. He looked at her and smiled when she reached the table.

"Right on time," he said. His voice was flatter than Treasure expected it to be.

Riley had cooked bacon, cheese eggs, and biscuits, her favorite. He pulled her chair out for her as she sat but said nothing. Well, at least, he smiled, Treasure thought to herself.

Riley took the seat next to her. They ate in silence as they had the night before. Treasure and Riley glanced at each other throughout dinner but never at the same time. Treasure hated this tension between them and decided to break the silence first.

"Riley, thank you for everything last night."

Riley could barely swallow. After a moment, Riley turned to Treasure. "No need to thank me. I didn't do anything. Anything at all."

Treasure couldn't stand the pained look in Riley's eyes, but she didn't understand why he was taking this so personally. "Riley, I don't understand. Are you angry at me for some reason?"

"No, Treasure, I'm not angry at you." He paused. "But I am angry. How many times have I told you that it's not safe for you to be in at the store late?"

"Riley, it was my normal closing time, and I left right after that." She paused and then continued, "to get ready for our date." She swallowed the last bit of eggs on her plate and put her fork down.

As soon as Treasure finished, Riley picked up her plate. He walked into the kitchen. Dishes clanged against tile and steel. The sound was so loud that Treasure expected to find broken dishes in the sink. Riley stood there for a moment and took a deep breath. Man, get yourself together. This is your fault, not hers.

Treasure was fuming. Is this man making this about him? Someone tries to muscle me and throw a rock in my window, and he's mad with me. She sat back in the chair and crossed her arms in front of her chest. He's got some nerve trying me this morning.

When Riley returned to the table, Treasure was furious or at least getting there. Her nostrils flared. Riley took a deep breath. He'd approached this conversation the wrong way. He walked past Treasure, grabbed a throw from the back of the sofa, and put it under his left arm. "Come take a walk with me. I want to show you something."

Treasure had half a mind not to go anywhere with Riley. She had too much to think about and too much to do. Worrying about his fragile ego was not on her agenda. But when Riley extended his hand, she couldn't resist his tired eyes and took it. His proposition intrigued her, but she still planned to set him straight--and soon.

Riley guessed that they both needed the fresh air. And he could tell his performance in the kitchen irritated Treasure. Well, irritation cuts both ways, sweetheart. He spent half the night imagining various ways to have this conversation, and this was not on the list. Riley needed a do-over.

She and Riley walked a good distance from the house, in silence, until Riley reached his favorite spot on the grounds--a towering oak tree surrounded by a field of clovers and honeysuckles. He used to sit under this tree as a child while his grandfather worked in the yard, climbed this tree, and when he was older, came here, to this tree, to talk to the old man.

Riley let go of Treasure's hand and caressed the tree's bark like an old friend. Very few people were privy to sensitive Riley, loving Riley. He seemed more himself out here than in Jackson, at work. Treasure looked at Riley and couldn't deny it to herself any longer. She loved Riley Taylor, and she was so far gone that, at this point, she didn't care that he didn't love her back. Treasure wanted to enjoy Riley for as long as she could, and then, lick her wounds and heal herself when it was over. Just like the last time.

Riley placed his hand on the tree trunk. "My grandfather used to bring me out here when he worked in the yard, or when I was getting on my grandmother's nerves. He'd throw a blanket down, and I'd sit. Sometimes, we'd watch the day go by and talk. Other times, I come out here alone. But it was always here. Here, I was safe."

"It's a beautiful tree, Riley," Treasure whispered as she touched his arm. She was unsure of what to say to him and followed his lead.

Riley picked up a fallen branch and threw it across the field. They watched as the branch wobbled through the air for a few seconds until it landed. He then unfolded the blanket and laid it down at the base of the tree and motioned for Treasure to sit. She sat down and waited. Riley let out a deep breath and told Treasure about his childhood under the tree. He felt lighter as he told her stories about hanging out with his grandfather and how many times, his grandmother threatened both of their lives for one thing or another. He and Treasure needed to laugh together. The night before had been so intense and was still unresolved, but the levity helped ease the tension between them and take their minds away from the nastiness of thugs and broken windows. Soon, Treasure could see Riley hanging upside down from the branches, his grandmother screaming for him to get down, and him, making circles in the dirt with sticks like he was doing now. Then, she saw a vision of Riley with a little boy playing in this very spot. She could see it in her mind as if it were as real as the man standing before her.

And just as quickly, Treasure thought her heart stopped.

Riley's voice dropped an octave, far different from the sounds of laughter as he walked her through his memories. He turned to look at the stretch of land before him he loved so much. Riley couldn't look at her while he was trying to say what he needed to say. He was still building up his nerve. He took a deep breath and said, "Treasure, I didn't know what to think when I saw the police at your house. The thought that something had happened to you nearly killed me."

Treasure said nothing. She expected him to be angry that she didn't call him from the store, but this was something else entirely. He was more hurt than she realized, and she hated that she had been the cause of whatever pain he was feeling.

"Only once before..." He stopped for a moment. "My entire world stopped when I got the call about my grandfather's heart attack. I didn't like it then, and I don't like it now."

Treasure got up and walked toward him. Riley still had his back to her, so she walked beside him and touched his arm. "I don't understand, Riley. What is it that you don't like?" Treasure paused. His looked straight ahead. "I was a little shaken up maybe, but I'm fine. Really, I am." Treasure frowned. Riley's reaction confused her.

"But I'm not." Treasure's hand felt like a branding iron against his skin. Treasure didn't understand what he was saying, or what he was trying to say. He finally turned to face her. Her brow furrowed, and still, Riley thought she was the most beautiful woman in the world. His heart thumped in his chest. Riley cupped her face was both hands. "You. Are. Mine." He placed his forehead on hers. "Treasure, my Treasure," he whispered. "Don't you know how much I love you?"

Pure desire and love shone in Riley's eyes. Words she never thought Riley would say. Treasure thought she was hearing things, or at least, was still dreaming.

The moment she imagined was happening, and all she could do was stare at him. Riley lifted her head to look in her eyes and say it plainly. "I love you, Treasure. You are mine. Mine to protect. If anything had happened last night..." His voice trailed off.

Tears sprang to her eyes. She opened her mouth to tell Riley that she loved him too, but she never got the chance. Riley grabbed the back of her neck, pulling her to him, and took her mouth so fast that she could barely catch her breath. This kiss felt different from any other kiss between them. This was a kiss of possession. Riley was exploring every inch of her mouth with his tongue, and Treasure's core contracted to its rhythm. He was feverish and harder than he had ever been in his life. Riley pressed his body flush to hers, his need, his hunger for Treasure overtaking him.

She gasped when her back came flush against the tree. Riley's tongue was drawing circles on her neck and sucking that sensitive spot at her jugular. Treasure moaned as Riley lifted her dress and found the damp slip of material of her panties.

Riley repeatedly whispered against her heated skin, "Mine."

Treasure hissed, "Yours," as Riley rubbed the sensitive flesh between her legs. The bark pressed at her back was rough, but the sensations of pleasure and pain were fusing in her mind. Riley loved her and that was all that mattered.

Riley lifted her dress and found the thin material of her panties dampened with her arousal. He inhaled, Treasure's scent now mingling with the honeysuckles nearby. Treasure gasped when Riley rubbed the sensitive bundle of nerves, and her legs opened on their own to give Riley more access to her womanhood. Treasure's legs trembled when Riley's fingers slid inside and massaged her.

"My Treasure," Riley said just before he took her mouth again. She felt his hardness against her. She reached to touch him but became frustrated by the barrier his jeans created. Treasure groaned in frustration as she yanked his shirt up, so she could at least touch his skin. Riley thought his heart stopped the moment Treasure's hands touched his skin. Her hands were on his chest, his back. She was branding him. Riley was hers as much as she was his.

Her arousal perfumed the air, and Riley dropped to his knees and pulled her panties down. Treasure blindly stepped out of them. He slipped her panties in his pocket and bit the inside of her thigh before burrowing his head between her legs. Treasure wantonly threw her leg across Riley's shoulder.

"Riley…" she whimpered.

Such nectar had never rested on his tongue. Treasure's leg trembled; her orgasm imminent. Riley didn't want her to come this way. He wanted to be inside her when she came for him.

When he stopped, Treasure whimpered. Riley stood up and kissed her. She could taste herself on his lips. "So sweet," Riley murmured, licking his lips. Treasure closed her eyes. Before Riley, she didn't think it was possible to nearly orgasm just from the sound of a man's voice.

"Baby, I need you," Riley whispered, "and I don't think I can wait."

Treasure said nothing. She pulled her dress off and tossed it to the side. Treasure's breasts bounced with every ragged breath and threatened to spill out of her bra. The breeze did little to cool her skin. If Riley didn't make love to her soon, she thought she would scream. She didn't think she could wait either. And had she not been so aroused, Treasure would have laughed at the sight of herself braced against an oak tree on Riley's property.

As much as he wanted her, Riley needed to summon some control. He wanted to savor this moment. His Treasure. Leading her to the blanket, Riley took deep cleansing breaths. As she sat, Riley took off his shirt and jeans. He then eased Treasure on her back, nestling himself between her legs. Treasure shivered under his touch, as Riley traced her collarbone with feather light kisses. He unhooked the front clasp of her bra with ease, and the hardened tips of her breasts were full and begging to be pleasured. Treasure moaned as he pulled and rolled her nipples between his fingers. Both of them were feverish with desire, as Riley left a trail of kisses along Treasure's neck. Riley lowered his head and laved her breasts with his tongue before pulling a sensitive nipple into his mouth. Treasure's back arched as Riley feasted on Treasure's breasts. He moved lower, placing kisses on her stomach, his tongue darting in and out of her belly button. He wanted to kiss every inch of skin. Treasure cried out in pleasure when Riley bit the inside of her thigh and then soothed it with a lick against her skin. She grabbed her breasts and squeezed them, pretending that her hands were his.

She cried out in need. Riley's mouth and hands were scorching her skin, but she forced herself to pause things. "Riley," she whispered breathlessly. "I need to tell you something."

Riley looked up at her, concern flashing across his beautiful face. "What, baby, am I hurting you? Do you want to go back to the house?"

"No, I just needed to tell you that I love you too." Treasure had never told a man she loved him. Hell, she thought, she never loved a man like she loved Riley. She was trusting him with everything she had--her heart.

Riley's heart soared in his chest. He kissed her hard in response as he slid over her body and entered her on a hard thrust. Treasure gasped and threw her arms around his back and held on. Riley was filling her completely, leaving no part of her untouched. Her nails dug into his back, as he thrust harder and deeper inside her. Treasure was gripping his shaft so tightly that Riley couldn't stop even if he wanted to. The friction of their bodies, her soft skin against his, sent electric shockwaves to his heart.

Riley lifted himself up so he could look at her. Her eyes slowly opened, and they stared at each other as they made love. No words between them, only the music of their lovemaking mingled with the sounds of nature around them.

He tugged on Treasure's earlobe with his teeth and whispered in her ear. "Come for me, baby."

Treasure exploded at his command. "Riley!" Treasure screamed, as he cradled her body.

The pulses of her womanhood triggered the most powerful orgasm Riley had ever experienced in his life. He let out a primal yell with a voice he didn't recognize. She was draining him completely, but when Treasure's back arched as she exploded again, Riley thought he would go blind from the pleasure. He closed his eyes and let the sensations wash over him. As Treasure's core pulsated around his manhood, Riley finally understood what it meant to be loved by a woman so completely and to love her in return.

CHAPTER 8

Riley and Kenzo met in the conference room of their office suite to look over the plans for their next project. A scale model of the intersection of Highway 18 and Highway 80 to Ellis Avenue lay before them. Riley's plan was to raze the abandoned properties first, particularly near operational businesses, which would make the existing real estate look more profitable as they brought in more retail and office spaces.

"Are you still planning on starting the program for small businesses in conjunction with this project," Kenzo asked.

"Definitely," Riley said. "The small business incubator will go in the old Saks building for now. That building just needs a few upgrades. Folks at the University think it will be good space for students in the entrepreneurship program. Plus, we can apply for additional funding with an educational partnership."

Kenzo made a few more notes in the margins of project paperwork in front of him. "Looks good. This is a major project for us, and I think the area is ripe for development. When are you bringing the investors in?"

"Next week. I've been reeling them in for a few months, and they loved the idea, especially now that the Metro Center has a new owner. The area is going to be a hotspot pretty soon. Briana is analyzing the real estate angle as well. I imagine that real estate values will double, maybe triple, if we develop it right."

Kenzo nodded his head. "Good. I like her. She's a hard worker. She beat me into the office all this week. Let's commit to making sure that the increased home values, if that happens, doesn't mean that we lose the character of area"

Riley and Kenzo decided to expand their business to include residential holdings, but neither of them wanted to leave commercial. They hired Chrishaana Yelddir, a seasoned real estate agent, to build that area of the business in tandem with their commercial projects.

Riley didn't respond, as he gathered his copies of the reports and slid them into his briefcase. "Anything else?"

"Not that I can think of at the moment," Kenzo said, also gathering his things into his briefcase as well.

Both men stood and began walking to the door. Kenzo asked, "How's Treasure?"

"She seems fine. I'm the nervous wreck. I finally understand why you needed to go to the Coast for Grace. Knowing someone is out there plotting on your woman over God knows what is enough to make a man crazy."

"Your woman?" Kenzo smirked at Riley. "That sounds serious."

Kenzo enjoyed this turnaround. Riley gave Kenzo much grief before he accepted being in love with Grace. Riley just decided to come clean. "Yeah, it's serious as hell. How did you do this twice?"

Kenzo placed his hand on Riley's shoulder. "Well, with Noelle, I was just young and stupid, and, unfortunately, she died before I could make it right. With Grace, I could finally be man enough to admit to myself when I'd found the right woman."

Riley nodded. "I hear you, Ken. I'm there."

Kenzo and Riley walked toward Riley's office, continuing their conversation. Riley's assistant, Carolyn, handed him his messages.

Kenzo laughed. "Because, honestly, man, I don't want to be there if you mess up again. My wife is a pretty good shot, and after that night at Treasure's, she's been worried and going to the gun range. By the way, I stopped by the boutique the other day. Nice place."

Riley rolled his eyes and took a deep breath. "Good to know. The security cameras are being installed at the store today, so I'm headed over there. The system at the house won't be upgraded until tomorrow. She wouldn't hire a bodyguard for the store, so I had Marcus arrange for surveillance. But he still hasn't found any leads."

Kenzo frowned. "That's unusual for Marcus. I'm sure he'll have something soon. Treasure still staying at your place."

Riley responded quickly. "Hell, yes. I didn't want her staying at her place until we, at least, got the security upgraded."

Kenzo laughed. "Yea, man. Loving a woman can be the best of times and the worst of times. But, how is that going? You...living with a woman? I never thought I'd see the day."

Riley could only shrug. "I didn't imagine it either, but man..."

"What?" Kenzo's eyebrow raised.

"Man, it's just..." Riley paused as if he was looking for the right word. "Different. But good."

Riley didn't want to admit to Kenzo just how good. He loved having Treasure in his bed every night and every morning when he woke up. Since he decided to take Treasure out of Jackson, they spent most of the week in Pocahontas. He loved the drive home. He and Treasure talked about their respective days and everything else going on in the world. Before, they ate out most the time, but Riley was enjoying eating at home. They either cooked together or took turns. And Treasure could definitely cook.

He walked over to his coat rack and retrieved his jacket. He was picking up Treasure from the boutique in about twenty minutes.

Kenzo smirked as he leaned against the door frame. He said nothing.

Riley grabbed his keys. "I'm out. Treasure's closes in about thirty minutes."

Kenzo wanted to needle Riley just a little longer and blocked the door. "Cool. One more thing, does she have any idea that she's not going back to her house?"

Riley didn't like the smug look on Kenzo's face, but he answered as honestly as he could. He turned to his friend. "No, she doesn't."

~

Treasure was setting up a new clothing display for Berko Bongani Collection on the far wall when the security technician emerged from the back of the store with his clipboard in his hand. Berko Bongani, a Jackson-based designer, recently launched his first collection of luxury athleisure wear for men and women. Treasure liked the fact that he used quality, luxurious fabrics and the garments were well made. She zipped up the jacket on the mannequin and ran her hand over the velvet to smooth it out. The cute squirrel and nut design in the Berko Bongani logo reminded her of Kimora's Baby Phat cat.

The security tech cleared his throat, snapping her attention back to this strange reality. "Ma'am, we're finished with the last few cameras in the back."

Treasure sighed and walked over to the security tech. This security upgrade was costing a small fortune, but it was easier than fighting with Riley and Grace about it. She scheduled the appointment near closing since there would be less foot traffic in the late afternoon. She dealt with the few walk-in shoppers easily as the technician installed the equipment. For the most part, he stayed out of the way, and Treasure pretended everything was normal.

Grace and Riley tried to insist that she hire a bodyguard, but Treasure drew the line at that. Having some man standing at the door of her boutique reminded her too much of the stores on Fifth Avenue in New York. Treasure always felt criminalized the moment she walked in the door, and she was adamant that her store would be comfortable and treat everyone like human beings. Treasure made it clear to Riley and Grace that she was not going to let anyone change her life or routine.

Plus, there was no need to pay a bodyguard. Except for the limited time she spent at the store, Riley never let her out of his sight. But she had her suspicions that he or someone was always hovering in the parking lot to make sure that nothing happened while she was there. All of them--Grace, Riley, Kenzo and Marcus--popped in and out all week. She laughed to herself. At least she convinced Kenzo to buy Grace the Gucci pumps she wanted. Treasure planned to gift them to her on her birthday, but she could always give her the matching purse. Kenzo never looked at the receipt, and she wished she could be there when he opened his credit card statement.

She and Riley were staying at his house since last weekend. A chill ran up her spine. Their confessions of love ignited a weekend of blissful lovemaking that continued all week. Even though Riley insisted that she stay with him, especially after everything that happened, Treasure didn't want to crowd him. She told him that she would stay only until she could sign off on the repairs at her house and all the security cameras installed at her home and the store. Riley didn't argue with her, which was surprising. He just nodded his head in agreement. She never wanted him to think of her as clingy or feel crowded.

But now, the cameras seemed to be too much, and Treasure really doubted that she would need them at all. Plus, they increased her anxiety. Treasure began to regret this as a panic-driven purchase that was going to eat into her yearly profits. It had been a week since the incident at the boutique and her house, and nothing. Treasure inwardly groaned. The complex already had security, and Grace called in a few strings to have the police patrol the area even more than usual. Riley insisted on taking her to work and picking her up every evening to make sure that she left on time.

Demonstrating the camera placement, he said, "Cameras at both entrances means you can see every angle in the parking lot, front and back." He walked toward her counter and continued, "We've also installed two monitors--one at the counter and the other in your office."

Treasure nodded her head and listened to how to work this new system, and she downloaded the app that would let her access the system remotely. She felt violated all over again. She thanked the technician and signed her purchase agreement. The technician handed her an envelope with her documents just as Riley walked in the door.

Riley waited for Treasure to finish and looked around the store. An emerald green and silver gown caught his eye. He walked over to inspect the dress further, finding the intricate beading of crystals and sequins fascinating. He wondered how much a dress like that cost. Riley realized the silver accents were tiny crystals. The dress was quite striking, fascinating really. He looked at the price tag and nearly bit his tongue.

"A Max Andean original," Treasure said as she walked up beside him. Riley's sticker shock thoroughly amused her.

"But $12,000! For a dress!" Riley was incredulous. No dress should cost that much ever. Most families didn't spend that much on food for a year.

Treasure stifled a laugh and rolled her eyes. "Yes, Riley. For a gown. If this were a piece of art, would $12,000 be too much?"

"But..."

"Not art? Look at the gown, Riley. Look at that hand sown beading." She picked up the gown's hem and invited him to hold it. "Feel the weight of the fabric. The silk and beading. All hand sown. And the woman who wears it is art wearing art." She snapped her fingers with a flourish. "Priceless."

"Do you really think someone in Jackson can buy a $12,000 dress?" If folks in Jackson were paying this much for a dress, he and Kenzo were in the wrong business.

"Maybe. But I have clients all over, Riley. A Max Andean will sell." Treasure surprised herself. Before, she would have bristled at his questions, but now, she could educate him about her business without being defensive.

Treasure was straightening the gown when Riley pulled her to him. "Hey, I missed you today," he said before kissing her. He sucked her bottom lip and brought her flush against his body. "Ready to go?"

Treasure's heart thumped loudly in her chest. Surely, Riley could hear it. She forced herself to pull away from Riley's embrace after feeling his hardness against her middle. "Let me get my bag, and then we can go home."

Riley and Treasure looked at each other and just stared. Treasure had said "home," not "your house," as she had most of the week. Treasure realized what she said immediately and noticed how easily the word slipped from her lips. As she rushed to get her purse, she thought about how at home Riley's became in a short amount of time and chastised herself for getting too comfortable. He's probably scared to death, Treasure thought, thinking I'm trying to overstay my welcome. She decided that she would tell Riley she was going back to her house Monday morning. Everything would be finished by then.

Home. Until that moment, Riley didn't realize just how good that sounded coming from her beautiful lips. Suddenly, it dawned on him that, with Treasure, he now had a home. He didn't even miss his condo or anything in it. What he missed now, wherever he was, was Treasure. She added love and a light to his life he didn't realize he missed having. Treasure brightened every space she entered, every corner he touched in his home and in his heart.

"I'm ready." Treasure searched Riley's face to see if he seemed irritated by her slip. She breathed a sigh of relief when he kissed her temple and took her bag from her.

Riley took Treasure's hand. He was ready to take his woman home.

~

E-Money parked his car in the lot directly across from Treasure's store. He parked close enough to see what was happening, but he still needed binoculars for detail. Zeus taught him a long time ago that details mattered. He didn't recognize the man with her, but it was clear that Treasure Jordan already had a man.

What the hell was Zeus doing? This woman was already pulling attention and manpower away from their real operations in the city, and she didn't even want Zeus. "Damn," he mumbled under his breath. Zeus wanted a woman who didn't look like she was going to come willingly. The way she looked at this dude meant Zeus had his work cut out for him. According to E-Money's sources, Treasure never returned home. He figured she stayed with this dude. Interesting, he thought. Would Zeus still want her then?

He checked his watch. It was still light outside, so he decided not to follow them. He didn't want to be seen, and he figured that he would have plenty of opportunities later seeing how lovey-dovey they were. He needed to check in with his boys and then Zeus first anyway.

His phone rang, and Zeus's name popped up on the screen.

"What's up, Zeus?" E-Money held his breath. Zeus had been on edge since he ordered this little operation. And obsessed, E-Money thought to himself.

"Where are you?" Zeus snapped.

Here we go, E-Money thought. He exhaled. "I'm in the parking lot at Treasure's. Watching. The boys..."

Zeus cut him off. "Meet me at the spot in an hour," Zeus ordered before hanging up.

E-Money took a deep breath. There was never a need for niceties with Zeus. When the man called you, you went, so what was there to talk about?

E-Money sat for a few more minutes and watched the couple drive away. At least his little visit worked. She's scared. He chuckled to himself at her new security upgrades. Probably did her house too, he thought. Shaking his head as he turned the ignition, he thought, Folks would never learn. No security system could keep anyone out when they wanted to get to you. She was an easy target, almost too easy, and he needed to find a way to ramp this up so it could be over and done quickly. Or Zeus was going to let this woman destroy them all.

~

Harp observed E-Money watching Treasure and Riley leave the parking lot with little interest. He never questioned Shotgun when she sent him on this little assignment, but as soon as he saw Riley's car, he understood. She had a soft spot for Riley and Kenzo. He shook his head. The last time they got involved with those two led to the murder of a dirty cop and breaking up an international sex trafficking ring. Wonder what they were going to get mixed up in this time? He picked up his phone and dialed. "You were right. Someone's watching them. But he didn't follow them home. I got the plate. Gotta go. Going to see where he's going." Harp followed E-Money's car out of the parking lot, careful to stay two cars behind him.

E-Money turned into the parking lot at the hospital on State Street and drove to the top level of the garage. Hardly anyone parked on the uncovered level, which suited E-money just fine. He parked next to an older model black Mercedes and switched cars. He text one of his boys to pick up his dummy car.

Harp didn't follow E-Money into the parking lot but parked at the curve of the entrance as if he was waiting for someone. He kept his eyes glued on the parking lot exit. Luckily, it was the only one. He chuckled to himself. Good plan, Youngblood, just bad execution. Harp wished one day he could hold a seminar to teach these young thugs how to be better criminals. You never switch cars in a parking lot that only has one entrance. He sighed.

E-Money's black Mercedes pulled to the exit of the lot and prepared to turn right on State Street. Harp pulled behind him and memorized the license plate. This was E-Money's primary car. It was too clean and not tricked out like most young thugs do, making it classy enough to be invisible even in its visibility. Harp watched him negotiate traffic like a pro. Someone trained you well, Harp mumbled.

E-Money navigated the streets well, turning on Fortification and then to I-55, going North. Harp exhaled. Trailing someone on the interstate was always easier. since drivers focused more on the destination than who was behind him like in stop-and-go traffic. Harp slowed as the car he was following turned on Lakeland Drive and quickly turned into the Smith-Wills Stadium parking lot. E-Money drove to the upper right corner of the lot and parked in one of the smaller bars. To avoid suspicion, Harp parked two cars behind him but at an angle to maintain his line of vision.

E-Money breathed a sigh of relief when he realized that he beat Zeus there. He always tried to be the one waiting rather than the other way around. Zeus was not a man to be kept waiting, and this situation was already sensitive. E-Money stepped out of the car and lit a cigarette. The sunset cast a purple and golden haze over the sky, and E-Money leaned against his car. He debated about whether he should go inside and wait but decided against it. He tossed the cigarette when Zeus's black Mercedes G-Class 550 truck approached.

Zeus cut the engine and exited his car. He nodded at E-Money and motioned for him to follow him into the bar. Neither man said a word as they walked into the building. He and Zeus were regulars and had plenty of people who lifted their glasses as they walked through. Zeus spoke to a few people as he walked to a table in the back, and E-Money walked to their waiting table. One of the waitresses brought two bourbons in highball glasses as soon as Zeus sat down.

"Bourbon, Mr. Newall." The waitress smiled politely at Zeus as she put the drinks down. Will there be anything else. Appetizer? She turned to E-Money and flashed him a smile.

Zeus smiled at her flirtation with E-Money. E-Money would never take such obvious bait. He focused too much on his money to get caught up in some random woman.

E-Money barely registered the waitress's tone. His eyes roamed the crowd, looking past her, "Nah, I'm good. Thanks."

"Alright then. Just let me know if there's anything you need." She emphasized "anything" while looking at E-Money as he ignored her. She turned around slowly and walked away, trying to casually turn her head to see if E-Money was looking. He wasn't.

Zeus took a sip of his bourbon and looked around, smiling at a few people. No one in the place figured that one of Jackson's most respected businessmen was sitting with the man running his criminal activities.

E-Money looked like just another young man he was mentoring toward a lifetime of success, a possible business partner even. Without looking at E-Money, his voice lowered to a whisper, "Where are we?"

E-Money told Zeus about the security cameras and the man he saw with Treasure. He watched Zeus carefully. Zeus calm expression hid clenched teeth. As he smiled at someone who called his name, Zeus hissed, "It's that damn Riley Taylor."

Vexed, E-Money asked, "Boss, what's the deal? Are you sure you want to pursue this woman like this? I mean, I can get you a girl..."

Zeus's head snapped toward E-Money. He hissed, "Boy, do I look like I want a girl? I need a woman. And that woman is Treasure Jordan." He downed the rest of his glass and grabbed the glass in front of E-Money. E-Money never drank. "But it looks like being nice won't get this done."

E-Money couldn't believe that Zeus was going to break every rule he ever taught him and the crew. And over a woman. I mean, she was fine and all, but to risk everything? "So, what do you want to do?"

Zeus swirled the bourbon in the glass as he thought about things. He could afford to be irrational sometimes; he had to have that woman. "Listen, carefully. You say she has cameras at the store. She'll probably have them installed at her house as well. Have G.K. see if he can tap into her system but pull back otherwise." He paused, giving E-Money a hard look and said, "until I give the word."

"Sure, boss."

~

Harp sat at the opposite end of the bar, watching the exchange between the two men. He couldn't tell what they were saying, and he really didn't care. It was the who that mattered, and he was far enough away that he could openly stare without any notice. Harp brought the beer bottle to his lips as the young man walked past him on his way out and didn't make eye contact. Harp shook his head. This is going to get ugly as hell, he thought. Harp motioned to the bartender to pay his tab and left a $20 bill on the bar.

As he walked to his car, he shook his head in disbelief. This had the potential to be huge, and his boss liked news like this to be delivered in person.

Sometimes, Harp really hated his job.

CHAPTER 9

The drive home was unusually polite.

Riley noticed Treasure's unusual silence on the way home, but he decided not to push her. Treasure kicked off her shoes and stretched her legs out on the sofa. Her feet were killing her, but the throbbing of her feet gave her something else to think about other than her present conundrum. Riley poured her a glass of wine and placed it on the end table before going to the kitchen to grab himself a beer. She swirled the wine in her glass before taking the first sip. She let the smooth liquid coat her insides while she thought about how she was going to tell Riley that she was going to start staying at her house in a couple of days.

When Riley returned with his beer, Treasure was rubbing her aching feet. He joined her on the sofa and placed his beer on the coffee table. He pulled Treasure's feet into his lap. "Here, let me do this. Just relax." He gently massaged her feet. At one time, Riley never thought he would even want normal, but now, Riley relished normal and loved every moment of it.

Treasure purred as Riley eased the tension in her feet, and she fought her eyelids to stay open. The newscaster's voice became background noise as Riley's warm hands casually kneaded her flesh and traced circles on her instep.

Between his ministrations and the wine, Treasure's entire body relaxed. She took a deep breath and closed her eyes. *You don't play fair, Lord.*

She forced herself to take a long look at Riley while he focused on the sports highlights. His chiseled jawline was perfect with just a hint of stubble. His suit coat lay next to him on the back of the sofa. He loosened his tie, but his shirt was just as crisp as he moment he put it on. Damn, he was sexy, and all he was doing was watching the news.

Treasure gripped the wine glass with both hands as her heart constricted. Tears spring to her eyes, but she dabbed them away quickly. She loved Riley more than she ever imagined she would ever love another person. The problem was that she truly believed Riley's declaration of love. She did. But if he ever stopped loving her, she doubted she would ever recover and become a bitter shell like her mother. She thought she could handle it until it was "over." She prepared herself for "over." But when he told her he loved her, she realized that it was forever that she couldn't handle.

The one thing she knew for sure was that the promise of forever and the reality of over would kill her.

Riley hoped that the massage would ease the tension between them as well. He turned to her and smiled, "Better?"

Lazily, Treasure responded, "Indeed."

"Hungry?" His eyes searched her face. Perhaps the wine and a little quiet had calmed Treasure's nerves a bit, he hoped. Riley had something on his mind as well, and he wanted to eat before he discussed it with her.

Treasure's stomach growled. She forgot to stop and eat lunch today, especially with the security team there. "I am. Listen, why not let me cook for once? We've either had takeout or you cooked. I'm a pretty decent cook. Any requests?" Treasure needed to think and that meant movement. She processed things better if she was busy. It was either cook or clean. And cooking would do that well enough. Maybe bake something. Perhaps, a pound cake would add a little sweetness to the conversation she dreaded having.

Riley smiled. "Chef's choice, but I did take out pork chops or salmon for dinner before we left this morning."

"Chops sound good," Treasure said, rising from the sofa. Yeah, he was making this really difficult without trying.

Treasure entered the kitchen and took a deep breath. Riley's kitchen looked like a country kitchen. His grandmother's cast iron pots hung from a rack in the ceiling and decorative copper baking pans mounted on a side wall looked more like art than kitchen tools. A baker's kitchen. Even though Riley upgraded the appliances, everything still had a vintage feel to it. She could almost see Riley in this kitchen cooking with his grandmother or sitting at the table waiting for her to bring him a warm slice of cake and glass of milk.

Treasure marveled at how easily she moved about Riley's kitchen in such a short amount of time. Effortlessly, she navigated the kitchen. She pulled out four sticks of butter and set them on the counter to soften. Treasure grabbed a large bowl from the cabinet and pulled a cake pan from the wall. She chose a basic Bundt pan and placed it on the counter.

She combined a few herbs, garlic, olive oil, thyme, parsley, salt, and pepper to create a marinade, and as she did so, she thought about how she would tell Riley that she was going to return to her house next week. Well, perhaps, she could stay until the weekend, she thought. That gave them a couple of days left to enjoy the solitude of his home. She was sure Riley wanted to get back to his condo in Jackson, the restaurants, the conveniences, and with the added security, there was no need to be afraid anymore. That's what this was all about, right?

She dipped the chops and laid them on the cutting board. Yeah, this was just because of the incident at the store and her house. Warranted, maybe, but definitely unplanned. No one would accuse Riley of wanting a serious relationship and settling down. His declarations of love, though, had to mean something, but she refused to take it to mean that he wanted a live-in girlfriend, or worse, think that she was going to use this time to get him to propose marriage. Treasure reached up to get the skillet from the rack. She placed it on the stove and poured in a bit more olive oil. She turned on the oven and preheated it for the cake. No, she definitely didn't want him to think that, and she didn't want to even think about it herself.

While the chops were marinating, Treasure pulled out the flour, sugar, eggs, and vanilla. She took a paper towel and greased and floured the pan. She smiled. Mama Blossom would be so proud. And then it hit her. Would Riley think this too domestic? Did she want him to think that? Treasure shook her head. I'm a mess! She couldn't think about that now. The butter had softened. By the time she had measured the sugar, the chops were ready for the skillet. She boiled water for the rice. She seared the chops on each side until the sides were golden. Adding a bit more oil, she reduced the heat and let the meat cook. Treasure stood over the stove for a few moments, lost in her thoughts about how they got to this place. Lord, how am I in Riley's kitchen with chops on the stove, and butter on the counter? You got to help me, Jesus.

Laughing to herself, she flipped the chops over and eased over to the mixer and finished the cake batter. She poured the batter in the pan and slid it into the oven. She flipped the pork chops again and poured the rice in the boiling water.

Treasure had twenty minutes before everything was ready, so she decided to make a salad. As she was pulling the salad ingredients out of the refrigerator, Riley strolled into the kitchen. Riley glanced at the stove and at the woman in his kitchen. He had to take a breath to summon some control. He never wanted someone so much or needed someone so much. Seeing her aroused him more than he ever thought possible.

Treasure sensed Riley enter the kitchen. Her skin heated as she remembered the first time she caught him staring at her in a kitchen. Thankful for the cool air of the refrigerator to give her skin some relief, Treasure pretended he wasn't there. Hearing him come behind her, she closed her eyes and counted his footsteps against the tile. One. Two. Three. Four. Holding a bag of shredded cheese in her hand, Treasure closed the door. She found Riley standing directly in front of her when she dared to turn around.

"Do you need any help?" Riley asked. Just seeing her was enough to send his desire soaring.

Treasure would have swooned if she could have. Why does everything he say sound like sex, she wondered. The sensual timbre and octave of his voice heralded what pleasures awaited her. Riley's eyes darkened with desire as he came within inches of her. He lowered his head and nuzzled her neck.

Her mouth went dry. She forced herself to speak. Her voice sounded weak and breathy, "I'm good. A few more minutes and everything should be ready." Riley's nose traced the curve of her neck. Between the coolness at her back and the heat Riley was generating, Treasure was a bundle of nerves and need.

Riley smiled against her skin. "Sure?" he asked. He cupped her face in his hands and kissed her sweetly on the lips.

"I'm sure, Riley," Treasure whispered. "Shoo, before you make me burn the pork chops."

Riley laughed and stepped back. He threw up his hands. "Okay, he said. "Everything smells wonderful. Is that a cake I smell?"

Treasure laughed. "Your subtle hints about wanting something sweet did not go unnoticed."

Riley eyes twinkled. "Oh, baby, I already have my something sweet." He kissed her on her forehead and walked out the kitchen.

Treasure found herself smiling as she plated dinner. Riley was already at the table waiting when she returned. When she sat down, Riley held out his hand.

Riley blessed the food, and they began eating. Dinner, like the drive, was unusually quiet and polite, but Treasure was glad that he seemed to be enjoying everything. She giggled when he took his first bite of the pork chop and closed his eyes in appreciation. But the cloud still hung over them as they both struggled to find the conversational rhythm they usually enjoyed. Finally, they surrendered to the silences, comfortable and uncomfortable, between them.

"That was amazing, sweetheart," Riley said as he brought her hand to his lips and kissed it. "I couldn't eat another bite." He smiled as he rose from the table to take their plates into the kitchen. She followed him to the kitchen to retrieve the pound cake out of the oven to cool.

"So, you don't want a slice of cake?" Treasure smiled.

"Maybe later. Come sit with me for a moment." Riley led her to the sofa and pulled her onto the sofa right night to him and put his arm around her. Treasure tensed up. She really hoped that she would have the courage to tell him her decision by the time he finished dessert. He turned her chin towards him. "Hey, what's wrong? You were a million miles away just then."

"Nothing, Riley." She leaned into his embrace and placed her head on her shoulder.

"Listen, I wanted to talk to you about something you said earlier." Riley took a deep breath. Treasure was always skittish about any talk of a relationship, but he truly believed that they were past all of that now.

Treasure knew where this was going. She just decided to beat him to it. "Riley, I..."

Riley stopped her. "Wait. I need to say what I need to say first. Please."

Treasure didn't say anything but nodded her head.

"At the store, you called this 'home.'

"I didn't mean..."

"Didn't mean what...that this felt like home for you?" Riley asked as he held her to him. "Treasure, this house has felt more like a home in the past week than it has since my grandparents died." Riley took a deep breath, steadying himself for the fight he knew was coming and once he said it, there was no going back. "I want you to move in with me. Stay here with me."

Treasure's internal jaw dropped. Surely, he was kidding! She turned to face him. "Riley, I don't know if we're ready for that. And I definitely don't want you to feel obligated. Don't get me wrong, being here with you has been wonderful, but we started dating a little while ago. The camera installation at my place is tomorrow, so I thought I would go back home next week. I'm sure you want to get back to your place in Jackson too. We'll be okay." She squeezed his hand.

Riley looked at Treasure's face. Her face was the picture of cool, but he felt her body tremble. He said nothing for a few moments and listened to her ramble about how she needed to get back to normal. Riley felt her running away all over again.

He touched her face, and she leaned into his palm and closed her eyes. The touch sent a warm shiver down her spine. "Treasure, look at me."

Treasure reluctantly opened her eyes. His eyes narrowed, and he stared at her intensely before he spoke. "Don't run away from me again. I love you more than anyone in the world, and my asking you to move in with me wasn't out of obligation, or even fear." He cupped her face in his hands. "I. Love. You. Wherever you are is home for me."

Treasure felt the tears brimming in her eyes. "Riley, this is going too fast. Too much is happening all at once. The store. My home. You."

"Fast?" Riley laughed sarcastically. "Baby, nothing about us has been fast, except that first weekend." He pulled her closer to him. "Treasure, baby, you were mine even then, and I am so sorry my stupidity cost us those years. But I know it now. You belong with me. We belong together. Here. We've lost enough time, and if you think that I'm going to let you keep running away from me, you are sadly mistaken."

Treasure eyes flashed in irritation. She resented his words despite its truth. "I'm not running away, Riley," she lied, "but this isn't the right time. I came here because someone threw a rock through my window, not because we had made a decision together to get to this level."

Riley lowered his forehead to hers. "Trust me, Treasure. Trust us."

Treasure closed her eyes and took a deep breath. She loved this man with every ounce of her being, but she just couldn't trust it. Not yet. Her business mind was saying one thing, but Lord, her heart wanted something else. Her heart and soul wanted Riley Taylor.

Riley whispered in her ear, "Go upstairs. I'll put the food away." He kissed her temple. "Be ready for me." His voice was deep and breathy in her ear, and Treasure's body responded immediately to his command. Without another word, Treasure ascended the stairs, anticipation running though her.

Riley stood rooted to the spot, watching her climb the stairs. When the faint sound of water running reached him, he shuddered. Riley never tired of making love to Treasure, and he didn't think he ever would. He fired off a text to Marcus as he walked into the kitchen. Marcus needed to come up with something soon, or he was going to take matters into his own hands. Riley began putting the food away. Just as he closed the refrigerator door, his phone vibrated in his pocket.

The cryptic text from Marcus read: Hey. Working on a lead. Will call in the morning.

He slipped his phone back in his pocket and cut a huge slice of cake and put it on a saucer. He smiled to himself. Proving to Treasure that she was definitely sweeter than a slice of pound cake was going to be delicious.

CHAPTER 10

Treasure stayed at Riley's another full week before she made the decision to go back to her house. She simply needed to restore normalcy in her life and so did he. Riley pouted for two days when she told him. This was one of the nights that Treasure would be staying at her house alone. Nights without Riley were the hardest. In a short amount of time, Treasure had grown accustomed to his warmth next to her body and making love in the middle of the night. More than once in the last few weeks, she reached for him while she lay alone in her bed. Treasure sighed. Even though moving home was best, she missed him already, and it was only noon.

Living at Riley's felt comfortable, natural even, so much so that sleeping in her bed alone seemed foreign. Since they drove together most days, Treasure and Riley either ate dinner in Jackson or they ate at either of their places. They spent weekends in Pocahontas. It was like a dance as they moved about the kitchen, laughing, chopping vegetables. Sometimes, he grilled. They talked. They laughed. They made love. Lord, have mercy, she thought, as a memory flashed before her. She sighed and shook her head. That man's hands ought to be classified as lethal weapons.

He actually pouted the first night she stayed at her house, but rather than drive all the way to Pocahontas, he stayed at his downtown condo when she stayed in Jackson. Treasure staying alone made Riley uncomfortable, but he knew that Grace had ordered more patrols in the area. Cameras captured a 360 view of her house and the surrounding houses, her lighting had been upgraded, and short of putting bars on her windows and doors, Treasure felt relatively safe. Plus, nothing more had happened either at her store or her home, but Riley was insistent that she stay vigilant.

She smiled to herself. She couldn't imagine that she and Riley were a real couple. The idea still fascinated her. Riley was like a different person, or he was being who he always was--a gentleman. And she, chuckling at herself, didn't recognize herself as a woman in love.

Yet, she kept looking for him to revert, to tire of her and long for his playboy days, but he was as attentive as ever. Riley met her at the store every evening to follow her home where he checked out the house first. Then, they decided whether to dine in or out--but always together. If they dined out, upon their return to her house, Riley checked the house all over again. She stood there at the door, waiting, covering her mouth to keep from laughing out loud. It was sweet, really, the way he looked in every conceivable hiding place before he let her move an inch further into the house.

She was completely, indescribably, in love with Riley Taylor.

~

A few weeks after his conversation with Zeus, E-Money found himself outside Treasure's Boutique again. He watched the hustle and bustle of Fondren on a sunny Saturday afternoon, the kind of day when people wanted to spend money, especially when they had it to spend. Shoppers proudly carried bags from store to store, smiling and laughing, without a care in the world. He imagined women pulling out their credit cards, swiping without any concern for how the bill would be paid. E-Money saw a young teenage boy on a skateboard. He remembered wanting one at that age. He shook off a twinge of jealousy he felt at kids who looked like they didn't have a care in the world, especially not junkie mamas or convict daddies. E-Money could buy a hundred skateboards now, but it still wouldn't be the same.

Treasure noticed a strikingly beautiful woman browsing in the store. Ebony-hued skin. High cheekbones. A dancer's body. She'd been looking at the Alexander McQueen gown in the display case at the center of the store. The dress was an elaborately beaded dress on a sheer fabric that made the wearer appear ethereal and nearly nude. The dress would look beautiful on her. Treasure walked over to the woman who looked up at her with a toothy grin that Treasure didn't like. Her senses went on high alert. There was something about this woman she didn't like. Treasure had a few clients she didn't like, but Treasure was always professional.

"Welcome to Treasure's Boutique. May I help you?"

The woman looked Treasure up and down. "Hello, I'm looking for a dress to wear to a wedding. Can you help me?" Treasure noticed that the woman casually rubbed her belly but didn't comment.

"Wonderful. I love weddings. Now, do you know what day and time? We can find a beautiful dress suitable for Mississippi weather. That's important." Treasure decided to throw herself in the hunt for a dress rather than focus on this woman's energy.

Smiling, the woman said, "It'll be soon, so let's say late July or early August."

Treasure thought that was strange but didn't engage in a conversation. "Okay. You'll need something light." Treasure moved about the store and selected dresses for her. By the way, I'm Treasure. What's your name?"

"Scarlett."

"Beautiful name."

Scarlett shrugged. "My mother loved Gone with the Wind. She's probably the only Black woman who did."

Treasure laughed. "No, I love it too, especially Hattie McDaniel. I have a drawing of her in my home." Switching gears slightly, Treasure asked, "So, Scaaarlett," emphasizing her name with a southern drawl, "who's getting married?"

Scarlett gleefully responded. "Me." My fiancé and I wanted to get married before I really start showing." She rubbed her belly again this time to make sure Treasure saw it.

Treasure smiled at her. "I understand completely."

"Riley suggested I come here to get my dress. Said you were the best shop in town."

Treasure's blood ran cold. After a moment, she had to ask, "Riley?"

"Yes, Riley Taylor. He's a real estate developer here in Jackson."

Treasure felt a lump in her throat but refused to show any emotion. She knew that this visit was intentional. "Wonderful," she said with a smile. I'm glad he thought of me. Why don't you try these dresses on, and I'll check on you in a few minutes, okay?" She closed the dressing room door without waiting for a response and walked as slowly and deliberately as she could to her office.

Safely behind the door, Treasure leaned against it and took a deep breath. She felt like she swallowed a stone. Her stomach churned. How could I have been so stupid? Treasure fought the tears back from her eyes. Riley Taylor was not going to make a fool of her--twice. She walked to her desk and sat down. Treasure spun her chair around so that she would face nothing that reminded her of Riley in her office. Truth was, she could still smell him in there. His scent permeated every fabric of her office. Treasure shook her head. She was a professional, and she had a client waiting for her.

With another deep breath, Treasure rolled her shoulders back and lifted herself from her chair. She was going to deal with Miss Scarlett now, and then, she was going to deal with Mr. Riley Taylor.

~

Treasure usually didn't leave work early, but today she felt that she earned it. After pasting on the most insincere smile she could muster, Treasure helped Scarlett try on several dresses while listening to her gush about Riley Taylor for an hour. She clenched her jaw so tight, her head started to pound at the temples. It didn't help matters that Scarlett looked good in everything, and Treasure realized that Scarlett was just Riley's type. Beautiful and Oblivious. Scarlett bought an ivory strapless gown with a thigh-high split. The cut of the dress hid her baby bump well, and the beading of the gown shimmered against her skin. Treasure "oohed" and "ahhed" over her in the dress, her wedding plans, her hopes for a little boy who looked like Riley.

Treasure thought, Lord, please get me through this. Treasure dropped her off at the counter so one of her employees, Brandi, could complete the sale.

"It was nice to meet you Scarlett. I hope everything works out for you." Treasure heard her voice tremble. Tears, she knew, were not far behind.

"Thanks, and I'll be sure to tell Riley that you helped me personally." Scarlett emphasized "personally" and looked at Treasure with a sinister smile on her face.

Treasure straightened her back and rolled her shoulders slightly. She should not have done that, she thought to herself. Her eyes glared at Scarlett while she kept her smile, "You do that." Now, she was angry and confused as to just exactly at whom. Riley. This woman. Or Herself.

She turned to Brandi, "Please make sure you take good care of Miss Scarlett, Brandi."

Brandi raised her eyebrow at her, her eyes holding questions that Treasure couldn't answer. Treasure kept her face still and without any emotion. Brandi had worked at Treasure's long enough to have witnessed Treasure's calm with the most difficult customers. But Treasure knew from the look on Brandi's face that she overheard the woman talking about Riley. Yet, Brandi followed Treasure's lead and placed the chosen dress in a garment bag.

Treasure walked deliberately around the store to speak to other customers before returning to her office. Scarlett may have her man, but not her dignity. Her man? A joke if she ever heard one. Treasure didn't look up when the chimes at the door signaled Scarlett's exit. As soon as she could, Treasure returned to her office and grabbed her purse. If she could get to her car and away from there, she would be okay. But once outside, Treasure thought that her car seemed so far away even though it was only a few steps from the door. Treasure's legs felt like lead, as she labored to reach the driver's side door. Tears stung her eyes and started falling before she could get to the safety of her car. Not here, Treasure. You can't do this here, she thought.

She held her face to the sun, willing her threatened tears back in her head. Treasure didn't know what to think or how to feel. She allowed herself to believe Riley's declaration of love, to believe in him, and even more, she allowed herself to love him. But Riley wasn't any different from before, or any other man she knew. And now he had a baby on the way. A baby!? All of her dreams of having a life with Riley flashed before her. None of it would be happening now. She pressed the ignition, and as the engine came to life, her shoulders slumped. How could she face him now? How could she have done this to herself?

Treasure exited the parking lot. She had no place to go. Riley would come looking for her when he came to the store and found her gone. He would drive straight to her house. Treasure knew she couldn't handle seeing him right now, and she really didn't feel like listening to whatever bullshit explanation he was going to offer. She'd fallen for him twice. He wouldn't get a third chance to break her heart.

Riley pulled into the parking lot in front of Treasure's store with a smile on his face. This was the best part of his day. Treasure's beautiful smile would greet him, and nothing else mattered. Nothing was better than that except the mornings he woke with Treasure in his arms. Riley paused as he approached the darkened storefront and cocked his head. Something was off. He pulled on the door and found it locked. He peered inside and saw Brandi at the register. Riley tapped on the door to get her attention. Did she just roll her eyes at him?

Brandi unlocked the door and opened it just enough to speak. She didn't want to let Riley in the store. "Yes," she said dryly.

Riley stepped back. "Hi Brandi. I'm here to pick up Treasure."

Brandi didn't move from the door. "She's gone for the day."

"What do you mean she's gone? Was she sick? Did something happen?" Riley pulled out his phone to call Treasure and to see if he missed her call. No call from her. He frantically checked both his emails. Nothing. What the hell?

Brandi opened her mouth to tell him just what happened, but she decided against it. "You'll have to ask her, Mr. Taylor. Now, if you'll excuse me, I need to close up." Brandi closed the door. Riley heard the finality in the click of the lock in his soul.

He dialed Treasure's number. After a few rings, it went to voicemail. He called again as he walked back to his car. Again, no answer. Dazed, Riley walked to his car and got in. He stared at the front of the store as if Treasure was somehow going to miraculously appear and this was a cruel joke or gross error. What the hell happened today? He text Treasure: "Baby call me. Where are you? Are you okay?" He saw the three dots but then nothing.

Riley was still waiting for an answer as Brandi locked up and drove away.

He threw his phone on the passenger seat and headed to Treasure's house. Maybe, he thought. His mind and his heart were racing, but he tried to remain calm. He started to call Marcus but decided to wait until he got to Treasure's house. What should have been a five-minute drive took at least fifteen minutes. The construction on State Street didn't make things any better. He had to take two detours and wait for a construction crew before he could get to her house, and when he arrived, he found it dark and empty. He hit the steering wheel in frustration. Riley didn't have a key, but he knew someone who would.

Riley called Kenzo. He didn't have time for greetings. "Man, I can't find Treasure. I need to speak to Grace. Are y'all at home?"

Kenzo looked at his wife who was sitting on the sofa curled up beside him. She'd been unusually quiet since he arrived, but Kenzo chalked that up to a case she was working on. "Yeah, we're here. Come on by. Do you want me to call Marcus?" Kenzo noticed that she tensed up when she heard Riley's voice over the phone.

"Nah, I'll call him and tell him to meet me there. Ask Grace if she's heard from Treasure in the last few hours.

Kenzo rubbed Grace's back. "Riley and Marcus will be here in a few. He's looking for Treasure."

Grace was silent. I bet he is, she thought.

Kenzo knew his wife. She knew something that she wasn't telling--even to him. "Have you talked to her?"

Grace rose from her comfortable spot and stood in front of Kenzo, just between his legs. She bent over and kissed her husband softly on the lips. "I have. Please don't ask me anything else. I'm not going to lie to you, but I'm not going to betray her either."

Kenzo said nothing. Man, you have really messed up, Kenzo thought to an invisible Riley. If Riley hoped Grace would give him some insight, then he was sadly mistaken.

"Now, husband," Grace whispered, "I'm going to start dinner. Any requests?" The doorbell chimes sounded, alerting them to Riley's arrival. Grace pressed her lips together and took a deep breath. "I'll be in the kitchen."

A confused Kenzo watched his wife saunter into the kitchen as he walked toward the front door. Whatever Riley had done, he was going to have to help his man fix it and quickly. This situation would cost them both.

Riley rushed past Kenzo. 'Man, something's happened to Treasure. I can't find her. She's not answering the phone. She's not at home." Riley paced the floor as Kenzo walked to the bar. Kenzo took a highball glass from the cabinet and opened the Maker's Mark. Riley needed a drink strong enough to handle what he was about to tell him. Riley plopped down into the leather club chair by the sofa. "Man, I show up at the store like I do every damn day. And she's not there. And an employee looks at me like I am persona non-grata? I need to talk to her. Maybe we can trace her phone." Riley looked around for Grace.

Kenzo sighed and looked toward the kitchen. Grace heard everything Riley said unless she'd gone deaf in the last three minutes. He handed Riley the drink and sat down on the sofa. "I'm sure she's fine. She's just..."

Riley cut his off. "She's just what? What? Are you crazy? They must have gotten her. Where the hell is Marcus? He's been slacking on this. She would have called me. Treasure wouldn't just disappear on me. This ain't us, Ken." Riley's eyes were darting around the room like a madman. He was frantic, and Kenzo of all people should know what this feels like. He downed the drink and stood up. Riley needed to talk to Grace.

"Grace!" Riley called out. "Grace!"

Kenzo shook his head. If Grace wouldn't tell him, she definitely wasn't going to tell Riley. "Riley! Calm down. Let me ask you something." He needed to get Riley to figure out where the hell Riley messed up. "When was the last time you talked to Treasure."

It took a few seconds for the question to register. "I called her around noon, and everything was fine. I went to pick her up at closing for dinner. Like we always do."

Kenzo recognized the agitation and fear in Riley's voice. He experienced the same over a year ago when Grace was working a case on the Gulf Coast, and she had a dirty cop in her command.

"So, something must have happened between then and when you went to the store. We'll have Marcus check the feed when he gets here. But you can't panic. Not yet."

Riley stopped and looked at Kenzo. Kenzo knew something. He was about to ask him when the doorbell rang.

Marcus walked in with his computer bag and sat down on the sofa. As he pulled out his laptop, he pulled up the security feed from Treasure's store. "I checked with the man I put on Treasure's store, and he didn't notice anything out of the ordinary."

"Well, something happened. It's like Treasure disappeared into thin freaking air." Riley took a glance at Kenzo. Surely, he told Grace that Treasure was missing. Or maybe she told him.

Marcus tapped into the security feed of Treasure's store and the parking lot and projected it on Kenzo's television. They watched in silence as shoppers came in and out of the store.

"Anyone look familiar?" Marcus asked. "Riley?"

Riley stared at the screen. "Not one person. Kenzo?"

Kenzo didn't recognize anyone either and just shook his head. Soon, they saw Treasure coming out of the store to her car. Riley studied the screen as if he was seeing her in person. "Go back to her coming out of the store again. Can you slow it down?" Riley walked directly up to the screen. Treasure walked slowly to the car. He saw her lips moving, but he couldn't make out what she was saying, but his heart broke the moment he saw her throw her head back. Then, she was in the car and driving away.

This was the moment his life stopped.

Riley stood there, watching the screen as Marcus rewound the video. No one took her. She left.

"I need to speak to Grace now." Riley's voice sounded defeated even to his own ears. Thinking she'd been harmed by some monster was one thing. Knowing that whatever made her leave was somehow because of something he did or didn't do, was another.

Kenzo sighed. He found Grace reading in their bedroom. She looked up with a raised eyebrow. Grace swung her legs over the side of the bed and stood up. Her husband didn't have to say a word. And neither did she. But Grace knew just what she was going to say to Mr. Riley Taylor. She hoped he would be ready for it.

Riley turned around as he heard Kenzo and Grace enter the room. Kenzo stood behind Grace and shrugged his shoulders slightly. Riley could tell that Grace didn't appreciate the summons, but he was desperate at this point.

"Riley."

Grace crossed her arms and glared at him, confirming that he was the reason Treasure disappeared. He thought about Kenzo's comment about Grace's gun when he saw how angry Grace was. Between Treasure's tears on that video and Grace's disdain, he remembered why he'd always kept things with women at a distance.

"Where is Treasure, Grace?" he asked quietly and firmly. He doubted seriously that Grace was going to violate Treasure's confidence.

"Treasure's safe. She just doesn't want to speak to you. When she's ready, she'll call you." Grace searched his face. Riley looked devastated, which was good. Serves him right, she thought. She turned to leave but stopped when she heard the sheer pain in Riley's voice.

Riley ran his hand over his head. "If you're not going to tell me where she is, at least tell me what set this off." He felt like he was aging by the minute, but he was ready to beg Grace, in front of his boys, if he had to. "Tell me what I did. Give me that much."

Grace heard Kenzo whisper her name. His voice was low enough for only her to hear, but she knew what he meant and what he was asking of her. She looked at Kenzo over her shoulder. She nodded and turned to Riley. He was waiting for any morsel of information she could give him, like a starving dog waiting on a piece of meat to drop to the floor. "Riley, she told me specifically not to tell you where she was, and I will not break her confidence." Riley's shoulders slumped, and Grace almost felt sorry for him. He really had no clue, so she decided to help him... just a little. "Treasure's never sounded so," she paused, looking for the right word. "Broken."

Riley felt the same. He couldn't lose the woman he loved over something he didn't even know he did. "But I haven't done anything but love her, Grace. And I do love her. But I can't make this right until I know what happened." His voice cracked and raised.

Kenzo heard the fear and frustration in his friend's voice. He understood completely. Images of Grace's kidnapping over a year ago flashed through his mind. "Grace, can you give us anything without betraying Treasure?"

Grace closed her eyes and took a deep breath. She offered him a cryptic nugget. "Riley, the only thing I can and will tell you is that your life as Jackson's resident playboy just caught up with you. Big time." She emphasized "will" to let all of them know, including her husband, that this was all she was going to say, especially without talking to Treasure again.

Confusion flashed on Riley's face.

"Just give her a couple of days." Grace spun around on her heel and left the room, touching Kenzo's arm as she walked past. Part of her hoped that Kenzo and Riley could figure things out. In all the years Grace and Treasure had been friends, Grace could not remember Treasure giving her heart to anyone—not even to break it. Her friend fell so hard and so completely for Riley that she threw all caution to the wind. Grace couldn't blame her after falling for Kenzo the same way. And she definitely couldn't blame her for wanting to be happy.

With Grace out of earshot, Riley looked at Kenzo. "Days? Is she kidding?"

Marcus called out, "Yo, I think I have something." Kenzo and Riley walked back over to where Marcus sat. "Grace said that your past was rearing its ugly head, so that just means a woman."

Riley rolled his eyes, "Man, come on, I know how I used to do, but that's over."

"But Grace also said you messed up 'big time'," said Kenzo. "Marcus, can you track her phone? I'm sure my wife told her to turn off the GPS, but can you find where she was last? Riley, you didn't recognize any of the women in the feed, right? But we know it was a woman who went in that store."

Riley responded, "Yeah." The realization hit him like a ton of bricks. Before that moment, he never apologized for his life. He was a young, single man who liked women. But this, this was different. His fear and anxiety gave way to irritation and anger. She should have called him. She should have trusted him.

"Listen, fellas, thanks for all of this, but I'm going home. She's not in any danger. Marcus, can you keep the men on the store and her house? There's still a threat out there, and I want to make sure she's safe." He pulled his keys from his pocket and studied them. Riley wished he had a key to Treasure's place, but there never seemed a need since they were always together. He wished she had the keys to his place. Then, maybe she would come home. At least, he would be able to talk to her, hold her, fix whatever he did. Right now, the silent treatment would be a blessing as long as she was with him.

Kenzo raised his eyebrow. "You sure."

Riley squared his shoulders and lifted his chin. "Positive." Without another word, Riley turned and walked out of the house.

He aimlessly drove around the city, hoping to spot her car parked somewhere. Riley drove by her house and left a note on her door. Riley stared directly into the security camera. He knew that she would be notified that he was there. He wanted her to see his face since he couldn't see hers.

After a few moments, he walked away, dejected but determined to find out who and what hurt her so bad that she wouldn't even talk to him before she believed whatever they told her.

CHAPTER 11

Grace couldn't sleep. Nestled in the curve of Kenzo's arm as he lay behind her, she stared at the wall in front of her. Her mind raced, trying to make sense of Riley's betrayal of Treasure. As angry as she was at Riley for hurting Treasure, something wasn't sitting right with her. None of it made sense. Part of her felt like he betrayed her too. Grace trusted him with Treasure's heart. Riley wouldn't have been that concerned if he didn't care deeply for her friend. But looking at him tonight, she could see the anguish in his face, the pain in his voice, and she was no longer sure about Riley's guilt. Sure, he lived his young bachelor days as a man-whore, but his commitment to Treasure's safety in the last few weeks please her. From what Kenzo told her, Riley was a man in love and was like a different person.

She created an imaginary white board in her mind like this was one of her cases. Treasure's life had been way too exciting for this to be coincidental. The shakedown. The vandalism. The random woman. Her heart raced. She opened her mouth to wake Kenzo, but as usual, he beat her to it.

Kenzo nuzzled her neck, "I've been awake," he said groggily. He shifted his hips so Grace could feel just how awake he was. She smiled. Kenzo always made her feel desirable and loved.

Grace turned to face her handsome husband. He started kissing her neck and caressing her breasts. Grace almost forgot what she was thinking and needed to say. She had to summon every ounce of control she had to stop him. She tried to pull away, but Kenzo had latched onto a sensitive nipple. "Baby, wait. I need to tell you something," she said breathlessly. "About Riley."

Kenzo looked up at her. "I don't want to talk about Riley. I want to make love to my wife." He resumed his torture of her flesh. Grace arched her back when he bit the curve of her waist and nestled himself between her thighs.

Focus, Grace, she thought. "A woman came into Treasure's store today."

Kenzo kissed her naval. "Isn't that what they are supposed to do?" Right now, Riley's woman troubles were the least of his concerns.

Grace sighed. Men were such simple creatures she thought. "Kenzo, the woman told Treasure she was pregnant with Riley's baby."

Kenzo stopped and moved to her side. Incredulous, he asked, "Seriously? I don't believe that at all. That's not Riley's style at all." Kenzo moved to sit up. It made sense now. He looked back at his wife. "And Treasure believed it. You believed it."

Grace remained silent but nodded.

"Grace." Kenzo shook his head. "I have to tell him what happened. You should have told him earlier."

Grace pulled the sheet up to cover herself. She suddenly felt exposed and frankly, a bit naïve. "She swore me to secrecy, but you didn't hear the pain in her voice. I felt her pain like it was my own."

Kenzo touched her cheek. "I know, Love, but did Riley look like a man that would hurt Treasure like that? Did you really listen to him, or was it too easy to believe the worst in him?"

Damn, Grace thought. "You're right. I'll call Treasure first thing in the morning. We need to think this through. Maybe I can find out who this woman is and why she's lying on Riley." She leaned forward and kissed Kenzo.

"Good."

Kenzo picked up his phone to call Riley, but a text from Shotgun, a childhood friend, stopped him cold. Her ties to Jackson's underbelly proved invaluable when she wanted them to be. She wanted to meet the next morning. Kenzo, Riley, Marcus, and Shay had all been friends once, but tragic events led Shay to a life of crime. Eventually, they saw less and less of Shay as she morphed into her street persona--Shotgun, so named because she carried a double-barreled shotgun on her hip. Notorious and no-nonsense, Shotgun had her hand in, or knowledge of, every criminal enterprise in Jackson. Helping Kenzo last year save Grace from a sex trafficker who'd infiltrated her special task force brought the crew back together again. She and Kenzo had always checked in over the years, but not the whole gang. Riley's indifference didn't bother her. Marcus, on the other hand, always made her feel like the criminal she pretended to be.

After confirming with Shotgun, Kenzo sent Marcus a text to join him. Marcus didn't really like Kenzo bringing in Shotgun, but Kenzo always covered his basis. And Shotgun could go places Marcus couldn't.

He called Riley. The call went straight to voicemail. Brother is probably passed out, he thought.

And, for once, Kenzo didn't blame Riley. Since he was meeting Shotgun so early, he would just check in with him then. Hopefully, he went to his downtown condo last night. He definitely didn't feel like driving up Highway 49 that early in the morning.

~

Treasure drove around the city for hours. She watched Riley's name appear on her screen and in her text messages until she realized he gave up trying to reach her. But when she saw his face in her door camera notification, she almost broke down and called him. He genuinely looked sad. She frowned. Had his baby mama told him what she did? She let out a scream and hit the steering wheel in frustration. She just wanted to know why Riley didn't tell her. But what could he possibly say to her about another woman having his baby that would make her heart stop breaking into pieces? She'd fallen completely in love with Riley. Treasure knew she couldn't go back to pretending that she didn't love Riley Taylor like she had before.

She had a vision of Riley and his new family at Kenzo and Grace's for a party, bouncing a little boy on his knee. Treasure felt bile rise in her throat. She grabbed her bottle of water in the cup holder. She needed something to calm her nerves. While she didn't believe Riley sent that woman into her store, a woman was claiming to be pregnant with his baby. And with Riley's reputation, she couldn't be sure that the woman was lying.

Treasure yawned. She just wanted to crawl into her bed and forget everything about this day. She had driven in circles downtown, ending up at the Civil Rights Museum on North Street before driving by the new mural at the. Old Capitol Inn, profiling Jackson-born artists. She had to smile. Only in Jackson would Eudora Welty and David Banner be in the same conversation. But her smile led to tears as she thought about her first real date with Riley at the art museum. How sweet he had been, she thought. Had he been seeing this woman then? She shook her head. Doesn't matter anymore, Treasure, she whispered to herself. Treasure drove away from the mural and her thoughts of Riley. When her phone rang, she almost tapped the decline button on her steering wheel until she spied Grace's name on her dashboard screen. She didn't want to talk to anyone, not even Grace but answered anyway.

"Hi, Grace."

"Hey," Grace said, trying to be as upbeat as possible. "What are you doing? Sounds like you're in the car." Grace sat up and swung her legs on the side of the bed.

"I am. Just driving. Trying to clear my head, but honestly, it's not working."

"Listen, I know you might not want to talk about it, but I need you to tell me exactly what happened today."

Treasure took a deep breath. This day was like a horror movie on a continuous loop. She didn't think she could speak the words again. "Grace, please, I don't need a cop right now. I can't."

Grace heard the anguish in her voice, and her heart broke for her friend. "I know, sweetie, but Riley was here and…"

Treasure cut her off, "You didn't tell him, did you?"

"Of course not, but he needs to know why you're angry. But I did let him know how angry I was. Treasure, he didn't look or sound like a man who would do something like this and not to you."

Treasure had played and replayed the scene in her head. What woman would do something so…so cruel. Even if the baby wasn't Riley's, clearly, he dealt with her on a personal level. And that was almost too much. "It's like I told you, she's gorgeous. Just Riley's type. Could probably be a model."

"Had you ever seen her before?" Grace asked.

"No." Treasure's irritation grew. "I know you mean well, but I'm not in the mood for an interrogation right now."

"Did she approach you, or did you approach her?"

"I approached her." She snapped, "That's what I'm supposed to do."

Grace didn't respond. Softening her voice, she said, "I know, sweetie. I'm just trying to visualize everything. Just bear with me. What did she say to you? Try to remember everything just as she said it and how she said it."

Grace, I.... Treasure's voice trailed off as a notification came in from her security company. She saw shadowy figures on the feed. They were trashing her place. What the hell?

"Grace, I have to go. I think someone is breaking into the store." She ended the call without waiting for a response. Her man might be gone, but no one was taking her store. Treasure was too hurt and angry to be rational. She turned on State Street, and sped northward. Part of her wanted to confront these thugs who thought they were going to muscle her out of a business she fought to build and maintain. The other part of her wanted to just fight, period.

Treasure pulled into the front of an empty parking lot. Even though the security system would notify the police department, she arrived before they did. Or maybe they had already run them off. She noted that the parking lot was deathly silent, lit only by the lights surrounding the names of the stores and a lone streetlight at the corner. Treasure hesitated as she opened her car door. She picked up her phone to call Grace but thought against it. She was perfectly capable of handling herself and her business.

Armed with her keys in her hand, Treasure walked cautiously to the front of the store. She checked to see if there was any evidence of a break-in. The front window was intact, but the door had scratches at the lock. She pulled the door and it opened. A car door slammed in the distance, and Treasure jumped. Jesus, she whispered. As soon as she stepped into the store, she found racks of clothes turned over, displays pulled from the wall, and shoes strewn everywhere. How could they have done this so quickly, she asked herself, as she looked around at the mess before her.

As her eyes adjusted to the darkness, Treasure stepped carefully through the mess of clothes and shoes on the floor, becoming angrier and angrier. She needed to reach the light switch to see whether she would be able to salvage the thousands of dollars of inventory on the floor. After weeks of nothing, they--whoever they were--picked today of all days to break into her store. This security system was Riley's idea, and look at what good that did her right now. She had no Riley. And now, no security. Serves you right for falling in love with Riley Taylor, she mumbled to herself.

Just as she was about to flip on the light switch, Treasure heard a noise in the backroom. She stopped in her tracks, her hand hovering at the switch. Treasure froze in her tracks and held her breath. She heard her heartbeat pounding in her ears. She stood as still as she possibly could, griping her phone tightly in her hand.

Treasure heard a loud crash in her office and glass breaking. She knew it was the crystal vase that held the flowers Riley sent her a few days ago. Perfect, she thought. She didn't want the reminder, but she would have liked to have thrown it at him herself. Treasure heard hushed voices. One sounded familiar but she couldn't place it. She strained to hear but couldn't make out what they were saying to each other.

Treasure quickly tiptoed around the counter, trying not to make a sound, but she didn't see a shoe in the dark and stumbled forward. She cried out as she felt her left ankle turn awkwardly. Treasure clenched her teeth as pain shot through her ankle. She couldn't afford to make any more noise. She hoisted herself up from the floor and placed her weight on her right foot. A shooting pain went through her left ankle when she tried to walk. She closed her eyes waiting for the pain to pass. Lord, help me get to this door, she prayed.

She needed to get out of there. Using the light from her phone to create a path, Treasure prayed that they wouldn't notice the beam of light. She hoped Grace was on her way already, but she decided to text her anyway. Treasure knew there was no need to call 9-1-1 since they couldn't track her cell phone. A dispatcher would have to ask her questions, which meant that she would have to answer them. And she didn't want to make any more sound than was necessary.

Just as she hit "send," light flooded the showroom.

Before she turned around, she knew who was standing behind her. Before Treasure could turn around completely, E-Money was there, his right hand swooping down across the right side of her face. His calloused knuckles against her cheek stunned her as her body fell to the floor limp. Treasure's head bounced on the floor, and E-Money didn't need to check to know she was completely knocked out.

E-Money was still looking down at her when his partner, Lucky, came out of the back room.

"Yo, man, she see you?" Lucky reached behind his back to retrieve the .45 in his waistband.

E-Money looked at his partner. Usually, his crew didn't leave witnesses, but he doubted that she would ever be able to recognize him. Their paths would never cross, not directly anyway. And Zeus didn't want her dead, just scared. For the first time, he lied to one of his men.

"Nah, I knocked the bitch out before she saw me." E-Money admired his handiwork. No real damage, but one helluva mess. "Hit the lights. Everything wiped down in the back?"

"Yeah, man. We good." Lucky returned his gun to his waistband.

"Good. Wipe down that light switch by the counter." E-Money didn't wait for Lucky to respond. He walked out of the front of the store into the darkness. E-Money lit a cigarette. He never questioned anything Zeus commanded, but this job was going to get them all hemmed up or worse.

E-Money leaned against his car, waiting for Lucky. As Lucky approached, E-Money heard sirens in the distance. He chuckled as he and

Lucky entered the car. Right on time, he thought, as he eased out of the parking lot on State Street. He saw a bright blue and orange patrol car with flashing lights in his rear view mirror going straight for the store. E-Money took a final drag on his cigarette and tossed it out of the window.

As he turned on Meadowbrook Drive toward I-55 S, E-Money listened to Lucky's random chatter. Lucky never needed a response, just a body to absorb the sound, which was fine with him since, tonight, he needed sound to drown out the alarm bells ringing in his head.

~

Grace and Kenzo arrived at the store to a parking lot full of the blinding blue lights of police cars and an ambulance. Grace took a deep breath and said a quick prayer for calm, her palms splayed across the front of her thighs to keep her hands from shaking. The feeling of dread washed over her. An ambulance could mean anything, but she knew it was for Treasure. Kenzo reached over and gave her trembling hand a little squeeze as he pulled the car as close as he could to the front of the store.

As soon as Kenzo shut off the engine, Grace jumped out and ran to the store. He exited the car, his phone in hand, trying to call Riley again. No answer. Voicemail full. Kenzo knew that Riley would never forgive himself if something happened to Treasure, especially if he wasn't there because he refused to answer the phone. Kenzo slipped his phone in his pocket as he stepped next to Grace while she was talking to Detective Tims. He could feel the tension in their conversation, and he had to admit a bit of pride watching his wife flexing her rank. Grace stopped talking as soon as the paramedics brought out Treasure's limp body strapped on a stretcher.

Tears brimmed Grace's eyes as she headed to the back of the ambulance and got inside. Kenzo called Marcus on his way to his car. He wanted him at the meeting with Shotgun to compare notes. He sent Grace a quick text to let her know that he was going to find Riley before coming to the hospital.

Kenzo just prayed he could find Riley in time.

~

Riley's head was pounding. Riley shifted his body on the sofa and swung his arm over his eyes. Or was it the door? He peeked from beneath his arm as if he could see the sound. Who would be knocking at his door? He groaned as he struggled to get up. Riley wasn't in the frame of mind to be polite, so whoever it was better have a good reason. Someone better be bleeding or dead, he thought.

"Who is it?" Riley called out.

"Open the door! It's Kenzo!" Kenzo hadn't heard from Grace, which was a good sign. The longer he didn't hear anything, the better the outcome. And it gave him time to get Riley to Treasure before it was too late.

"Kenzo? What the hell are you doing here?" Riley leaned against the door. "Grace put you out already?"

Riley smelled like he bathed in bourbon, but he was going to have to get it together and quickly. No wonder he didn't answer the phone, Kenzo thought. "It's Treasure, Riley. Someone attacked her at the store. We need to get to the hospital." Kenzo tried to say it as calmly as he could. He didn't want his friend to panic. Riley needed to be strong right now for whatever happened. Kenzo paused to see if the words were registering in Riley's brain.

Riley stared at Kenzo as if he were trying to register what Kenzo was saying. Treasure? Attacked? Riley stammered, "Wh-wh-what happened?"

Kenzo saw confusion flash across Riley's face. He said, "I don't know, but the ambulance took her to the hospital. We showed up at the store as soon as we could. The ambulance took her almost as soon as we got there."

Riley grabbed his phone and keys from the bowl by the door. As he did, Kenzo turned and headed toward the car. Riley was close on his heels.

Neither man spoke on the way to the hospital until Kenzo finally decided to break the silence.

Kenzo turned on State Street. "Man, I've been calling you all night."

Riley hung his head. "I cut my phone off. Didn't feel like talking to anyone."

"I found out why Treasure went ghost on you today."

Riley's head snapped up, but he remained silent. He waited.

Kenzo let out a breath. He hoped that his earlier defense of Riley proved correct. "Some woman came into Treasure's store and told her she was pregnant with your baby."

Riley's eyes widened. "What the hell? Man, c'mon. Did Grace tell you that? You know I don't roll like that." He rubbed his hands down his face. "What woman?"

"Some woman named Scarlett," Kenzo said. After Grace and I talked, she was trying to talk to Treasure and then something happened, and Treasure said she had to go to the store. And I was trying to call you to tell you.

"Man, I don't even know a woman named Scarlett." Riley shook his head in disgust. If something happened to Treasure over this bull, there was going to be hell to pay.

By the time Kenzo and Riley pulled into the emergency room parking lot at the St. Dominic's, Riley was a nervous wreck. He just needed to lay eyes on her and make sure she was going to be okay. Kenzo had barely slowed the car into a parking space before Riley jumped out and ran inside the emergency room entrance. He saw Grace talking to two officers at the information desk.

"Grace!" Riley called her name. "What happened? How is she? Where is she?"

Grace dismissed the officers and turned to face Riley. His eyes were frantic, and his voice was rising. "Wait, Riley. I'm waiting on the doctor now. She hit her head. The think there might be some swelling, but she's breathing on her own."

Riley's heart constricted in his chest and a lump formed in his throat. Grace had gone into cop mode, but he could tell she was as scared as he. "Swelling? What does that mean? Brain damage?"

Grace's bottom lip trembled as she nodded "yes." Kenzo stood by Grace's side. He clasped her hand and gave it a squeeze.

An older black woman came out of the double doors leading to the back of the emergency room. Riley stopped her. "Ma'am, can we get some information on Treasure Jordan. An ambulance brought her in nearly an hour ago?"

"The doctor will be out shortly. Please. Have a seat. It shouldn't be too much longer." The nurse walked into another set of doors.

Riley was about to follow her when Kenzo placed his hand on his shoulder. "Stay cool, man. No news is good news right now."

Riley nodded followed Kenzo and Grace to the small waiting area. Grace and Kenzo sat down, but Riley couldn't sit. He paced the floor, praying and checking the clock on the wall behind the information desk every few seconds.

The next few moments felt like an eternity. Between ambulances and walk-ins, the waiting room filled up rather quickly. Every time the doors to the triage opened, Riley would look expectantly in that direction. Finally, an older black woman with silver locks tied up in a loose ponytail approached them.

"Mrs. Dallas?"

Grace and Kenzo stood up. "Yes, I'm Mrs. Dallas." She motioned to Kenzo. "This is my husband, Kenzo Dallas, and this," motioning to Riley, "is her boyfriend, Riley Taylor." Grace leaned on Kenzo for support.

The doctor introduced herself. "I'm Dr. Carmichael. I treated Ms. Jordan since she arrived." She patted Grace's shoulder. "Ms. Jordan will be fine. We're going to keep her tonight for observation though. She has some serious swelling on her left ankle, but it's not broken. It's wrapped and will be elevated for tonight. Scans show that she does have a grade one concussion. There is some swelling, but not as bad as we initially thought."

Riley swallowed, "Has she said anything?"

Dr. Carmichael smiled, "No, but she should wake up in the next 24 hours. Her brain and body need to rest. But don't worry, the baby is doing fine and has a strong heartbeat. We're being really careful about the types of pain meds we're giving her."

Riley's knees almost buckled under him. He heard Grace gasp while Kenzo exhaled.

Riley's head cocked to the side in confusion. "Wh-wh-what did you say?" His voice was a strangled whisper he barely recognized as his own.

Dr. Carmichael looked at the stunned faces before her. She reached out to touch Riley's arm. If the three people standing in front of her didn't look so stricken, she would have laughed. "I take it this is a surprise."

Grace blinked. "Yes, Doctor, quite the surprise. I don't think she knew either." She turned to Riley. "Treasure never would have gone back to the store if she knew."

Dr. Carmichael nodded. "I see. Well, yes, Ms. Jordan is fairly early in her pregnancy. So early, in fact, that it wouldn't have shown up except in a blood test at this point."

"When can we see her?" Riley asked, his voice raspy and barely above a whisper. A baby? Riley walked to the closest seat and sat down. He hung his head and leaned forward. He and Treasure were going to have a baby, and she doesn't know it. She's not speaking to him, and was so mad at him, she put herself in harm's way.

Dr. Carmichael glanced at Riley and spoke to Grace. She touched her arm. "She's being transferred to a room now, so soon. A nurse will let you know what the final room number is.

Grace smiled weakly as the doctor walked off. She could only imagine what was going through Riley's head right now. He fell into a chair and held his head in his heads. Riley looked lost, and for the first time tonight, she realized that he truly loved Treasure. She took the seat next to his and placed her hand on his back.

"She's going to be fine, Riley." Grace motioned to Kenzo to find some coffee. She wanted some time alone with Riley to find out what he was thinking.

Riley sat up and looked at Grace. Tears brimmed his eyes. "Grace, what if it had been worse? What if I'd lost her?" He dropped his head in his hands.

Grace exhaled. "I know. I'm having them pull the security tapes. Hopefully, we can track the assailants that way, and then we can find out who's targeting her and why. Right now, we just have to focus on making sure that she and the baby are safe."

Riley shook his head in disbelief. He whispered, "the baby," to himself. How could I have been so careless? She deserved better than this, he thought to himself. He threw his head back. Marcellus drilled it into his head to use a condom from the moment a girl turned his head. Riley had always been proud that he always used a condom. Always.

Calmly, Grace said, "Did Kenzo tell you why Treasure was so angry and hurt today? And before you answer, let me apologize, I should have told you earlier. But she made me promise not to tell you."

Riley's jaw clenched and his jaw jumped. He should be angry, but the fact was that he was glad Treasure had a friend like Grace despite all of this. "Yeah, he told me. Whatever that woman said today is a damn lie."

Grace opened her mouth to speak but Riley gave her a look that stopped her cold. She wanted to, at least, explain why Treasure was so quick to believe the worst. But she realized that Riley didn't want to hear any explanations right now.

"Grace, the only woman I've ever slept with without a condom is carrying my baby right now."

Riley didn't care if Grace believed him. All he needed, right now, was to see Treasure. Touch her. Hold her. Riley wanted to be the first person Treasure saw when she opened her eyes. He wanted to be the one to tell her that she was pregnant with their child. Riley knew the moment she conceived. Riley smiled at the memory. He just hoped that she would be just as happy.

Then, he would find the man responsible for putting his woman and his child in harm's way.

CHAPTER 12

Shotgun navigated her metallic black Escalade down Robinson Road, negotiating the potholes with ease. This early in the morning the streets were beautifully quiet, giving her a bit of peace. And you could see the beauty in those grand, rundown houses that lined the street. Large homes with vaulted ceilings, large windows, and hardwood floors hidden under dirty carpets. A shame. But the gentrification had begun. You could see it in pieces. A house here. A storefront there. Though some of the changes were good, but she often wondered how long it would take for the hood folks to realize their neighborhood was gone.

Soon her thoughts turned to what she was about to do. Being Shotgun day in and day out weighed on her, but she couldn't show it. Weakness on the streets, or even with her people, the ones she trusted, could prove deadly. She had been in the game too long not to know that simple truth. She listened to the local university's jazz station and let the smooth sounds wash over her. It was a welcome change from what her crew listened to most of the time. Tonight, Shotgun needed calm. Helping Kenzo last year to save his wife's life opened a part of her memories she buried deep inside.

Hanging out with Kenzo, Riley, and Marcus made her remember too many memories of her children before things went so badly. And no matter how she distanced herself from everything and everyone in her previous life, if any one of them needed her, she would be there.

And that's why she was driving to the train station at 4:00 in the morning. She absentmindedly ran her fingers through her hair. Shotgun knew that this meeting, unlike any other, was going to change everything.

But she knew it had to be done.

~

Kenzo didn't tell anyone--not even Riley--that he also called Shotgun that night at Treasure's house. It had taken some time, but Shotgun had come through with some information that would get to the heart of all of this.

She texted Kenzo to let him know that she had information that he needed but could only be discussed in person. When she told him to meet her at train station at four in the morning, Kenzo knew something was wrong. He picked up Marcus and drove to the station, parking in the far corner of the lot across the street.

Marcus moved to the backseat as soon as they parked. He hadn't seen Shotgun in about a year, but she was always just as beautiful as he remembered from school. Her long black hair curled around her right shoulder like a lion's mane, and Marcus remembered when he used to watch her curl a lock around her finger when she was thinking or daydreaming in school. He closed his eyes. Those days were over, and he needed to accept that.

He and Kenzo saw the lights of Shotgun's Escalade at the same time. When the truck pulled up, Shotgun sent Kenzo a text to get in her truck.

Kenzo frowned as he read the message. Something was wrong. "She wants us to get in her truck." He opened his door and got out. When he noticed that Shotgun was in the driver's seat, his hair stood on edge. Usually, she had a driver and was never alone like this. Marcus took a deep breath and exited Kenzo's car. Here we go, he thought as he and Kenzo got into Shotgun's passenger side.

Shotgun didn't like surprises, and it seemed that dealing with Kenzo was always full of those. "I thought it was just going to be you. Kenzo, you know I don't do surprises. Surprises get folks killed."

"Well, hello to you, too" Marcus said sarcastically. His jaw tightened. The last time they saw each other was over a year ago when he tried to convince her to go straight one last time. Her refusal broke his heart.

Kenzo chuckled. "Shay, you know me. And you know Marcus. Don't trip. It's too early in the morning." Marcus hated what Shay had become. Kenzo had to convince him to come to the meeting in the first place. Knowing and seeing what she had become were two different things.

Shotgun's brow lifted at the use of her birth name. "Alright, alright. I'll let it go this time, but next time, if I allow a next time, you need to at least give me some notice." She glanced at Marcus in the back seat and back at Kenzo. "And stop calling me Shay."

Kenzo laughed and held up his hands. "Okay, okay. So, what's the word?"

Shotgun took a deep breath. "I wanted you in my car because I know it's clean. Your car might be bugged, and I can't take the risk."

"Bugged?" Kenzo and Marcus said at the same time.

"Yes, fools, bugged. You ever heard of Zeus?"

Kenzo said, "No, who is he?"

Marcus replied, "Rumors, but it's more myth than anything."

Shotgun rolled her eyes. "Zeus is not a myth. He's got his hands in everything above and below the line."

Marcus sat up in his seat. "Who are we talking about here?"

Shotgun closed her eyes. She needed Marcus to stop talking. She didn't need Marcus here period. Shotgun didn't answer Marcus but turned to Kenzo. "My man, Harp, is posted outside the store. He parked close enough and far enough that even your men didn't notice him, Marcus." She smirked at him.

Marcus bristled but said nothing. Someone was going to have to answer for this one, for sure. The last thing he wanted to deal with was Shotgun's people being better than his own.

Kenzo needed both of them to focus. Wearily, he asked, "What did he see, Shay?"

Shotgun told them everything Harp told her about the young man outside Treasure's store and how Harp tracked him to a bar at Smith-Wills Stadium. She took a deep breath before continuing. "Listen, what I'm about to tell y'all goes no further than this, even though I know you're going to tell Riley. Where is he by the way? Shouldn't he be here for this, especially since you brought this one." She nodded her head at Marcus.

Marcus bristled. "What do you mean, 'this one'?" He took a deep breath.

Shotgun ignored Marcus. "You need to play this close to the vest, Kenzo. I don't want to tell you to keep anything from your wife, but if she doesn't ask, I sure wouldn't tell. Do y'all understand me?"

Kenzo and Marcus nodded.

Shotgun stared at them. "Say. Yes." When they responded, she continued. "So, the young one, is called E-Money, Zeus's top lieutenant. Real name is Ernest Walker. He handles the underworld crew, but it's a smooth operation. Legal businesses clean the money. They have laundromats, car washes, beauty supply stores. You know, lots of cash transactions in places no one really pays attention to. They can run the drugs, women, or whatever they want, without raising any eyebrows."

Marcus leaned back. "So, basically, the stuff you do."

Shotgun glared at Marcus. He saw the hurt flash across her face. The eyes that were always bright and full of life held sadness. Marcus immediately regretted his comment, but more than that, he regretted hurting her.

She whipped her head around, eyes blazing, and hissed at him. "I don't have to answer to anyone for the choices I had to make. Get out of my car." Then she turned to Kenzo, "You too. Out!"

Kenzo, turned to Marcus. Through gritted teeth, he commanded, "Apologize." He turned to Shotgun like she was a wounded animal and softened his voice. He touched Shotgun's arm, "He didn't mean anything by it, Shay." Turning to Marcus, "Did you, man?"

Marcus looked out of the window and sulked. "No. I apologize. Sorry, Shay."

Kenzo took a deep breath. Shotgun gripped the steering wheel and hissed, "Fine, but Kenzo, don't bring this motherfucker with you next time. If there is a next time."

"Duly noted," Kenzo said, sighing. "So, what else is there? Something's got you spooked, for real. What's the deal with this Zeus character?"

"It's Seth Newall."

Kenzo felt like the wind had been knocked out of him. The name hung in the air like heavy fog. Marcus whispered, "Damn" under his breath.

Shotgun waited for them to recover. Very few people knew who Zeus really was, and she was one of the few. Their dealings had been minimal by design, but she had a thick folder on all of his affairs. Shotgun made sure their interests and paths didn't cross unless she wanted those paths to cross. Zeus was a big fish in a small pond, but big, nonetheless.

Kenzo shook his head. "Nah, Shay, your intel is off. Seth Newall is one of the most successful businessmen in the city, black or white. A philanthropist! Can't be? Are you sure?" Shotgun had to be positive about this. Kenzo held his hand in his hands. "So, he's been muscling businesses, running drugs, women, all of it? Why hasn't he come up on Grace's radar then?"

"How do you think he got that way? Kenzo, have you forgotten? Did you forget how the streets work? How Jackson streets work? The North Side and the West Side don't mix. And they definitely don't trade secrets." Shotgun continued, "He didn't come up because he didn't want to come up. Plus, the girls who work for him don't know they work for him. And the pimps don't know it either. All they know is E-Money."

Kenzo could only nod his head. She spoke the truth. He couldn't deny it one bit. Marcus was stone silent in the backseat, which suited Shotgun just fine.

Kenzo stared at Shotgun in disbelief. He and Riley once looked up to Newall as a mentor, and even when the relationship soured, Kenzo still admired what he was able to do in Jackson. "Wait, it still doesn't make sense. Are you sure? Why would he go after Treasure? From what Riley told me, he's been after Treasure for years?"

Shotgun's jaw clenched. Through gritted teeth, she snapped. "Yes, I'm sure. I put Harp on it. He made a positive ID. I trust him with my life, and I trusted him with Grace's, remember." She continued, "I don't know. But you need to find out. But I'll tell you this, E-Money doesn't make a move unless Zeus tells him to, so if he's pushing up on Treasure now, he's under orders."

They sat in silence for a few moments, each weighing the gravity of what they now knew.

Kenzo's mind was reeling. He closed his eyes to think and let out a breath. "Someone attacked Treasure tonight at her store. She's in the hospital. Riley is there with her. She's going to be fine, but still..." He paused, his thoughts processing Shotgun's info with Treasure's attack. "You think Seth Newall would go this far? I did find it strange that they didn't just kill her since she surprised them."

Shotgun shook her head. "Damn." She tapped the steering wheel. "That's sloppy as hell." This was worse than she imagined. "Listen, Ken, you need to tell Riley, because he and Treasure need to be on guard. She paused, "But, he cannot go half-cocked against Zeus. This is strictly chess, baby."

Marcus let out a deep breath. "Man, this is crazy."

Shotgun sighed as she looked out the window. "But, yeah, he would. And they didn't kill her because that wasn't the order. Trust me, even if she recognized them again, they would never do a day." Shotgun absentmindedly twirled a lock of her hair around her finger. "Kenzo, how did you and Riley both choose women with targets on their back?"

Kenzo laughed nervously, "Just meant to be, I guess. I sure didn't plan it that way."

"I bet," Shotgun replied. "Listen, I got business to handle, so I'll call you when I have something. Be careful. I'll put Harp on the store just to be careful."

Marcus exited the car without saying a word. Hearing that she had business didn't set right with him at all. He stood by the car and waited for Kenzo.

"Thanks, Shay. I appreciate the info." Kenzo exited the car and closed the door. Shotgun drove off, leaving the two men standing in the parking lot. Marcus spoke first, "You know we'll have to sit on Riley, right? He's going to kill Newall."

Kenzo didn't answer but opened his door and got in. Marcus followed. As they drove back to Marcus's house, both were silent. Marcus was thinking about the woman he once knew, and Kenzo was thinking about how he was going to tell Grace, Riley, and Treasure that the enemy was much worse than they could ever imagine.

~

Shotgun parked her car in front of her house. The sun was coming up, and Shotgun took a moment to appreciate the sunrise. She always thought sunrises were better than sunsets. Sunrises held hope. Sunrises were another chance to survive, and in her line of work, a sunrise meant she survived to see another day. And maybe one of those sunrises would start the day she would be Shay again. Tears pricked her eyes. Seeing Marcus, hearing the disgust in his voice, hurt her to the core. She wiped her hands down her face and shook the memories out of her mind. Shotgun couldn't worry about that right now. She whispered to herself, "Dreaming will get you killed. That was never life and it never will be."

She retrieved a phone from the hidden pocket inside the bodice of her catsuit and dialed the one number she knew by heart. When the voice on the other end answered but said nothing, she spoke fast and in shortened sentences. "Operation Black Valkyrie compromised." She didn't wait for a response and hung up. She knew the man on the other end would call in the morning, or hell, he might just show up on her door. No telling. Shotgun shook her head.

She had to be ready to explain her actions or face whatever consequences that were coming her way.

CHAPTER 13

The rhythm of the dull, throbbing pain at her ankle roused Treasure from sleep. Treasure didn't know how long she slept, or even which hospital she was in, but Mama Blossom always said pain was a good thing. Pain meant you were still alive, and if you were alive, you survived. Thank you, God, she prayed.

Opening her eyes was even painful. Her left eye opened fine while her right eye struggled against the weight of the lid as if it were peeling it open. She touched the right side of her face and winced. Her swollen cheek smarted at the slightest touch. Tears welled in her eyes as she tried to make sense of the pain shooting through her body, her surroundings, and who wanted to hurt her so.

Treasure found a source of the warmth. Riley held her hand but had fallen asleep. His neck is going to be sore, she thought. Treasure didn't think she should wake him. What could she say to him? As much as she was happy that Riley was here, that he would come after she ignored him all day and night surprised her. And there was still the matter of that woman and his new baby. The "baby mama drama" type of woman she was not, and judging from her baby bump, it meant that he was seeing both of them for months.

Riley woke to a start. He blinked, gazing into Treasure's beautiful, big eyes. The bruise on her cheek had turned an ugly purple, and her eye was puffy.

"Hey," Treasure said weakly. Her mouth was dry.

"Hey, baby," Riley said. "How are you feeling? Do you want anything?"

Treasure looked around the room before answering. "Yes, water. My mouth is dry."

He reluctantly left her side and grabbed the water pitcher. As he handed her a cup of water, he causally remarked, "You keep scaring me, you know."

Treasure took a huge gulp of water. "I feel terrible. My ankle and my head are both pounding. How long was I out?" Treasure tried to sit up, and when Riley assisted her with the controls on the remote, he was close enough for her to get a whiff of his natural scent and the cologne he wore. She inhaled, knowing this was neither the time nor the place for her libido to kick in, especially since Riley had other obligations. She willed tears not to fall. "What are you doing here, Riley," Treasure whispered.

The words to answer her question escaped him. Elation at the sight of her collided with the fear that he almost lost her. Riley did the only thing he could. He leaned forward and cupped her face in his hands and kissed her sweetly on the lips. Treasure's lips were so soft against his. He couldn't help himself, deepening the kiss. His tongue swept across her mouth, and Treasure's lips parted for him. Treasure moaned softly as Riley explored every inch of her mouth with his tongue. Riley needed Treasure to feel every ounce of love he had for her. Riley felt Treasure's tears fall down his fingers. He reluctantly ended the kiss and still holding her face in his hands, brushed her tears away with his thumbs. Treasure closed her eyes as she let the tears fall. Riley placed his forehead on hers. When he could finally speak, he answered her question with one of his own. "Where else did you think I would be?"

Treasure closed her eyes and let the tears fall. Despite the pain he caused her, she wanted him here so badly.

He whispered against her skin, "Don't cry, baby. It's okay. I'm so sorry. Please don't cry."

"Riley," Treasure choked, her voice full of emotion. She needed to tell him that she knew about the baby, but she couldn't bring herself to say the words out loud. The nearness of him, his tenderness, was almost too much to bear.

Riley kissed her again, chastely, and stepped back. He poured her another cup of water. "Drink some more." As she sipped, Riley decided to answer her question.

"First, I'm here because I love you, and second, I'm here because I love you." He emphasized "you" the second time and looked at her hard.

Before she could say anything else, Riley's eyes softened. "Grace told me what happened at the store."

Treasure shifted her eyes away from him and looked in the direction of the window. "Grace shouldn't have done that."

"No, she shouldn't have," Riley conceded. "You should have. Baby, look at me."

After a few seconds, Treasure turned to face Riley. His eyes were full of a love she didn't understand. How could he say his loved her after all of this?

Riley wiped a tear away with his thumb. Treasure closed her eyes. The tenderness of his touch would be what she missed the most. But miss it she would.

He palmed her cheek, and Treasure automatically leaned into his touch. "Treasure, my Treasure," he whispered. "There is no possible way that any woman other than you is pregnant with my child. No possible way." He didn't want to tell her yet that she was the one carrying his child. They needed to settle this first.

He leaned forward and took her hand. "Do you remember that first night at your store? I told you then that I wasn't your father and you're not your mother. You believed the worst of me because of something your father did, not because of anything I did. I have loved you as completely as I know how. But I can't do that if you keep running from me."

Treasure held her head down.

Riley lifted Treasure's chin. "Now, let me be clear. I don't care what any woman says or said." He paused. "I haven't made love, touched, or anything else with another woman, except you, since Kenzo and Grace's wedding." He could see Treasure counting the months in her head.

Incredulous, Treasure stammered, "But...but...that was six months before we..." Treasure didn't know if she should believe him. This was Riley Taylor after all.

Sheepishly, Riley added, "Yes, believe me, I know. You ruined me with just one dance." He smiled at her, reminding her of their dance at Kenzo and Grace's wedding. "Do you remember our dance?"

He rubbed her cheek with the back of his hand. Then, his tone became serious. "Treasure, you should have trusted me, or at least given me the opportunity to defend myself. We could have avoided all of this. After all we've meant to each other, you believed a woman you didn't know over the man who loves you and who you said you loved. We deserved better than that. Do you really think so little of me?"

Treasure closed her eyes, convicted by Riley's words. But it still didn't explain why some woman claimed to be pregnant with his child. Treasure's lip quivered. "But why, Riley? I just don't understand why any woman would be that cruel to any woman and to me in particular."

"I don't know, sweetheart, and I only care that she hurt you. But I promise you that I will get to the bottom of it. Right now, I need you to relax. I told the nurses that I would let them know when you woke up, but I needed to talk to you first. Besides, there's something else."

Treasure nodded, but a chill went through her. Treasure didn't know how much more she could handle. "What is it? The store?" She closed her eyes. Lord, help, she prayed.

Riley flashed a smile at her. "Treasure, the store is fine, or it will be. Brandi and Simone are there now cleaning up. Grace is there too." He chuckled. "Grace went into straight cop mode so fast, I think even Kenzo had to take a few orders."

Treasure tried to laugh but her cheek and head hurt. She groaned in pain.

Riley lovingly patted her arm. "Easy?" he asked.

Treasure nodded. "Well, what is it? What did the doctors say?"

Riley took a deep breath. "When they brought you in, you had a severe sprain."

"I turned my ankle when I stumbled over a shoe trying to leave the store."

"And a concussion."

"I got hit."

Riley's jaw clenched. He could give less than a damn about some lying woman, but the man who put his hands on his woman should pray that the police find him before he did.

"Riley?"

"Well, since you couldn't answer any questions, the doctor ordered a full blood workup on you." He took a deep breath and held her hand a little tighter. "We're pregnant." Softly, he whispered, "So, sweetheart, trust me, you are the only woman having my baby." He rubbed the back of her hand with his thumb.

Treasure blinked. She opened her mouth to protest and then closed it. "Pregnant?" Treasure was in disbelief. They always used protection, even the last time they made love. Well, there was that one time. Riley saw the memory flash across her face. He turned her hand over and kissed her palm.

Treasure couldn't believe it. She was pregnant with Riley Taylor's baby. Treasure closed her eyes and let the gravity of what was happening wash over her. How was she going to be somebody's mother? "Riley, I..." The tears she held back fell silently down her cheeks.

Riley had hoped she would be happy. "Baby, please don't cry. And don't worry. We'll be fine. I promise." He kissed her lips and then, her forehead. He pulled his handkerchief from his pocket and blotted her tears from her face. "I know it's not how you would have wanted this to happen, but we'll be fine.

Treasure didn't know how to explain what she was feeling. Carrying Riley's child was something she dreamed of, but not like this. An unplanned pregnancy. Would Riley propose marriage just because she was pregnant? She knew what kind of man he was, and she was almost sure that's what he would do. Marrying because of a pregnancy was the last thing she would do.

At that moment, Dr. Carmichael walked in. "Well, hello Ms. Jordan? Nice to finally meet you. You gave everyone quite a scare last night. How are you feeling today?" She smiled in Riley's direction.

"My head is pounding, my ankle is throbbing, and I just found out I'm pregnant," Treasure said flatly. "But other than that, I'm fine."

Dr. Carmichael's eyebrow raised as she heard the pain beneath the sarcasm. "You will be."

She didn't even blame Treasure, really. "I know it's been quite the ordeal, Ms. Jordan, but pain is a good thing. Means you're still feeling something. The alternative is much worse."

Treasure looked heavenward. I hear you, Mama Blossom, she thought. She kept her tone appreciative and her words cordial going forward.

As Dr. Carmichael conducted her examination, she casually instructed Treasure about her condition and what to do next. "Having a concussion is serious business. And we have to be especially cautious since you're pregnant. And you need to make an appointment with your obstetrician as soon as possible."

"Yes, Ma'am," Riley piped in.

The women looked at him as if they'd forgotten he was there.

Dr. Carmichael smiled before continuing, "Ms. Jordan, you'll need to keep both your head and your leg elevated. I'm going to release you, but you must take it easy. No charging at windmills, okay? Someone will need to stay with you until your checkup in about a week, but I think you have that covered." She glanced in Riley's direction.

"Yes, ma'am," he said. Treasure started to object, but one look at Riley's chiseled jaw changed her mind. They were still staring at each other when the doctor gave her final instructions.

"The nurse will be in to finalize your discharge. She paused for a moment. "This should go without saying, but I'll say it anyway. No sex until after the checkup. An accelerated heart rate will elevate your blood pressure, which isn't good for a concussion." She clicked her pen twice.

"Once the concussion heals, you're free to resume normal activities." Speaking of, Ms. Jordan, are you related to Corinne Jordan?"

Treasure nodded, "She's my mother."

Dr. Carmichael smiled. "I thought so, you look like her. Tell her I said hello."

She rested her hand on Treasure's shoulder. "You take care of yourself and your baby, Ms. Jordan." She turned to Riley, "Mr. Taylor, take good care of this one."

"Trust me, I will." Riley didn't take his eyes off Treasure as he spoke.

Treasure nodded through teary eyes. She couldn't believe that she was going to be a mother. And she would have to tell her mother before someone at the hospital said something. And her father. Riley seemed thrilled, but fear gripped her heart. She couldn't protect herself these days, and now she had to protect a baby growing inside her. What did she know about being a mother?

As if Riley read her mind, he placed his hand on her stomach. "Baby, all you have to do is take care of this right here. I'll take care of the rest." He placed a featherlight kiss on her lips and then laid his head on her stomach. Treasure lay her hand on his head.

She had no doubt that he meant every word. But the thought worried her that Riley, for all his pronouncements, would eventually see her and the baby as more obligation than blessing.

~

Exhaustion had taken over Treasure's body. She'd been confined to Riley's bedroom for nearly a week, until today, when Riley took her to her follow-up appointment with Dr. Carmichael. He treated her like a porcelain doll since she left the hospital. Riley carried her from the car to his bedroom where she remained until today. Treasure wanted for nothing. He cooked or ordered her favorite dishes, bathed her, dressed her, and even let her watch her reality shows without his usual commentary that they were infecting her soul.

When her parents visited, Riley effortlessly charmed her mother until she was giggling like a schoolgirl and even her father was shaking Riley's hand like they were old friends. She and Riley decided to wait to reveal their baby news until later. Treasure knew she couldn't handle telling her parents right now, especially with the break-in and her attack.

Riley gave Treasure just what she needed. Peace. But what he didn't give her was himself. As much as he did for her, his touches were distant. She wondered if he was as overwhelmed as she was.

She tested her ankle by putting a little weight on it and limped to the row of large windows in the bedroom that opened to a balcony overlooking Riley's property. Treasure always thought Riley's bedroom rivaled any spa she visited. She walked to the ceiling-to-wall windows and ran her palm against the brocade of the drapes. The material felt good against her skin, and Treasure closed her eyes. She felt every groove against her skin. The texture soothed her, made her disconnect from the pain in her heart and the body. She thought about fabrics and their textures. She loved that part most of all. Fabrics were like people to Treasure--soft or hard, easy or rough, warm or cool. Complicated. Plain.

Riley's bedroom was massive and nearly took up half of the upstairs floor, and the balcony was the length of the room. She decided that a few moments on the balcony would be good for her. Even though her body was healing, Treasure still had so much on her mind. Riley's distance was foremost among them.

When she opened the French doors, the warmth of the sun and a cool breeze greeted her. She braced herself on the back of one of the chairs by the doors and stepped down. Treasure sat down and took a deep breath. She placed a hand on her stomach as her eyes landed on Riley's favorite oak tree. She closed her eyes, the memory of their confessions of love and the life they made flashing before her.

Treasure sat in the comforts of her memories for fifteen minutes before she heard Riley enter the bedroom.

Riley almost panicked when he didn't see Treasure in the bed. He scanned the room and saw her on the balcony. He watched her for a few more seconds. She was absolutely beautiful with the sun shining on her face. He remembered watching his grandparents sit quietly on this balcony on Sunday evenings. No one violated those quiet moments between them. Riley wondered if he and Treasure would have those sacred moments. Treasure teetered between confusion and fear most days, and he didn't want to push her too fast. Today's appointment gave him hope, and even now, she looked more like herself than she had all week.

"Hey," he said, leaning against the door frame.

"Hey, yourself," she replied, smiling weakly at him. "I just wanted some fresh air. Getting out today made me realize how much I needed some sun." She held out her hand. "Come sit with me."

Riley sat next to Treasure and took her hand. They enjoyed the view together, neither one daring to break the companionable silence between them. Riley absentmindedly rubbed the back of her hand with his thumb. The intimacy of the moment centered both of them. Treasure closed her eyes. The softest touch from Riley touched a piece of her soul, and at that moment, she just knew that they would be okay.

Riley asked, "Is everything okay?"

Treasure smiled at him again. "I'm fine, Riley. It's just a beautiful day, and I just wanted to capture a piece of it."

Riley nodded and looked ahead. "You should be in bed, Treasure," he said softly. "You still need to rest and elevate your ankle."

Treasure remained silent. Her ankle throbbed slightly, but she soothed herself with the rhythm of pain. She knew he was right, and for once, Treasure would comply without comment. "Yes, sir, Dr. Taylor." She chuckled and pretended to be annoyed. As she braced herself on the chair's armrests, Riley quickly came to help her stand.

He pulled her to him and held her tightly. He missed her laughter and her touch. Just a small chuckle made his heart soar. Treasure leaned into his embrace. Being her own rock all these years had taken its toll. Riley felt Treasure's body surrender to him the moment the thought crossed her mind.

"Just let me take care of you, Treasure," he said. "Both of you."

Treasure hugged him tightly and Riley pressed his hand in the small of her back. Treasure flinched slightly as pain radiated from the large bruise in the center of her back. "Am I hurting you?" *When I get my hands on that sonofabitch,* he thought. A lump formed in Riley's throat. Riley forced himself to speak. "C'mon, let's get you into bed."

Riley delivered a quick kiss to her forehead before scooping her up to carry her, turning sideways to enter the bedroom from the balcony.

Treasure always felt so light and so cared for in his arms, but she felt compelled to put up a little protest. "I can walk, Riley,"

"You need to get off this leg," he replied. Without another word, he placed her gently beside the bed. "We just need to get you out of these clothes first." Riley's heart constricted in his chest. Even though she tried to hide it, Treasure looked miserable trying to balance herself. She placed her weight on her good leg as the toe of her other leg barely touched the floor.

Treasure winced as Riley lifted her shirt. The slightest movement highlighted every bruise and sore muscle she had.

Riley whispered, "I'm so sorry, baby. Easy. I'm so sorry." Riley wrapped his arm around her waist to hold her up and placed kisses along Treasure's collarbone. If he couldn't take away her pain, perhaps he could replace it with something pure.

He slid his free hand in the waistband of her leggings and knelt to remove them. Struck by what he could have lost without even knowing he had it, Riley placed kisses across Treasure's belly, imagining that in a few months how it would grow with the life inside it. As much as he wanted and needed to be strong, Riley simply couldn't hold the tears back any longer. Tears joined his kisses across her belly. He hoped the life growing inside her could feel how much Riley loved him or her.

Treasure felt Riley's tears against her skin. She leaned back on the bed for balance. "Riley," she whispered. She placed her hands on the sides of his face and called his name again. His pain was palpable, and all of her earlier doubts and fears she had dissipated. Silent tears flowed down her cheeks.

Riley looked up, his eyes awash with tears, at the woman he loved more than anything in the world. "If anything had happened to you, Treasure, it would have killed me."

Treasure didn't think it was possible to love Riley any more than she did. Riley rose, never taking his eyes from hers, picked her up and placed her on the bed. Riley pulled her face close to his. "Do you understand, woman, that I love you more than anything in this world? More than I have loved anyone or anything?" Before she could respond, he kissed her, taking her mouth and pressing his body against hers. The gentle kiss turned into one with every passion Riley had. As much as he tried to stop, he couldn't. His desire for Treasure controlled him, and he needed her more than he ever had before.

Treasure felt his desire for her, and any soreness she might have felt in her body was secondary to her need for Riley. Her panties dampened with her arousal as Riley's tongue explored her mouth. Treasure grabbed at his shirt and yanked his shirt out of his jeans. She needed to feel his skin. She slid her hands underneath Riley's shirt, caressing his pecs and squeezing his nipples. Riley moaned against her mouth. Treasure's touch was a like a hot brand, marking him, rewiring his body to respond only to her touch. No woman had ever come close to owning his soul like this. And no woman ever would.

Riley broke the kiss and mourned the loss of her lips against his. . He and Treasure stared into each other's eyes for a few seconds. His eyes darkened with desire. Treasure's full breasts threatened to spill out of her bra. He snatched his shirt over his head and took her mouth again, unclasping her bra, freeing her breasts. He leaned forward and captured a swollen nipple in his mouth and swirled his tongue around it before sucking it hard. Treasure's pleasure-filled moans ignited a powerful desire within Riley. His manhood strained against his jeans, fueled by the scent of her arousal and her pleasure-filled moans. As he caressed and laved her breasts with his tongue, Riley gently pushed her back and swung her legs around in the bed. Reluctantly, Riley pulled back to quickly disrobe and join her on the bed. He needed Treasure so badly that his hands were shaking, but he didn't want to hurt her, or the baby. He gently grabbed Treasure by the waist. Treasure's sharp intake of breath sobered him. He stopped and eased to her side.

"Baby, did I hurt you? We shouldn't be doing this right now." As much as he wanted to make love to Treasure, he couldn't risk hurting her or the baby.

Treasure stifled her laugh since Riley looked so painfully serious. She caressed his face in the attempt to assuage his fears. "I'm fine, Riley. The only thing hurting me right now is not being with you. I'm fine. The baby's fine. Dr. Carmichael cleared me this morning, remember."

She reached down between their bodies, stroking his manhood. "Make love to me, Riley." Treasure kissed his collarbone softly before delivering a long lick to his neck. Riley shivered.

"Woman, I swear, you don't play fair."

Treasure smiled against his neck. "Not today, I don't." She bit his neck at his jugular, his sweet spot. Riley's sharp intake of air spurred her to continue. His hands roamed over her body as defenses broke down.

"What my Treasure wants, my treasure gets," Riley whispered against her skin. Treasure's touch was driving him insane. She was simultaneously nibbling on his ear and stroking him at the same time. He gently eased her backwards, kissing her and nestling himself between her legs. Feverish with desire for her, he kissed and nipped every inch of her flesh as he traveled the length of her body. Treasure opened her body to him, and he teased the ball of sensitive flesh with his tongue. Riley made love to her core like a starving man, his moans sent vibrations through her body. As he pressed his mouth to her, Riley reached up and fondled her breasts. When he squeezed her nipples, Treasure exploded on his tongue, screaming his name.

He needed to be inside her. As her orgasm subsided, Riley eased over her and entered her warmth slowly, deliberately. Treasure gasped and arched her back. Riley filled her completely, and every thrust drove her to a higher plane of pleasure.

Riley closed his eyes and steadied himself, summoning every ounce of control he had. But Treasure's core was gripping him, contracting around him. Riley couldn't stop moving against her, and her moans drove him to a frenzy. Every thrust, every movement against her, had his entire body on fire. Riley dropped his head and took her earlobe between his teeth. He whispered in her ear, "Treasure, my treasure." His thrusts became deeper and deeper inside her. "You feel so good, baby."

Treasure wrapped her legs around Riley's waist and pulled him deeper insider her. Riley and Treasure stared into each other's eyes as Riley's thrust drove her orgasm.

Riley leaned down and kissed her. "Come with me, baby,"

Treasure's body responded on command. The most powerful orgasm of her life ripped through her body. She raked her nails across Riley's back as he threw his head back and let out a primal yell. Treasure's orgasm triggered his, as her core pulsed against his shaft. Riley trembled. Every nerve ending and cell in his body called her name. As their orgasms subsided, Riley lowered his forehead to hers.

"I love you, baby." He kissed her forehead one final time before easing away from her warmth.

Riley's love healed her spirit in a way she had never imagined possible.

"Don't move," Riley commanded. He retrieved a warm towel from the en suite bathroom. His tenderness overwhelmed her at times. When he finished cleaning her and himself up, he propped her ankle up on a pillow and slid next to her in bed.

"Better?" Riley asked.

"I am now," Treasure responded coyly.

Riley rolled his eyes. "I meant your ankle, but how's your head?." He kissed her shoulder. "But I'm glad you're all better." Riley emphasized "all" and laughed.

Treasure laughed and suddenly, all the easiness that they shared before the attack came back. She missed laughing with him, being emotionally intimate with him.

"I missed you, Treasure." Riley said quietly after the laughter died down. He drew lazy patterns on her skin.

Treasure nodded. "I missed you, too."

Just as exhaustion took hold, Riley's doorbell rang. What the hell, he thought. Riley didn't want anyone at the house right now, and definitely not right now. He checked his phone. Seeing Kenzo, Grace, and Marcus. standing on his front porch meant business. "Damn," he muttered under his breath.

He looked at Treasure, who was already asleep. He eased out of the bed and got dressed. A feeling of dread washed over him as he dressed. Kenzo and Grace could be a friendly call, but Marcus's presence changed the dynamic. He looked back at Treasure before heading downstairs. He just hoped that Marcus had the answers he was looking for to stop this madness once and for all.

~

Riley kissed Treasure's forehead before leading her into the en suite bathroom. Treasure watched him turn on the faucets on his claw foot tub and pour oil and Epsom salt into the water. Soon, the room smelled warm and exotic. He grabbed some towels and set them on the stool by the large shower. Then, he turned to her and smiled. Without saying a word, Riley walked behind her and began undressing her. Treasure winced as the slightest movement highlighted every bruise and sore muscle she had. Riley, whispered, "I'm so sorry, baby. Easy. I'm so sorry." Treasure stepped into the shower and let the pulsating water soothe the tension in her body. Her mind was another matter.

Treasure closed her eyes. She didn't have the strength to speak, to move even. She was still too dazed to really talk about anything. The store. The attack. And definitely not Riley and the baby.

Riley quickly undressed and stood behind her. He lathered a towel and washed Treasure's back, paying attention to the large bruise between her shoulder blades. Riley took a deep cleansing breath. He could feel Treasure's body tense under his touch. Tenderly, but quickly, he finished bathing her.

Treasure said very little since leaving the hospital. In fact, Riley didn't think Treasure said more than ten words, and most of those were one-word answers to his questions. He asked if wanted to check on the store. She refused. Treasure was past being wounded. She was broken.

The attack stole a piece of her spirit, and Riley silently vowed to help her get it back.

CHAPTER 14

Shotgun pulled up to a small rundown, brick building at Gallatin Street. This part of downtown would probably never get the revitalization treatment. Surrounded by construction supply businesses, tire places, and a few gas stations, the building was, just as the structures surrounding it, in need of a good power washing. But then, Shotgun, thought to herself, a clean building would definitely be suspicious in this area. She checked her watch. It was 5:30 a.m. Thirty minutes until her meeting. Jackson streets were relatively quiet that early in the morning, so being recognized wasn't the issue. Creating a power position was. And she needed all the power she could get for this one even though she had no power here. Shotgun had broken serious protocols, and consequences would be exacted. Of that, she was sure.

She saw a lone, unmarked black sedan parked down the street. Shotgun took a deep breath and cut her engine. Might as well get it over with. She exited her truck and walked to the entrance. The door was slightly ajar, and Shotgun patted the shotgun at her hip. She counted the weapons on her person in her head. A .25 in the small of her back. A knife between her breasts and at her back. A small gun on her right ankle. Luck favors the prepared, she muttered under her breath.

Shotgun entered the building. Immediately, she saw her contact sitting in a large chair in the center of the warehouse, reading a copy of the *Jackson Free Press*. Without lowering the paper, he called to her.

"Ms. Johnson, good morning," he said, peering over his newspaper. "Come. Sit."

Shotgun hesitated for a second. The room was too quiet for her liking. She preferred chaos. Chaos she could handle. Silence made her uneasy. Silence meant fates were already sealed. Chaos always meant you had a chance. She walked to the vacant seat, sat down, and waited. After a few moments, the newspaper came down and the face she dreaded stared at her.

Chief's face was always different. Only the voice remained the same. The only constant was that he always came South though in whiteface. "The complexion for the protection," he always said. Shotgun always thought he resembled Eddie Murphy as the old white man in *Coming to America* in the short brown-haired wig he wore. Shotgun wanted to laugh but thought better of it, considering the subject of the meeting.

"Now," he said, "tell me what the hell happened that made you compromise a mission that's been in the works for the last five years."

"You asked me to look after Grace when she came to town. Neither one of us knew that she was going to marry one of my oldest friends. He asked me to look into something and it collided with the Black Valkyrie operation. Seth Newall had Grace's friend Treasure Jordan attacked."

Calmly, "I see."

Shotgun straightened her back. "Listen, Chief, I have worked this operation for five years. I have had Grace's back like you asked, but it's time for all of this to end. I have run these streets long enough to amass every bit of intel you need to put Seth Newall away. Now is the time. I have a business to run and it's time for me to get out of the snitch business."

Chief raised an eyebrow. "Ms. Johnson, you are in no position to tell me when an operation is finished. Do you remember that when I found you, you were doing random contract hits, putting your sisters at risk?

Did I not get your record clean, your sisters out of Jackson, and set you up in this little criminal enterprise at the government's expense at the government's pleasure?"

"Yes, but I'm telling you, Seth Newall has gone too far. You won't be able to arrest him, because I know Riley and Kenzo. And now I know Grace. Grace will blow this operation through the local police, and if that doesn't work, Riley will ask me to kill the man outright." She paused. Firmly, she said, "And I will do it."

Chief laughed. "I bet you would." His face became deadly serious. He took a sip of coffee. "Convince me then."

Not only did Shotgun relay everything Newall and his henchman, Ernest, had done to Treasure, but also his forays into pandering, gambling, and the drug trade in Jackson. "Zeus hides in plain sight, simply because no one would believe that the great Seth Newall would engage in any criminal activity."

Taking another sip, Chief remarked. "A RICO case for sure. But do you have the proof?"

Shotgun nodded and retrieved a flash drive from her pocket. "Everything is on this drive. Pics, documents, even some voice recordings. A few of my men and I were able to get a meeting with Zeus about six months ago. I muscled in on one of his territories, which necessitated a meeting between us. It's on there as well."

"How did you manage that?"

Shotgun smiled. "I hid the recorder in my hair. His boys could pat me down and try to cop a feel, but they knew not to mess with my hair. They got mamas. They know better."

Chief laughed heartily and shook his head. "Have mercy. Black women and their damn hair. Y'all won't swim, exercise, and will cut a man if he touches your hair."

"Indeed." Shotgun swept her hair around her shoulders for effect and smiled broadly.

The smile in his eyes turned into a frown. "One last question and then you can go." Sarcastically, he asked, "Did you tell your friends about your involvement with the Agency?" His eyes narrowed as if he were expecting her to answer incorrectly.

"No, I didn't," she responded. She thought about Marcus and how he spoke to her that night. Things would have been so much easier if she didn't have to carry her secret alone.

"Good. Don't. For now." Chief stood. "I suppose that it will come out soon enough, but that will be delicate surgery. I'm sure Kenzo has given Grace your intel. And I'm sure she doesn't know what to make of your relationship with her husband." Chief halfheartedly chuckled. The odds were astronomical but what can you expect from a little big city like Jackson. Two of his best agents linked to the same man. He shook his head.

Shotgun looked at Chief squarely. "Nothing to make out. Kenzo and I have always been like brother and sister. She knows that. But since I'm technically a criminal, I'm not invited to Sunday dinner. Kenzo won't put her in that position, and I won't put him in that position."

She rose from her chair. Quietly, she remarked, as she turned to leave. "But a civilian Sunday dinner would be nice, you know?"

Chief didn't respond. As she disappeared around the corner, Chief thought about how much alike she and Grace were even though they trained in different sectors and for different purposes. They both wanted more out of life than the State Department or the Agency could give them, and for once, Chief envied their youth, their hopefulness. He shuddered murmured under his breath, "Let me get the hell out of Mississippi before I start dreaming about porches and sweet tea."

~

Riley listened intently to Kenzo as he explained Shotgun's information. As soon as it registered that Seth Newall was behind everything that had happened to Treasure, he felt his blood literally boiling in his veins. He already disliked Seth Newall for business reasons and then that night of the Black Men United event when he disrespected Treasure, that was it for him. But he was madder still that Kenzo and Grace kept it from him for the past week.

Grace sat there quietly, watching Riley get angrier and angrier while Kenzo and Marcus were oblivious to the powder keg about to explode before them.

Kenzo leaned forward, "We," motioning to include Grace, "thought that Treasure could somehow get Newall talking and get him to confess on tape. Grace would handle the logistics and security"

Riley cut him off. "First of all, you must be out of your rabid ass mind, Kenzo, if you think I'm going to let Seth Newall anywhere near the mother of my child. And second, I don't know why y'all have known about this for a week and haven't said a word to Treasure and me."

Grace sat up. Riley's anger made him dangerously calm. "Riley, listen to me, Treasure is my best friend in the world. Kenzo wanted to tell you immediately. I told him not to..."

Riley opened his mouth to speak, but Grace kept talking.

"I told him not to, because Treasure needed rest and you needed to take care of her. You both needed a bubble, and with her pregnancy and a concussion, I didn't want anything to happen to her or your baby." She emphasized "your" so Riley would understand that withholding this information was in their best interests.

Riley scowled. He knew Grace was right but damn if he was going to like it. "So, let me get this straight, Seth Newall, one of Jackson's most prominent businessmen, is a criminal kingpin who goes by the name Zeus. And his chief second, this E-Money character, is the one who broke into the store and attacked Treasure."

Grace answered, "Yes."

"But you can't pick him up because you have no real proof other than what Shotgun told you?"

Grace sighed. "Unfortunately, yes, that's the sum of it."

"But if I go break this motherfucker's skull, you'll arrest me, right?"

"Riley, man," Marcus interrupted, "this is why we held it. You can't go guns blazing on this one."

Before he realized it, Riley was shouting. "Why the hell not? It was good enough when we went to the Coast to save Grace! Right, Kenzo? We had a freaking arsenal in that hotel!"

Kenzo said nothing. He understood Riley's passion. When someone is after the woman you love, there are no limits to what you'll do. "The situation was a bit different, Riley, but I understand. You know I do, but just like you had my back on the Coast, I have yours now. Seth Newall isn't just some big fish we don't know. This is a big fish we know, man, in a city who loves him. This has to be delicate. Strategic. Trust me on this."

"I don't want to hear that shit man. Y'all come in here talking about using my woman as bait for a damn psychopath, and you expect me to just accept that."

Treasure heard voices in her sleep. At first, she thought she was dreaming, but when she heard Riley's voice raised, she knew something was terribly wrong. With a bit of a struggle, she limped to the dresser and found a shift nightgown and pulled her robe from the bench by the bed. As she got closer to the stairs, she realized that the entire crew was downstairs, which meant she was the topic of a conversation and no one bothered to send her an invitation.

"Hey, what's going on? Having a party and no one woke me?" Treasure quickly assessed the strained faces in the room. Riley was clearly upset, but his face softened when he saw her. When he turned to get her from the stairs, Treasure held up her hand. "No, Riley, I can make it."

Riley stood by the bottom of the stairs, worried that Treasure was going to hurt herself but more than that, that she was going to go along with this crazy plan.

Grace came over and hugged her, almost knocking him out of the way. "Hey, mama, how are you feeling?"

Treasure smiled. "Still processing, but enough about me, though something tells me that all this hollering is still about me." Grace led Treasure to the sofa and Riley followed behind them. When Treasure sat down on the love seat, Riley pulled the ottoman over to elevate her legs and placed a throw over her. Grace smiled at Riley's care for her friend. She sat on the adjoining sofa closest to Treasure.

No one said anything. Marcus picked imaginary lint from his jeans, while Kenzo and Grace gave each other apprehensive looks about where to begin. Oh, now, you want to be quiet, he thought.

"The night of your attack, Kenzo and Marcus met with Shotgun." He felt Treasure tense up beside him. "Turns out that the person behind your attack is Seth Newall."

Treasure's eyes widened. She looked at Riley and then, at Grace. "I don't believe that. Seth Newall is a lot of things. He's a leech and a womanizer, but a criminal?" She shook her head and turned to Grace. "Do you believe this?"

Grace shrugged. "As law enforcement, we don't have a great deal of proof yet. Nothing links him directly to your attack, or any criminal activity. We're still analyzing the security footage and need your ID once we have a suspect. But knowing how the streets operate, I'm inclined to believe it. Shotgun can get into places we can't." Grace glanced at her husband. She trusted him completely, but his friendship with a known criminal, even if said criminal helped save her life, never sat right with her.

Kenzo ignored the look Grace gave him, but he was pretty sure everyone in the room heard the double meaning. He made a note to discuss it with

Grace later. "Treasure, Riley said that he's been after you for a while. Can you think of anything that happened recently that would make him want to hurt you?"

Treasure closed her eyes. She turned over the last few weeks in her mind. "The last time I even spoke to Seth Newall was at the Black Men United event. He approached Riley and me and asked me to speak to some girls they were also working with." She stopped. She didn't want to bring it up, especially in front of everyone, but she gave full disclosure. "Seth did insinuate that there was something or could be something between us." She heard Riley try to suppress a growl at the reminder.

Grace's mind was racing. "And the first incident was soon after, right?"

Treasure nodded silently.

"And you said you felt like you'd see the guy at the store before, but you couldn't place him."

"Yeah," she said. Riley gave her hand a reassuring squeeze.

Grace pulled out a folder from her purse. She pulled the jackets for all the Ernest Walkers and E-Moneys in Jackson. She opened the folder and turned it to a photo array of some Ernest Walker suspects. Grace hoped that Treasure could pick someone from this group. "Look at these men. Do you recognize the man who threatened you in the store or attacked you?"

As Treasure reached for the folder, Grace added, "it's more likely that they're the same."

Treasure didn't need to study each photograph. As soon as Treasure saw E-Money's face, she shivered. She pointed to his face. Him. That's the bastard who came into the store that day, and he was the one who knocked me out." Riley rubbed her back. Even though he attempted to comfort her, she could feel his anger rising in his spirit.

"Tell us about that, Treasure," Grace said. Quickly, she added, "If you can." I need every detail from the time you got off the phone with me."

Treasure recounted the events as best she could. Riley had never heard the whole story. He thought it was best not to even discuss it until her concussion healed, but hearing her detail her fear, having her relive it, infuriated him. Riley knew he was angry at Seth Newall and this E-Money character, but he realized he was angry for other reasons. As he listened to Treasure, he realized that he was angry at himself for not being there when she needed him. And if he were honest, he was even a little angry at Treasure for putting herself in that situation. He sat there, stone faced, listening to her recount every detail. Treasure seemed almost detached as Grace guided through her memories.

"Was there anyone else in the store?" Grace asked.

"There must have been. I heard voices in the back, which is why I turned to leave, but I didn't see anyone else but this guy," Treasure said, pointing at the photograph in front of her.

"Can you pick him up now since Treasure's identified the guy?" Riley asked. His agitation with all of this was visible to everyone.

Grace looked at Riley and then at Treasure. "Riley, all of this, right now, is unofficial. If this boy is connected to Seth Newall, that means he has access to certain protections. We need to have all of our proverbial ducks in a row before we do anything official."

Riley's voice raised. "So, we're supposed to wait for...for what... this thug to come back and try to finish the job?" He stood up and began pacing the floor.

Kenzo stepped in, "No, man, but Grace is right. You know she is. I'm sure we can put this together in a few days."

Marcus added, "Now that we have a face and a name, I can go from there."

Riley grunted and nodded. He turned to Marcus, "Get with Shotgun. Like Grace said, she can get into places we can't."

Marcus began to object. "Riley, I can handle..."

Riley cut him off. "Marcus, we all know the deal, but this is my woman and child we're talking about."

Marcus nodded and rose to leave. "I'm out. I'll call her in the morning."

Riley stared at Marcus. His eyes narrowed. "Now, Marcus, before you leave my driveway."

Kenzo and Grace exchanged looks. Kenzo saw the question in her eyes. He shook his head slightly to let her know that they would discuss it later.

Treasure looked at Riley. She felt his anger coming off him in waves.

Kenzo stood and held his hand out for Grace. "We're leaving, man. Let's see what Marcus and Shotgun can come up with in the morning."

Riley didn't even turn around. He said, "Alright, man" and walked to the door.

Grace bent down to hug Treasure and whispered, "We're going to get this guy. And Seth Newall. I promise you."

Treasure nodded but didn't say anything. She was too worried about how Riley would react. After sharing such a beautiful afternoon, Treasure now wondered if they were back at square one.

When Kenzo and Grace left, Riley remained in the doorway. He needed to calm down. The monster had a name, or names. And he felt powerless to do anything about it. At least, not right now without going to jail. He looked over his shoulder and met Treasure's large eyes.

"Riley?" she asked, expectantly.

Riley turned around and faced her. He wanted to just be grateful, grateful that Treasure and the baby were safe. But he just couldn't hide the hurt any more.

"You should have trusted me," he whispered.

Tears sprang to her eyes. She felt his pain in her heart. "I'm sorry, Riley. I should have."

Riley shrugged and wiped his hands down his face. "Listen, I don't want to rehash it. Are you ready to go upstairs?"

"Yes, but please let me say this, Riley. Things were going so well, and I admit, I was waiting for you to break my heart. I was preparing myself for heartbreak even as I was falling more and more in love with you. So, when that woman came into the store and told me she was pregnant with your child, it was easier to believe the worst in you because I was waiting for the worst to happen anyway."

Riley looked at her and asked, "And now?"

"Now?"

Riley sighed, exasperated. "I need to know if you still feel that way." He gave her a hard stare. "And I need to know right now, because I have no problem proving that I love you every day of my life. What I have a problem with is proving it while walking on eggshells, wondering if a mistake, a misunderstanding, is all it takes for you to walk out the door."

Treasure finally understood how her actions affected Riley. She'd never considered how any of this made him feel. "Riley, baby, I'm so sorry. I didn't mean to hurt you." Treasure held out her hand, and when Riley took it, his warmth radiated through her. "I promise, I will never doubt you or your love for me again."

He lifted her to her feet and held her tightly. Treasure nestled her head on his chest. She closed her eyes listening to the rhythm of his heartbeat. Riley kissed the top of Treasure's head and whispered, "Do you love me, Treasure? I mean, really? Do you? Do you want a life with me and our baby?"

Treasure looked up at Riley. A life. With Riley. A life with Riley and a baby. Teary-eyed, Treasure nodded "yes."

"I need to hear you say it, Treasure," Riley said softly.

"I love you, Riley, and I want a life with you and our baby."

Riley kissed her and gently scooped her up in his arms and headed for the stairs. For just a few hours more, Riley needed to love her. In the morning, they could face the ugliness of Seth Newall together.

But right now, he needed to love his woman.

CHAPTER 15

Grace leaned back in her chair. She combed through Ernest Walker's jacket for an hour. She threw her pen on the desk and rubbed her eyes. His rap sheet was full of petty crimes, but nothing major. Doesn't make sense, she thought. Nothing in his record suggested that he was violent or part of a criminal enterprise. She spun her chair around to face the window. The sun warmed her through the glass. Her mind scanned every piece of evidence. Pulling Walker's jacket was easy, but any local pull of Seth Newall's information would mean questions. Only one person she knew could get access to the information undetected. She picked up the phone to call Chief just as her assistant entered her office.

"That voice is on line one," said through clenched teeth. Her usual cheery demeanor always shifted when she heard "that voice" as she called it.

Grace smiled. "Thank you, Deloria. Will you call to see if Kenzo is in the office. I may surprise him in a little while."

"Grace Harrington Dallas."

Chief chuckled. "My, my, my. That just rolls off the tongue, doesn't it? How is my favorite couple?"

Grace smiled. "Yes, it does, and we're wonderful. How are you? I was just about to call you on a case I'm working." Grace often wondered if

193

Chief had a chip implanted in her head or some bug in her office. He always knew way too much. As infuriating as it was, knowing she could always count of him comforted Grace.

"I had a feeling you might. Gather what you have. I'm on the way." The line went dead.

Grace's brow wrinkled. Something was off. She never even told him what the case was or what she needed. But somehow, she knew that he already knew everything she needed. Grace grabbed her jacket and her keys, headed to her husband's office. Maybe he and Marcus had come up with something.

She could have called him, but it was too tempting to simply go to his office since it was in the same building. Plus, she smiled to herself, she needed a Kenzo-break to get through the rest of her day. He'd left before she woke, so she was overdue for seeing her husband today.

~

Shotgun studied the walls of her makeshift offices. Her men outside eyed the white man who walked inside suspiciously but said nothing as she'd trained them to do. Her men knew that what they needed to know. She would tell them eventually when they needed to know it. They accepted her direction without question.

Shotgun watched the Chief as he spoke to Grace. There was a light-heartedness in his tone that she rarely got from him even after all these years. Of course, she understood. Convincing yourself and those around you of the character you'd created was easy. The true problem was remembering who you really were. . Becoming Shotgun had been so consuming and life altering that even she had to remember, at times, who she really was, and even those who should know better, like Chief, could forget.

"Alright. Let's go," Chief said as he rose from his chair. "You might want to change into something else." Chief looked at her over his glasses. Shotgun looked down at herself. Wearing her signature catsuit, Shotgun bristled but said nothing. Chief noticed her reaction. "Ms. Johnson, we're going downtown in the Standard Life building. And as much as I appreciate open carry, your catsuit and weaponry will bring some unwanted attention." He paused, before adding, "Agreed?

Shotgun opened her mouth to tell him what he and the State of Mississippi could do with their "unwanted attention," but Chief never gave her an opportunity.

"Yes? Good, that's settled. I'll be waiting in the car." The dismissive tone in his voice irked Shotgun's nerves. His damn declarative interrogatives, she thought, as she rolled her eyes.

Chief turned on his heel. With his hand on the doorknob, he turned. "Let's get this done, so we can all move on as soon as possible."

Shotgun found her voice. "So, we're just going to walk into Grace's office and say what, 'Your husband's oldest female friend is not a complete criminal but an undercover agent with an agency that doesn't officially exist? Man, no disrespect, but are you insane? She won't believe this! I wouldn't believe this!" She was a decibel away from shouting, but the thought that her life would never be the same after this revelation, hit her all at once.

Chief turned slowly and sighed. He stared at her for a moment. "You changed the rules of engagement when you told them about Seth Newall, which I didn't authorize by the way. So, this is where we are. You compromised yourself and Black Valkyrie. So, yes, that's exactly what we're going to say."

"But...But...Newall had gone too far. I couldn't have Treasure Jordan's death on my conscience. Could you?" Shotgun's voice nearly raised to a near frantic pitch.

Chief's eyebrow raised. After a moment, he sighed, dropping his shoulders in resignation. "Which proves my point," he said, shaking his head. "You and Grace have the same sense of justice. You, my dear, just took the long way home, but you got there. Before I found you, you killed for righteous indignation and money. Child molesters. Women beaters. Politicians with abhorrent policies. It was quite beautiful really. But you were young and passionate even in your brokenness."

He gave her a sardonic chuckle, but with soft eyes. "A conscience. You always needed to know the why of the hit." He took another sip of coffee. "Made you a helluva recruit but you're out after this, kid."

Shotgun rolled her shoulders back and stared. She couldn't argue with him. He was right.

Chief accepted her silence and left her office. Shotgun shimmied out of her catsuit and boots and slipped into a blue tank top and black Rock Revival jeans. She dropped into her chair and eased into her black Tims. As she stood, she caught a glimpse of herself in the full-length mirror hanging on the back of her door. She imagined herself as a civilian as she had so many times before. She'd been a criminal and an undercover agent since she was sixteen years old. Shotgun had never had a chance to be regular.

Chief had given Shotgun an out, but now that she faced the possibility, she didn't know if that's what she really wanted, or if she was just too afraid to try.

~

Riley couldn't focus on anything. The specs for the Highway 80 land deal he drew up were just staring at him. He worried about Treasure's insistence that she return to the store and that he return to his office. She was ready. He wasn't. Admittedly, Riley enjoyed their bubble no matter how they got there.

Riley stood and walked to his window. The view of Capitol Street always centered him, reminded him of his purpose but his thoughts never strayed from Treasure. Riley was deep in thought when he heard Kenzo's familiar knock on his door.

"Hey, you got a moment," Kenzo asked.

"Several. I was taking a break from the Highway 80 project," Riley replied. He walked to the leather sofa and sat down. "What's up?"

Kenzo took a seat in the leather club chair across Riley. "I couldn't focus either. Just thinking about Seth Newall and how we're going to get this guy."

Riley didn't respond but rested his head on the back of the couch. He knew what he wanted to do--kill the bastard. After a few moments, Riley lifted his head. "Has Grace come up with anything that she can use officially?"

Kenzo shook his head. "Not yet, but if I know her, she probably called in a few favors to get the info she needed." His head cocked to the side, as his wife's perfume invaded his senses and just as he was about to turn around, Grace answered.

"I did."

Kenzo stood as Grace walked into the room. She eased into his embrace and kissed him quickly on the lips before speaking to Riley.

Riley cleared his throat. "Did you find out anything?" he asked. They could kiss at home or in their offices. He desperately needed answers.

"Not yet, but what bothers me is that this Ernest Walker has virtually no criminal record, just petty juvenile crimes. But my contact is getting me Newall's financials. There's no way to get them properly without arousing suspicion."

Riley nodded, but then asked. "How long is that going to take? You know, Treasure went to the store today." He rubbed his hands down his face.

"I know. I called her. She's coming here in a few moments. We're taking you fellas to lunch."

Riley jumped up. "How? She can't drive! Jesus, Grace!"

Grace rolled her eyes. "Riley, she's fine. The security detail you hired will bring her straight here." She paused. "A piece of advice, Riley? Please don't smother her. Treasure is fiercely independent, and she needs to get some normalcy back. Care for her, but don't control her."

Riley opened his mouth to speak, but he heard Treasure's laugh just outside his door.

Treasure burst into Riley's office as best she could, slightly limping. "Hey, y'all!" Treasure's grand smile brightened the room. Happy to be out of the house and getting back to her store, Treasure had been on cloud nine all day.

Riley jumped up to greet her, kissing her face. From the second Grace told him Treasure was on the way, his heart was in his throat. He hugged her. "Are you okay?"

Treasure laughed. "Riley, I'm wonderful. Today's been good. Only one problem all day."

Riley's brow furrowed and his possessive grip tightened. "What happened?"

Treasure smiled. "I can't decide what I want for lunch, but I'm starving!" She leaned around Riley and smiled at Grace, "What did you decide? I don't care where it is, but I want to sit down and see people again!"

Riley threw his head back in feigned frustration. "Woman, you had me going there for a moment." He kissed the top of her head and led her to the couch. "Why don't we just go to the new hotel on President, the one that opened up near the museum, or we could do the University Club?"

"Sounds good to me," Kenzo said.

As they prepared to leave, Grace's phone rang. "Hi, Deloria? Glad you called. We're just about to go to lunch." Grace stopped walking so abruptly that Kenzo nearly bumped into her. "On my way. We all are."

Grace looked into the expectant faces in the room. "We need to go to my office. Now. That call may change everything." She reached out and grabbed Treasure's hand. "You okay?"

Treasure looked up at Riley and then at Grace. The smile on her face turned firm and resolute as she answered Grace's question. "As ever."

~

Grace led the group into her office suite. Deloria was standing in front of her desk wringing her hands, clearly nervous about their unexpected visitor.

"He just went in," she said nervously.

"It's fine, Deloria," Grace said, patting her arm. "Why don't you head to lunch. We'll be fine here." Without waiting for a response, Grace walked briskly into her office.

"I believe I will," Deloria replied. She grabbed her purse and jacket, said her goodbyes, and left quickly.

"Chief! I didn't expect you this fast. What are you doing here?" Grace hugged the old man before he could feign a protest.

"Well, I was in the area with another agent and thought I'd stop by," Chief said as he pulled back. "Let me look at you." He placed his hands on her shoulders. "Yes, indeed, I believe marriage agrees with you." Chief laughed. He turned and shook Kenzo's hand vigorously. "Take care of this one."

Kenzo laughed, "She wouldn't have it any other way."

Riley and Treasure entered. Riley was the first to spot Shotgun sitting quietly at the far end of the conference table in Grace's office. "Shay?"

The entire room looked in Shotgun's direction. She waited to see how long it would take someone to recognize her presence in the room. She stood to stunned faces. Perhaps, the most satisfying was the shock on Riley's and Kenzo's faces. Grace pressed her lips together, making them disappear into her mouth. Treasure's eyes darted around the room, trying to gauge everyone's reaction. Shotgun exhaled when she noted Marcus's absence from the group.

Grace was the first to recover. "I see now," she said quietly through a tense smile. She turned to the Chief. "Your little birdie?"

Chief smiled sheepishly but offered little explanation. "Let's all sit, shall we?"

Grace gestured to the group to sit at her table. Grace took her seat at the head of the table. Kenzo sat to her left; Chief took the seat at her right. Shotgun took the seat next to Chief as Riley led Treasure to the seat next to Kenzo. Riley sat next to Shotgun at the other end of the table. He leaned toward Shotgun and whispered, "Girl, you know you've got some explaining to do. Does Marcus know?"

Shotgun looked at Riley and shook her head "no." Dealing with Marcus was the last thing she wanted to do or even think about. In a half-hiss, half-whisper, Shotgun replied, "And he can't know until all of this is over. It'll be the only way I can make this work."

A nervous silence settled at the table as they all stared at each other. Treasure had never seen Grace so outdone and was slightly tickled. But she saw why Grace initially tensed up at the thought of Shotgun. She was flat-out gorgeous with perfect bone structure, reminding her of Naomi Campbell when she walked the runaways in the 80s. Treasure looked at a shell-shocked Grace and decided to break the tension in the room.

"So, Chief, Grace said you had some information on the bastards trying to ruin my life and my business." Treasure stared directly at Chief and then Grace, who looked as though both had forgotten why they were there.

Riley smiled. Treasure was getting her spunk back, but if she thought she was going to be bait, she had another thing coming.

Chief chuckled. "Yes, Ms. Jordan, I think I have some useful information." He turned his head slightly toward Shotgun without looking at her directly. "Thanks to Ms. Johnson, the investigation of Seth Newall has to be sped up a bit. Seems his infatuation with you, Treasure, has created a most fortuitous wrinkle, and since Ms. Johnson is so fond of these gentlemen and by extension you and Grace, we have to move fast."

Treasure thought she heard Riley growl when Chief said "infatuation." No. Definitely a growl.

Kenzo looked at Shotgun. "Why would you be investigating Seth Newall in the first place?"

Riley shot a look at Kenzo. "Who the hell cares, man?" He then turned to Chief. "What do you have that can put him away without putting my family at risk?"

Riley's choice of words hung in the air. Treasure and Grace glanced discretely at each other.

Chief responded. "Seth Newall's base is Jackson, but he's one of the most dangerous sex traffickers in the country, operating different routes between California to Florida. Texas is his switch off point." Chief left the table and pointed to the map on Grace's wall. "Girls and, sometimes, boys, are taken from California to Arizona and East Texas and then funneled through the Deep South.

Grace glared at Chief. He was talking about it so calmly as if he hadn't just betrayed her and her task force. "So why didn't he come up in my investigation, and he's right here in Jackson? And why didn't you tell me he was a target?" The hurt in her voice was evident. Kenzo patted her leg under the table.

Chief sighed and faced her. Flatly, he said, "You know the drill, Grace. Simultaneous operations. Different agents."

Riley switched the focus of the conversation, turning to Shotgun. "So you've been some kind of secret agent all this time and Seth Newall has been your target?" He turned to Kenzo, "Did you know?"

Kenzo shook his head. "Not at all."

Riley looked between Chief and Shotgun. "So why didn't he come up and what put him on your radar?"

Chief headed toward his seat at the table as he responded. "The name 'Zeus' kept popping up but like some mythical god. No one had a picture. No one would talk. Not even low-level traffickers because they'd never seen him. He might as all have been the Wizard of Oz."

Treasure asked, "So, how did you figure out Seth Newall was Zeus? Doesn't make sense."

"No, it doesn't," Chief replied with a laugh. "But criminals are sometimes like lost keys. They are never where you think you put them."

Shotgun piped up. "I was in the area a few years ago on another assignment." She paused. They didn't need to know that it was a planned hit. "Zeus's name popped up on a wire once, but that was enough. My orders were to create a criminal enterprise that would draw this Zeus out to see if it was the same one."

Grace asked, "And it was?"

"Unfortunately," Shotgun replied. "But in Jackson, he does comparatively penny ante stuff, but it's significant, especially with the women he's working on the West Side.

Riley threw up his hands. "He's a damn pimp, too?" He glared at Kenzo, "I told you he was shady as hell. Didn't I?"

"But neither Newall, nor Zeus, came up in my investigation." Grace tried to maintain her professionalism, but she was beginning to feel like she'd been sabotaged from the moment she came to Jackson.

Shotgun heard the question even if no one else did. "Newall has been excellent at hiding his identity. Even the people who work for him don't know they work for him except a small few. His second here, Ernest Walker, is the only one who knows who he is for real, and if the others do, they will act as if they don't." She paused before adding, "If they like breathing."

"Well, what I want to know is if you have nothing linking him to Treasure's harassment, the vandalism, or her attack, then how do we get him? He's clearly not going to confess," Riley interjected.

Chief opened the folder. All eyes were intently focused on him. "The only way to bring down Seth Newall, or any big fish like this, is to get someone close to him to turn."

Grace nodded her head. "You think Ernest Walker is going to turn on Seth Newall? After all this time?"

Chief turned slightly in his chair and stared at Grace with a frown. "Grace, my dear, do you remember the Hollingsworth case?" He addressed Kenzo directly. "An entire family of criminals. By the time they left her interrogation room, the sons signed confessions and agreed to testify against both their parents to save themselves." He looked casually at Grace, "So yes, I believe you can get Ernest Walker to save himself and turn on Seth Newall. This is just another case. Remember that."

Riley leaned forward and gestured toward the folder. Frustrated, he asked, "What else is in that folder?"

Chief grinned. "What Ernest Walker doesn't know and what you can use against him is that his father died in prison because he was taking the rap for his younger brother. A younger brother who was about to go to college, who was a top football recruit coming out of high school, and

"And who made his nephew into a criminal," Riley quickly added.

"Exactly," Chief added.

Kenzo piped in. "How does this Walker boy not know that Seth Newall is his uncle?"

Grace read through the information in the file. "Different daddies. And by the looks of it, Seth's and his brother's mother died when they were young. When Walker's mother died of an overdose, he ended up in foster care."

"That is so sad," Treasure remarked to no one in particular. As an only child, Treasure knew what it was like to feel true loneliness, and she had both parents.

Riley leaned back in his chair. He could tell Treasure felt for the kid. "Sad as it is, Treasure, we can't be concerned about that right now. He and his uncle both need to go to jail. So, Grace, what's the plan? You already said Treasure's unofficial ID can't get him picked up."

Grace looked directly at Riley. "We have some footage from the surrounding stores. Unfortunately, the footage from the security company gave us only a glimpse of the perp but the image wasn't good enough to get a warrant."

Both Riley and Kenzo said, "Damn" at the same time.

Grace continued. "I still say that the only person who can draw out Seth Newall is,"

Riley cut her off. "No."

Treasure's neck snapped at Riley. "Riley! I can make that decision for myself. I need to get my life back, and if this is what I need to do, I'll do it." She didn't need Riley to make that decision for her. "Grace, go on. What do you think?"

Grace took a deep breath. "I don't have it all figured out yet, but I think we are going to have to turn Walker against him. Won't be easy. Clearly, he sees Newall as a father figure."

"But in order to do that, Walker has to come to the shop again. I can almost guarantee you that if I'm in the shop alone, he'll come back."

Riley got up from the table and gripped the back of the chair. Furious, he shouted at Treasure, "Are you serious right now?!" Riley couldn't believe Treasure. Had she forgotten that she was pregnant?

Kenzo got up and went to Riley. He whispered in Riley's ear, "Man, calm down. Don't do this here."

Treasure glared at Riley. Through clenched teeth, Treasure said, "First of all, what we are not going to do Riley Taylor is you hollering at me. Sit down, Riley."

When Kenzo returned to his seat and Riley sat back down, Grace calmly took control of the room. "Listen," Grace said. "Chief, Shay, and I will strategize a plan that will minimize the risk...for everyone." She turned to Kenzo, "why don't you take Riley and Treasure to lunch?"

Kenzo nodded. His wife was in her element, and Kenzo knew to let her work. "Sure, Love. Good idea." He leaned toward her and kissed her cheek. I'll bring you something back."

Grace stood to walk the trio to the door. She hugged Treasure. "It's going to be fine. I promise you. Go feed my godchild. I got this."

"I'm not worried," Treasure replied. She cocked her head toward Riley, "But this one here? I'm not so sure." She and Grace smiled in Riley's direction, but his conversation with Kenzo was so intense that neither man noticed them.

Grace patted her arm and went back into her office, leaving Treasure standing there waiting for Riley and Kenzo to finish their conversation. Treasure watched Riley's features contort with tension and anger. She could see the muscles in his jaw tighten as he talked and tried not to yell. Kenzo's efforts to calm him didn't seem to be working.

Treasure was about to say something when Riley glanced in her direction and caught her staring. She smiled and mouthed "I love you." Riley's eyes softened. He ended his conversation with Kenzo and walked over to Treasure. He kissed her sweetly on the lips.

"Let's go, sweetheart," Riley whispered against her forehead. He took her hand and led her to the elevator where Kenzo was now waiting.

"Voyages?" Riley asked.

"Yes!" Treasure nearly shrieked. She'd missed going to their favorite restaurant, the site of their first date. "I hope Leon has a good shrimp dish on the menu."

Riley laughed. "I'm sure he does." The laughter felt good and eased their tensions. The three talked about Voyages favorites and wondered aloud about what they might have on the menu this time. Their easy banter allowed them to forget, if just for a little while, everything they learned in the last hour. Soon enough, they would deal with reality, but right now, Riley wanted to hear Treasure's laugh and her face as she enjoyed a good meal.

He needed a bit of that heaven before he unleashed hell.

CHAPTER 16

Treasure walked into Grace's office determined to find an end to this madness. She found Grace standing in front of her case management board. She and Riley's pictures, along with Walker's, Newall's, and a still of Scarlett from the security video. Treasure found it a little jarring that she was not only part of a criminal case but the victim of one. She rapped on the open door to Grace's office. "Hey, Lady," she said.

Grace turned around, a dry erase marker in her hand. She drew lines and made notes directly on the board. "Hey. Perfect timing."

"I hope you have something good to tell me. I need something to keep Riley on this side of a jail cell." Treasure rolled her eyes and smiled, vainly attempting to mask her fear. Grace knew Treasure well enough to know how truly scared she was, but Grace was friend enough not to point it out just yet.

"I do, actually. So, Scarlett's name isn't Scarlett."

"Damn," Treasure said with a sigh. "She lied about her name too."

Grace smiled. "She lied about everything. Her name and," she paused, "being pregnant." She walked to her desk and grabbed a folder. "Her real name is Blake Ross." Grace handed Treasure the folder.

"There's not much here," Treasure said, thumbing through the pages.

"No, there's not, but what we do know is that she works for E-Money, which means she also works for Seth Newall. The problem is that she doesn't know about Newall, so she can't help us on that front."

Treasure walked closer to the board as she tossed the folder on the conference table. "So, Scarlett's real name is Blake, and she does what for E-Money?" Treasure had an idea, but she needed Grace to confirm the thoughts in her head.

"She's one of Walker's top, high-class prostitutes," Grace said. "But I think I've figured a way to turn E-Money."

Finally, some hope, Treasure thought. "Turning E-Money won't be easy. I know you're bad, sis, but I just don't see Walker snitching on Seth. He clearly idolizes the man."

"Believe me, I know, but we do have information that Walker doesn't have. The only thing is that we have one shot to use it. Once we tell Walker that Newall is his uncle, he's going to alert Newall. And believe me, they will close ranks."

Treasure's brow furrowed. "But just being his uncle isn't enough. Do we have anything else?"

Grace laughed and snapped her fingers. "Girl, this is what I do!" She pulled another folder from her desk. "This is Walker's father's jacket and prison records. On the surface, it's basic, but there's a slight notation from the prison therapist that he took the rap for his brother who was going to college."

Treasure's mouth dropped open. "So, Seth killed someone and let his brother take the fall?" She instinctively touched her belly. "Damn, and the brother had a baby too." They sat in silence for a moment before Treasure asked, "And you think this will be enough?"

"It's the best shot we have. Plus, we have a still of Walker outside your store the night of your attack. The image was blurry, at first, but the techs cleaned it up. It's still iffy, but it's enough to bring him in for a line up. And we have earlier footage of him outside over the span of several days."

Treasure looked at the board while Grace continued speaking.

"So, with your positive identification regarding the attack coupled with turning Blake Ross against him, we'll be positioned to incite enough anger against Seth Newall. We'll see how strong the loyalty is then."

"And we only have one shot?"

"Yes, so we must definitely make it count." Grace turned back to the board.

"So, are you and Shotgun working on this together?" Grace initially bristled at Shotgun's involvement, but Treasure hoped they could find a happy medium for everyone's sake.

Grace took a deep breath. "We were always cordial since she's Kenzo's friend, and she helped save my life." She sighed. "But I don't like being in the dark even though I know how shadow operations work," she paused and interjected, "I thought Chief and I were closer than that."

"I understand. Have you talked to him about it?"

"No, not yet. I will though. But only after we close this case. I'm not going to worry about trivial things when I have a godchild on the way." Grace smiled.

Silent tears flowed down Treasure's cheeks. Grace handed her the box of tissues on her desk and placed her hand on her shoulder.

"I'm sorry. I just seem to cry at the drop of a hat these days," Treasure said, wiping her eyes.

Grace patted her arm. "Between your pregnancy hormones and having to deal with this, of course you're crying. But we're going to get through this. I promise."

Treasure nodded through her tears. She hugged Grace, and said, "I'm going to stop in and surprise Riley before I go back to work."

Grace laughed. "He's probably going to convince you to go home and rest. And I can't say that I'll blame him. You need to get as much rest as possible now." Grace nodded toward Treasure's ankle. "How is it?"

"Still sore, but it's fine. Doctor says it's healing fine. I'll be running in heels in no time."

Both women laughed as Treasure shifted her purse on her shoulder. "Call me if you need me, you hear me?"

Treasure nodded and left. As she rode the elevator to Riley's office, Treasure threw her head back. Grace had a plan and seemed confident in it, but for some reason, Treasure was still uneasy. *Lord, be a fence*, she prayed. *Being a strong black woman is wearing me out, so I'm giving it to you.*

When the elevator signaled that she'd reached their floor, Treasure exhaled and smiled. Seeing Riley always gave her a reason to smile, and she definitely needed a smile today.

~

Riley signed the final document on his desk in his study. He looked at the stack of documents before him and rubbed his neck. He decided to have his attorney courier the papers to his home after her impromptu visit at his office. For once, Riley was thankful that Treasure was upstairs sleeping. He could tell that pregnancy symptoms were beginning though he was glad that morning sickness hadn't started yet. His sister's nausea was awful during her pregnancies, and he hoped that Treasure didn't suffer like Diahann did.

A yellowed envelope peeked out from beneath the pile. Riley fingered the edges before retrieving it. He traced his grandfather's familiar script across the front of the envelope with his finger. The contents of the letter didn't shock him as much as the fact that he planned on reading it. Riley had found a stack of letters from his grandfather when he died, instructing and outlining everything from how to do things at the house to what to do with his first big paycheck. Marcellus's instructions were clear in the first letter: Don't open the other letters until you need them. The man didn't ask for much, so it was the least he could do to honor his wishes. Today, Riley opened the one letter he never planned to open.

Marriage

Riley's hands were shaking when he pulled the letter from the safe. There were only two letters left to read, and he figured he would read the last letter in about seven months.

Dear Riley,

If you're reading this letter, you've found your good thing. I'm sorry I'm not there to meet her. I just know that your grandmother and I would love her. I don't have to ask if she's beautiful, but I do hope she's smart and feisty like your grandmother. The right woman will make you know what's important in life. The right woman, son, will make you a man. The first time I saw your grandmother, I knew she was mine. She was everything I knew I would ever need or want. As much love as you saw between your grandmother and me, Riley, it wasn't always easy. Marriage can be sweet like those honeysuckles by that oak tree you love so, but it's also hard work like clearing the northern pasture. Just never let it sour between you. Riley, your only job is to love her and make her happy so that the most difficult times won't destroy you.

You were the joy of my heart, and I need you to listen to me on this. If you follow the advice my father gave me and some I learned along the way, you'll be married a good long while.

Don't take her for granted. A good wife will cook for you and make sure that you have a home to come to, but she's not your maid, or your slave. Appreciate and acknowledge that what she does is because she loves you, not because she has to do those things.

Respect that she has her own life. Like I always said, always get a woman who has a life of her own. She won't suffocate you or lose herself in you.

Tell her you love her every day. Kiss her every morning, again before you leave the house, when you return, and definitely before you go to bed. Make love often. And for crying out loud, don't be selfish. (You know what I mean.)

When you have children, don't forget that she's a woman first. Court her. Bring her flowers, jewelry, whatever she likes, at least once a week. And take her out once a month even when the children come. And make sure she gets time to herself without you and the children.

And speaking of children. You are not a babysitter. You are their father. Be a parent.

Make her laugh.

Trust her and be trustworthy.

Apologize. You're wrong. Life will be easier if you accept it.

Give her and your children your full attention. Be present. Work will always be there. Don't let your family learn to live without you. No dollar you earn will make up for missed time with your family.

Don't love her like you want to love her. Love her as she needs to be loved.

Your wife is your pride, and how you love her is as public as it is private. I hope the woman God entrusted to you makes you as happy as your grandmother has made me all these years. I hope you can see the faces of your children in her eyes. I hope she is the woman you want standing next to you on your darkest days. I hope she is the woman who pushes you to become the best version of yourself. And do the same for her.

Remember Matthew 6:21: "For where your treasure is, there your heart will be also." If she's your treasure, love her with every fiber of your being for the rest of your life.

Love,

Daddy Marcellus

Riley pulled his handkerchief from his pocket and wiped tears from his eyes. Rereading the letter from Marcellus brought everything into focus. And that scripture. Riley shuddered at the coincidence of it. Of all the scriptures, his grandfather could have used, he picked one that said "treasure." Riley shook his head as he carefully placed the letter back in the envelope and lay it on the table. He checked his watch. It was nearly 7:00 p.m., and he knew Treasure would be starving when she woke up. He knew just what to cook for dinner. "Well, Granddaddy, I hope I'm off to a good start," he whispered quietly to himself.

Treasure smelled something wonderful coming from the kitchen. After a few seconds, she recognized it as Riley's Chicken Marsala. As she stretched, she caught sight of the clock. It was nearly 8:00 p.m. I didn't plan on sleeping this long. She grabbed her robe from the foot of the bed and headed down the stairs.

Riley transferred the chicken back into the sauce and reduced the heat. When he looked up, Treasure was standing in the doorway.

"Smells good." Treasure walked gingerly into the kitchen. "Anything I can do."

Riley wiped his hands on the towel and kissed her forehead. "Yes, go sit down. It's almost ready."

Treasure grinned. "I could get used to this, Riley Taylor."

Riley wanted her to get used to it, because he planned to do it for a long time. "I hope so." As she walked to the table, Riley took a deep breath. The papers on his desk, his grandfather's letter, weighed heavily on his mind. He hoped Treasure would allow him the peace of mind he so desperately needed.

After dinner, Treasure began clearing the table. As she stacked the dishes, Riley stopped her, touching her hand. "That can wait, sweetheart. I need to talk to you about something." She placed the dishes back on the table. Whatever it was that he needed to talk to her about was serious. His eyes were nervous, but his jaw was resolute.

"Okay," she agreed.

"Let's go into the den." Riley slowly led her into the den and deposited her on the sofa. As he propped her ankle on the ottoman, he looked deep into her eyes. "I'll be right back." He disappeared into the study and returned with a stack of papers seconds later.

Riley didn't regret the decision he made, but he was afraid that Treasure wouldn't understand it, or why he needed to do this. "Treasure, while you were sleeping, I had my lawyer send these over." He handed her the first document. "With everything going on, I needed to make sure that I provided for you and the baby if something ever happened to me."

Treasure's eyes widened.

Riley continued. "This is my will, life insurance, and investments. I've left everything, all I have, to you and the baby, including the house. You're the beneficiary of everything I have."

Treasure's jaw dropped. "Riley, I don't know what to say."

Riley touched the side of her face. "I love you, and I wanted you to know that no matter what, I will always make sure that you and our baby are safe and taken care of." He touched her belly and gently rubbed.

Treasure closed her eyes. Riley's warmth radiated through her. "Riley, this is a sweet gesture, but you didn't have to do this. I know today shook us both, but nothing is going to happen to either one of us."

Riley shook his head. "You don't know that, and neither do I. But this, I had to do." He paused. "For my peace of mind. I hope you can understand that."

Treasure fought back tears as she placed the papers on the coffee table. "Riley, you didn't have to do this to prove anything to me. I know you're not that guy." She looked down. "Even if we didn't work out. I know you'd always take care of the baby."

He brought her hand to his lips and kissed it. Riley turned on the television, and he and Treasure settled into the couch. Riley threw his arm around her, and she leaned back on his chest. Treasure was glad Riley couldn't see the pain and sadness in her face. He seemed so content after showing her how much she and the baby meant to him. She didn't have the heart to tell him that none of that mattered. Such things are temporary, and just as quickly as he gave her financial security, he could take it away. She knew Riley loved her to her very soul. But what she wanted, what she didn't know she wanted until then, was the emotional security only a commitment of forever would provide.

Riley felt Treasure's tension. Somehow, she appreciated his gesture but it fell flat. He rubbed her arm absentmindedly and thought back to his grandfather's letter. Love her as she needs to be loved. His heart constricted in his chest. How could he have violated the rules already before they were even married?

~

Simone came into the break room with a plate of liver and onions. A wave of nausea swept through Treasure, and she discreetly ran to the restroom, covering her mouth. Keeping her pregnancy a secret would prove impossible since her morning sickness seemed to be an all-day affair. What college student eats liver and onions, she thought. Treasure decided to stay in her office for a few moments, at least until Simone had finished her break. As she reviewed her monthly inventory reports, Treasure's phone rang. She knew it was Riley before she even picked it up. No doubt checking up on her. She shook her head as she read his name across her screen.

"Hey, Riley. And before you ask, I'm fine."

Riley laughed. "Am I that predictable?"

Treasure, smiling, said, "Yes, you are, but I'm used to it."

Riley laughed again. "And you secretly love it." He paused, remembering the true purpose of his call. "What time will you be ready?"

"Around the same time. I'm hiding in my office." Treasure said casually, as she continued reading a sales report.

Riley became alarmed. His pulse rate quickened. "Why? What's wrong?" he asked.

Treasure rolled her eyes. "Oh, nothing. Simone brought liver and onions for lunch. I haven't told them, but even without being pregnant, the smell is horrible."

Riley frowned. "I see. Did you..."

"Yes," Treasure replied, cutting him off. "But I'm fine really. Listen, I'm going to go back out there. They'll be looking for me in a minute."

"Okay, sweetheart, I'll be there at 6."

"I'll be ready." Treasure and Riley said their goodbyes, and Treasure walked out of her office, popping a mint in her mouth and hoping the smells of Simone's lunch was out of the air.

~

Riley gripped the steering wheel, glad that he didn't have to hide his nervousness during the ride home. And for once, he was glad that Treasure fell asleep as soon as they pulled out of the parking lot. He looked over at

Treasure sleeping peacefully beside him, snoring slightly. He realized how calming it was just having her with him after a long day and just knowing that in the morning, she would be there.

Treasure woke as soon as Riley pulled the car into the circular drive. "I'm sorry. I didn't realize I was so tired."

Riley leaned over and kissed her forehead. "Just a little cat nap." He exited the car and hurried to her side. Riley opened the door and helped her out of the car. "Feel like you can come somewhere with me for a moment."

"Where? We just got home. I don't feel like doing anything. I just want to lie down." Treasure adjusted her purse on her shoulder.

"Just a few moments, and I promise, you can sleep until the morning." He held out his hand, "If you want."

Treasure saw a pleading in Riley's eyes, and she knew that whatever he wanted was important to him. She said nothing as she placed her hand in his. Riley led her toward the grounds, and she was glad that she was wearing flats. As they walked further into the grounds, Treasure saw lights in the direction of Riley's favorite oak tree.

"Riley, what did you do?" Treasure looked further ahead and spied a pathway of lights. The pasture was twinkling like a fantasy, fairy land.

Riley smiled. "You'll see."

Riley took her arm, and as they approached the end of the pathway, a small table and chairs sat at the base of the oak tree. Lights wrapped around the base of the tree and throughout the branches. Treasure thought her heart would burst. "Oh, Riley, this is beautiful," she said. Her face lit up, and Riley's heart thumped loudly in his chest. He didn't think he would ever tire of making her smile like this. "What's the occasion?"

The lights and stars highlighted Treasure's natural beauty. His voice dropped to that familiar sensual octave that made Treasure tremble. "You are so beautiful, Treasure." He pushed a curl of hair that had fallen in her face. He traced her cheek with his finger. Treasure closed her eyes, letting the electricity of his touch move through her. He raised her hand to his lips and kissed the inside of her palm.

Riley and Treasure stared intensely at each other and the air thickened around them. Riley eventually broke the charged silence between them. "I knew you felt bad about not going to Paris with Mrs. Bridgewater because of everything going on, so I thought tonight, I'd give you at least the Parisian café experience."

Treasure laughed. "You know, she was not happy, but she understood. I connected her with all the designers and boutiques, so she's fine. And I'm sure Mr. Bridgewater is glad that he's off the hook for my expenses."

"Let's sit. "Thirsty?" He opened a bottle of sparkling white grape juice and began pouring. "Since you can't have wine these days..."

The grape juice chilled her throat. "I could, but this is better for me, I know." She smiled as they clinked glasses.

Riley laughed. "I'm sure Mr. Bridgewater is happy about that. I can only imagine what Sister Bridgewater has spent on food alone. My sister had a small wedding, but my father acted like it cost a fortune. One day, I caught him watching *Father of the Bride* with Spencer Tracy. He looked absolutely vindicated and miserable at the same time." Riley laughed heartily as he told Treasure about his sister's frantic phone call that their father had gone insane and had made her and her fiancé watch the movie again with him one evening after dinner.

Treasure shrugged with a slight chuckle. "I can only imagine what Randall Jordan will say, but it won't matter. As many society weddings as I have ordered dresses for, coordinated, and just witnessed, I wouldn't want anything that fancy. Intimate, but definitely not tuxes and tails." She took another sip of her juice and turned her head toward the vastness of the land stretched out before them. The conversation was entering a plane she didn't want to discuss. She absentmindedly touched her belly. She and Riley loved each other deeply. Treasure was certain of that simple fact. And though she wanted to get married, she promised not to force the issue or make Riley feel obligated to marry her. Treasure sat quietly, sipping her juice from her champagne glass, letting the night air cool her skin.

"The stars are beautiful tonight," Treasure remarked quietly, "reminds me of our first date."

Riley looked toward the stars. "Yes, but even better, because it's real." Riley hoped she understood the deeper meaning in his words. "I have something for you, baby."

"For me? Riley, you didn't have to do that." She paused and grinned broadly, "But what is it?"

Riley placed a small metallic gold bag with a black bow on the table in front of her. Treasure's brow raised. "Pretty bag." She reached inside the bag, finding a small, square box beautifully wrapped in black paper. "This is heavy. I can't imagine what this is."

"Open it." Riley bounced his knee nervously under the table.

"Yes, sir," she responded, excitedly. She ripped the paper off the box and opened it. A lock. A padlock and key. She picked it up and held it. "Riley..." She looked up and Riley was standing by her side. He took the lock and key from her. "I was researching about Paris and found out about this bridge where couples would place padlocks with messages on it and throw the key in the Seine River. Then I found out that Paris banned the padlocks, but I figured that we could still throw the key in the river when we go." He paused, "On our honeymoon."

Treasure remembered walking along the Pont des Arts bridge during a visit shortly after her first tryst with Riley years ago. "The Pont des Arts bridge? They're banning...wait. Did you say 'honeymoon'?"

"Yes, our honeymoon." Riley smiled as he lowered himself to one knee and looked deeply into her eyes. He opened the ring box, presenting a flawless three-carat cushion cut diamond in an antique setting in platinum, intricately designed with diamonds in the shape of infinity symbols. Tears flooded Treasure's eyes. "Treasure, I love you more than anything in the world, and I've loved you since the moment I met you even when I didn't know it. Will you do me the honor of being my wife?"

Treasure wiped tears from her eyes and took a deep breath. This is what she wanted, but she needed to be sure. She needed Riley to be sure. "Riley, I…"

Riley refused to move. "Sweetheart, I know what you're thinking. And no, this is not because you're pregnant. I'm asking you to be my wife because I love you. And because I…" he said as he rose to his feet, "need you, Treasure." He touched the side of her face. Treasure leaned into his touch. "Marry me, Treasure, and I promise you that forever won't be long enough to show you how much I love you." His eyes searched Treasure's. Her brown eyes glistened with tears, and Riley wiped her tears with his thumbs. "Please say something," Riley said with a strangled whisper.

Treasure reached up and touched Riley's cheek. "Yes."

Riley fought his own tears as his shaking hands slid the ring on Treasure's finger. The diamond sparkled, reflecting the surrounding lights, as Treasure held up her hand to fully appreciate her new engagement ring.

"Do you like it?" Riley asked. His heart thumped in his chest.

Treasure threw her arms around Riley's neck. "I love it, Riley, and I love you."

Riley slammed his mouth on hers and kissed her so deeply and completely that she almost lost her breath and her balance. When she stumbled, he caught her, wrapping his hand around her waist. He reluctantly broke the kiss, and whispered against her forehead, "I love you so much, Treasure." After a moment, Riley stepped back. "Ready to go back to the house?"

Treasure shook her head, and Riley scooped her up and carried her back to the house. As Riley entered the foyer, Treasure joked, "Riley, aren't we supposed to wait for the wedding night before you carry me over the threshold?"

Riley held her firmly in his arms and stared at her. "As far as I'm concerned, you're already my wife. Ring or no ring. Everything I am and everything I have, it's yours." Riley gently eased her to her feet but pulled her close to his body and kissed her again. Treasure eased her arms under his arms and splayed her hands across his back. Riley's tongue explored every each of her mouth, and she kissed him back just as passionately. Treasure gasped when he cupped her behind and pulled her even tighter against him. Riley's lips moved to her neck. His hands under her shirt. He whispered against her skin, "Baby, I need you. Now."

"Yes," Treasure said, trying to catch her breath.

Riley picked up his fianceé and climbed the stairs. His fianceé. He could think of no better way to christen their engagement than by making love, and he wanted tonight to be one both of them would remember for the rest of their lives.

CHAPTER 17

Grace walked into the interrogation room with determination. Terry, her senior detective, followed behind her. Her heels clicked on the concrete floor as she locked eyes with E-Money, who sat there with a smug smirk on his face. This should be fun, he thought. The silence and tension in the room was thick. Grace sat down in the seat directly in front of E-Money on the other side of the table while Terry stood at the end of the table.

Inside, Grace's nerves jumped. She had one shot to get this right. And the stakes were high personally and professionally. She didn't even look up at him.

"Hello Mr. Walker, my name is Grace Harrington Dallas, a special investigator with the Jackson Police Department. Do you know why you're here?" Grace stared him directly in the eye. She had to admit it. She missed this part of the job. She tapped her nails on the folder that contained E-Money's life story. The dull tapping effectively calmed her nerves as she and E-Money continued to stare at each other. Terry walked around E-Money and stood behind him.

"No, but I can't wait to hear why," E-Money said. He shifted his body, leaning forward in his chair. Zeus had taught him well. Say nothing. Offer not even an emotion. He counted the cement blocks in the room since they dumped him in here three hours ago. He was up to sixty-five.

If Grace didn't know his history, she would be convinced that the man sitting before her was a true-to-the-bone criminal. But there was something in her gut that still saw something that could help him, give him a chance. She opened the folder. "Mr. Walker, here's a picture of you outside Treasure's Boutique. Here's another. And another." She put the pictures side by side in front of E-Money. "But you never go inside. Any reason you're visiting a women's clothing store on so many occasions?"

E-Money looked at her and smiled. "Is it a crime to shop in Jackson now? Or is it just a crime if you're from West Jackson?"

Grace looked at Terry standing behind him. That's how you want to play it, she thought. "Don't play that game with me, Mr. Walker. But stalking, harassment, and making terroristic threats are crimes, and it seems your actions as of late fall into all three categories." Grace stood. She pointed at the first picture of him outside Treasure's the first night he came to her store. Luckily, they were able to pull the still from a neighboring store. "This is you going into Treasure's the night you threatened her. And shortly after that, a rock landed in her living room."

E-Money sat still as stone, staring at Grace.

She pointed out the dates of the other photos as E-Money feigned a lack of interest in what Grace laid before him. "No response, huh? Alright, then."

Grace read from E-Money's juvenile record. "Says here that your father died at Parchman while serving life for murder. And your mom died of an overdose when you were eight."

E-Money shrugged. "Public knowledge, Lady." If this is all she's got, I'm cool, E-Money mused. "So what? My daddy was in jail. You think he was the only daddy in there."

Grace knew this was the moment she needed to get inside his head. "Yes, but he wasn't everyone's daddy. He was yours." How much did your mother tell you about your father?" She just kept talking. Right now, she thought she could work him until he lawyered up. Once he did that, the interview was over. She needed to get as much in his head before he said the word.

E-Money sat motionless. He didn't like trips down memory lane, especially when he wasn't the one driving. He wiped his hands on his jeans beneath the table.

Good, she thought. And sad. She saw his emotion cracking through the façade. "Did you know your father had a brother?"

E-Money's eyes flickered with a hint of surprise, but he recovered. He didn't know any of his father's people, and even when she was high, his mama never said anything about having an uncle.

Interrogation was like delicate surgery. A good interrogator needed to pay attention to every twitch, sweat bead, frown, and smile.

E-Money was beginning to sweat.

Grace softened her eyes. "Do you want to know who your uncle is, Mr. Walker?"

E-Money said nothing, but his eyes searched hers.

"Seth Newall." Grace let the name hang in the space between them. She watched the muscles in E-Money's shoulders as his arms tighten to his side. His fingers spread out on the tops of his thighs. Good. She could tell the nerves were beginning to set in. Terry moved slightly just in case E-Money jumped. Grace asked, "Seth Newall, or do you call him Zeus?"

Whoa, he thought. She dropped Zeus's name so sweetly that E-Money eyes bucked before he could stop himself. If she knew the name "Zeus" and had made the connection to his government name, E-Money knew that it was a matter of time before this got ugly. And he knew he would be the fall guy. But E-Money was a soldier. He just needed to figure out how to get out of this and get to Zeus. "I know who Seth Newall is, but I don't know this Zeus you're talking about." He sat back in his chair. Out of his periphery, he saw the male cop move slightly to his right.

Grace looked at Terry, who grabbed a chair and turned it around before sitting down. Terry's steady voice chilled him. "Look here, boy. We know you know Seth Newall and that he put you up to terrorizing Ms. Jordan. If I were you, I'd save myself. Your uncle didn't take his brother's son in even after your daddy took a murder rap for him. He made you a criminal. Didn't send you to school. Put you in the gutter with hoes and hoppers, like you weren't his family. His blood. Are you really going to throw your life away for him."

E-Money's mind raced even though he tried to maintain his cool exterior. He should have killed that Treasure Jordan broad. He'd been sloppy, but so had Zeus. E-Money maintained his cool facade. "Am I under arrest?" he asked.

Grace's brow raised. She played enough poker. Here was the turn. "Not yet, but you will be. Soon." Just as she finished her sentence, the door opened.

An older disheveled man in a threadbare suit came in. "I need to see my client. Now."

Grace smiled. "We're just finishing up our chat." Grace picked up the photographs and returned them to the folder. "Talk to your client, counselor. We'll be back for the line-up. You're free to join us." Grace was intentionally smug. "We'll be back to get him in a few moments."

Grace and Terry left the room quietly. Grace turned to Terry. "What do you think?"

Terry chuckled. "That boy didn't get scared until you said Zeus. He could take the Seth Newall uncle thing, because he doesn't believe it. But when you said 'Zeus,' oh man! He nearly peed his pants.

Grace laughed. "Well, let's get this line up done, and we can really make him twist."

~

Treasure didn't need but two minutes to identify E-Money. Even through the one-way mirror, his black eyes and angular jaw proved menacing. Terry conducted the line-up, because Grace didn't want his lawyer to say she was unduly influenced. She returned to the store, much to Riley's dismay, but Seth Newall and Ernest Walker had taken enough of her time and her life. Since Grace promised to update her after E-Money's arraignment, she decided not to worry about it anymore. She just hoped that he wouldn't get bail.

Her cell phone rang. Thinking it was Riley, she answered absentmindedly. "Hey, baby, I'm almost done here."

"Well, that's good to know," the voice on the other end said.

Treasure's blood ran cold. She recognized the voice and checked the screen for confirmation.

Seth Newall

Black Men United

"Hold on for a moment, Mr. Newall" she said, as she muted him and texted Riley and Grace. Riley had been waiting outside, and Grace replied that she was on her way but to keep him talking. When Riley burst through the door, he reached for the phone. Treasure held up her hand and put a finger to her lips. She texted Riley instructions to record while she put Newall on speaker.

"Yes, Mr. Newall, what can I do for you?" Treasure hoped Newall didn't hear the tremble in her voice."

"I just heard that you've been having some trouble, and I wanted to check on you," Newall replied, his voice purring with confidence.

Treasure held Riley's gaze with pleading eyes. What she did not need was Riley ripping into Seth Newall, who was clearly fishing for information. "Well, they've caught the young man, so I'm sure everything will be getting back to normal."

"Good. Do you know his name?" Seth Newall knew that Ernest was in custody, but he needed to know how far his exposure was. Was he still a faceless thug, or had he become the public's newest enemy?

"No, I don't," Treasure lied. "I'm sure even if I did, you wouldn't know him. He's definitely not one of your boys," emphasizing "your." If you want to play, we'll play, she said to herself.

Seth's voice dropped to a low rumble. "You just let me know if you need anything. Anything. I'll always be here for you, Treasure. You know, we CEOs have to stick together."

Treasure said her goodbyes and quickly hung up the phone. Riley was so angry that Treasure thought he might have a stroke right there in her store.

"I can't believe he had the nerve," Treasure said to herself.

"I can," Riley replied as he called Kenzo. "Let's go. Grace needs to hear this, and maybe put that Walker boy in protective custody. I wouldn't put it past Seth, or Zeus, or whatever he calls himself, to have that boy killed."

Just a few weeks ago, Treasure wouldn't have dared to agree with Riley, but not now. Murder was clearly not out of the realm of possibility. She grabbed her purse and work bag and set the security system. Riley had let the security guard go home early, so they were cautious as they left the building.

A car backfired on the far side of the parking lot, and Treasure grabbed Riley's arm. Lord, I can't live like this, she prayed. Riley opened her car door, and as if he read her thoughts, held her so close she could feel his heartbeat. "This will be over soon, sweetheart, I promise."

~

E-Money lay face up on his cot in his cell. They assigned him to a cell at the end of the line, which suited him fine. The attack didn't scare him. That was part of the game. His name carried weight after all these years, so his attack didn't make sense. And this was a warning, not a kill attack. Of that, he was sure. He winced as he raised his arms to fold them under his head. A few cracked ribs and a black eye, but no shank. Even E-Money knew he should be dead.

And that's what bothered him.

He heard a guard coming toward his cell--another benefit of being in the last cell. He listened to the guard's footsteps, the clanging of the keys on his hip.

The guard appeared at the cell, and E-Money didn't move. He kept his eyes on the ceiling as he breathed to the rhythm of the throbbing coming from his left side.

"Walker, get up. You got a visitor," the nameless guard said firmly. E-Money could tell he was fairly young, about his age, but E-Money didn't care to make friends just yet. He recognized the guard as one of the ones who took him to the infirmary, but E-Money didn't remember the guard's name and thought it best not to before he got the lay of the land.

E-Money eased his arms from behind his head and rolled to his left. He couldn't get up too quickly or his head would start pounding again. "Who is it?"

"You think they tell me? Let's go!" The guard waited impatiently as E-Money walked slowly to the cell gate. He put his hands through the slot as instructed. The clicking of the handcuffs sounded amplified against the concrete walls. The guard took his arm and led him down the hallway. Either the lights were too bright, or E-Money's eyes were still sensitive. E-Money tried closing his eyes and just walking blindly through the hallways, but his balance was off. More than once, the guard had to catch him from falling.

When the guard stopped, he led him to a cell where the lady cop and her partner were waiting. His lawyer, in that same crumpled suit, he had on earlier, stood at the door. "Mr. Walker, are you okay? I heard about the fight. We might be able to get you into protective custody or released on bail."

E-Money barely looked at him. "They already moved me." Zeus should have sent an attorney for him. He shouldn't have to deal with some attorney who was barely holding on to his practice, or an overworked public defender. Zeus wouldn't have let this man fill out a job application, let alone handle any legal shit. He had real lawyers on retainer for shit like this. E-Money didn't even remember this man's name, but he remembered that wrinkled-ass suit. Especially since all of this was because he wanted some bitch, he thought.

"Damn," he whispered when he saw Grace. He started to ask the guards to take him back to his cell, but his attorney had already started talking.

"Ms. Dallas. I hope you've come to your senses and decided to drop the charges against my client. Where is the D.A.?"

Grace didn't respond right away. She and Terry examined E-Money's beaten face and then glanced at each other. Clearly, Seth Newall was nervous, which was good. Deals worked out better when folks were nervous. She watched as E-Money, clearly still sore from the fight, lumbered toward the table and sat down. She called to the guard, "You can take the cuffs off." Turning toward E-Money, she asked, "We won't be having any problems, will we, Mr. Walker."

E-Money looked at her and shook his head. But he remained silent. If she thought she was going to get him to snitch, she had another thing coming.

Eventually, Grace turned to E-Money's attorney. "The D.A. will be here when necessary. You're here as a courtesy. Listen and advise your client well." She turned toward E-Money.

"Mr. Walker, I hope you've had time to consider the information I presented to you the last time we talked. But in case you're still debating whether your uncle is Seth Newall..."

E-Money glared at her and cut her off. "Seth Newall is not my daddy's brother." He heard his suit's mouth drop.

The suit stammered, "The...the...Seth Newall?"

Grace held up her hand and smirked at E-Money. "Yes, he is, which means instead of raising the son of the man who sacrificed his life for him, Seth Newall trained you to run his criminal enterprise. Is that family to you?" She pulled out two pieces of paper from her folder and laid them out before him. "This is your daddy's birth certificate. See? His mother is listed as Emmaline Jeffries." She watched him pretend not to study the names in the little boxes.

E-Money couldn't confirm or deny anything about his father's people, even his grandmother's name.

Grace pressed on, realizing how little he knew. "Your grandfather's name is there, Frederick Walker." She slid the second sheet beside the other. "And this is Seth Newall's birth certificate. Same mother. Different father."

E-Money leaned forward and studied the birth certificate. Emmaline Jeffries jumped out at him as if it had been written in neon. He forcefully slid the papers across the desk. Exasperated, he asked, "What do you want me to do with this?"

"I want the man who ordered you to attack Treasure Jordan." Grace set her face hard. Game time. "Tell you what, why don't you ask him? He knows you're here, but I didn't see his name on the visitor's log." She turned to Terry, "Did you?"

Terry leaned back. "Nope. Which could mean a couple of things. Seth Newall probably cared enough to have some thugs beat you as a warning to keep your mouth shut. Or maybe, you're cut off and that beating was a

Dear John letter? Either way, he ain't been to see his number two man and didn't even send one of his top attorneys." He gestured toward the suit. "We all know you're screwed."

"Look, you're going to jail for your attack on Treasure Jordan, but you can save yourself from more time, if you roll on Seth Newall and his Zeus operations."

E-Money took a deep breath. "Y'all must be crazy. First of all, those little sheets of paper don't mean shit. You could have made that with Photoshop. Second, I don't know any Zeus. And third, even if I did, I ain't nobody's snitch."

Grace heard the false bravado in his voice. Leaning forward, she lowered her voice an octave. "Alright, Mr. Walker. I'm trying to help save you from more charges and quite possibly, your life. Do you know what a RICO charge is, Mr. Walker? I can have you, your whole crew, and Seth Newall picked up in a matter of moments and charge every last one of you with the same crime. Who do you think Newall is going to save? Are you really that confident in your boys?"

E-Money stared at Grace. He knew she was right. And so was the dude cop. But he couldn't let them know that he knew that. He needed to talk to Zeus. Today.

"So, what's it going to be, Mr. Walker? Give us what we need, and we can protect you. From the looks of things, you need protection."

E-Money remained stone-faced as he looked directly at Grace.

Grace slid her case folder in her briefcase. "Mr. Walker, I'm feeling merciful these days. You have twenty-four hours. Your attorney knows how to reach me." She rose from the table. "Guard!" She called. "We're done here."

She and Terry watched E-Money and his attorney walk out of the room. "Get a wiretap on all E-Money's calls, and make sure that if he has any visitors, the conversations are recorded. I can guarantee you that Seth Newall is going to make an appearance very soon. I'd stake all my badges on it."

~

Grace had everything she needed. Sure enough, Seth Newall visited E-Money at the jail under the guise that E-Money was a former mentee of his with Black Men United. Newall tried to get a private room but jail officials blocked it since E-Money's charges were violent. Seth Newall prided himself on getting perks everywhere, but Grace thought he needed to get a feel for the cramped common room. What neither one of them knew was that Grace watched the entire visit from a closed-circuit television set up in the adjoining room.

"Got your message, Zeus," E-Money hissed. "After all the years, you think I would snitch on you? Man, I'm in here 'cause you wanted that Jordan woman. I told you this was a bad idea."

Seth Newall leaned forward. "Who do you think you're talking to Ernest," he hissed. "I didn't tell you to beat the woman up or let her identify you. All you had to do was scare her, put a little pressure on her, make her dump that Riley Taylor." Seth leaned back a bit in his chair, "The woman was a nice touch though, I must admit." He paused, "But it backfired."

"Yeah, well, that's what happens when you make business personal, right. Isn't that what you taught me, Zeus? And now, I'm in jail over some dumb personal shit. Your dumb personal shit."

Seth said nothing. E-Money was right. His lust for Treasure and his hatred for Riley Taylor had been a bad combination. "Listen, I'll get you out of here. Just be cool."

E-Money looked at Zeus, stared at him to see if there was any resemblance to himself. "Alright, Unc," he said, waiting for Zeus's reaction.

"What did you say, Ernest?" Seth asked slowly and deliberately.

The two men stared at each other for a full minute before E-Money decided to answer. "I said, 'alright, unc.' You know, as in uncle. Because that's what you are right. My father's brother."

"Who told you that?" Seth asked, avoiding the question.

"Doesn't matter. I just wanted to know if it were true and why you never told me." The images of his father's and Seth's birth certificates imprinted on his brain. "Your mother's name," he said. "Emmaline Jeffries, right?" Guess what? My father's mother has the same name. What are the odds?"

Seth said nothing. His mind raced trying to figure out who gave E-Money this information, information that had been buried so deep that even he forgot at times. And just who was trying to put a wedge between him and E-Money? After a few minutes, he rolled his shoulders and repeated his question. "Who told you that?"

"So, it's true." E-Money shook his head. "All these years. Is it true that my father took the blame for the murder you committed?"

Seth's mind scrambled as he processed what E-Money asked him. He needed to play this cool and softened his face. "Listen, Ernest, I've taken pretty good care of you over the years. Don't you have everything you want and money in your pocket? I've treated you like my own son."

E-Money threw his head back and laughed. "Like your own son. Hell, I'm your blood, and you let me run the streets. I wasn't good enough for your real Black Men United program, but I can carry a tray though, right?" He remembered the night Zeus told him to threaten Treasure. He rose from his seat, "And now, I'm going to jail because you wanted a woman who didn't want you." E-Money's head started thumping. "You know what, get one of your fancy lawyers to get me out of here and give me enough money to start over somewhere else. You'll never have to worry about me again."

Seth leaned back in his chair. "I'll see what I can do."

As he watched E-Money walk through the doors to the cells, Seth shook his head. Ernest had been one of the best lieutenants he had, and Seth had never questioned his loyalty. Losing him would be hard, but Seth would make sure that the death he ordered was painless. He took out his phone and made the call.

Little did he know, Seth Newall made the call that would completely destroy him and his empires.

~

Treasure nervously combed through the dress racks for markdowns. The pricing gun felt heavy in her hands. And every click of the gun made her feel more normal despite everything happening around her. She still needed to prepare for her annual clearance sale to clear out her inventory. Treasure loved her three-day clearance sale. When Grace and Kenzo married, they focused a good deal of their philanthropy work on helping sex trafficking survivors establish new lives. Treasure helped out with clothes regularly, but for the sale, she went all out for them. The women had special hours to shop in addition to receiving gift cards to have their hair and nails done at a nearby salon. She expected around forty young girls and women, and she wanted to make sure that everything was as perfect as she could make it.

Plus, it helped her forget that her back office and storage room resembled something out of a James Bond movie. Between her cameras and the ones Grace hid throughout the store, every inch of her store was being recorded, except the dressing rooms. She even had an earpiece so small that you couldn't see it in her ear. And if Newall could see it, she could always say she needed a temporary hearing aid because of the attack. She was thankful for the few unsuspecting customers who came into the store, making everything seem normal. "Whatever normal is," Treasure muttered to herself.

Riley, Grace, Kenzo, Marcus, and several agents posted in her backroom waiting for Seth Newall to arrive. She didn't even bother to argue with Riley about his being there, and if Riley was there, Kenzo was there. Grace told Kenzo he was responsible for ensuring that Riley remembered that he was a civilian, or else. Riley had to respect her authority in that room, no matter what happened. Grace's only concern should be making sure that Treasure was okay, not whether she would have to shoot Riley, or, at the worst, arrest him. Treasure laughed to herself as Riley begrudgingly promised to behave.

Treasure fiddled with her engagement ring as she thought about seeing Seth after all his manipulations and crimes against her. She was still twisting it around when the chimes on the door signaled that someone had entered the store. Her spirit told her it was Seth Newall, and she half hoped that her spirit was wrong. She wanted to think she was just being paranoid. But there he was standing in her store like the predator he was in a tailor-made Hugo Boss suit. She took a deep breath and plastered a smile across her face.

Seth reached for her to embrace her in a friendly hug, and Treasure moved quickly away from him. The thought that he might touch her made her flesh crawl. "Hello, Mr. Newall. How are you? And Gail?"

Seth smiled. Treasure Jordan always remembered to ask about Gail, he thought. "We're fine. But I'm not here to talk about me. How are you? The store looks wonderful." He looked her up and down and noticed the wrap on her ankle.

I'm better now. Things are getting back to normal," Treasure replied. She moved closer to the counter to lean on it for support. "Especially since he's been arrested."

Seth walked around the store, and as Treasure watched, she realized that he moved the same way E-Money did the first night he entered the store. "Good." He walked toward her, his arms behind his back. His voice lowered an octave. "You know, Ms. Jordan, I was beside myself when I heard about your attack."

"Thank you for your concern, Mr. Newall, but I'll be fine once this is all over." Treasure moved to pick up her pricing gun and papers from the floor. If she kept moving, he wouldn't be able to get close enough to touch her.

"Yes, I'm sure you will." He looked toward the back of the store. His voice entered a sultry, seductive octave that made her flesh crawl. "Are you here alone? You shouldn't be alone at a time like this," Seth looked around the store. "I'm surprised that Mr. Taylor would let you be alone in the store." His lips curled in a sinister sneer. For the first time, in all these years, Treasure saw Seth Newall for who and what he was.

She heard Grace tell her to defend Riley to keep Newall talking. She heard Riley cursing in the background.

Treasure looked down, pretended to defend Riley, "Well, we both understand business..."

Seth Newall cut her off, approaching her. His head seemed to hang low like a big cat stalking its prey. "That's the problem with these young bucks. No understanding of what it means to have a woman, to protect her."

Treasure bristled. "And you do, Mr. Newall?"

Seth smiled. "Yes, I do. And I can show you better than I can tell you."

Treasure frowned. "What does that mean, Mr. Newall?" Treasure needed him to say it plainly--and on camera.

"After all these years, you can call me Seth, don't you think?" he asked.

Treasure heard Grace hiss in her ear telling Riley to sit down. Grace whispered, "You're doing fine, Treasure. Keep him talking. I got this fool back here." Treasure almost laughed but caught herself.

"Well, Mr. Newall, I mean Seth, what do you mean?" Treasure attempted to be coy, but she sounded fake, even to herself.

Seth looked at Treasure. Perhaps, this ordeal enlightened her on RIley Taylor's failures. She seemed to be wavering more than she ever had, which was good for him. And for her. He realized that she didn't invite him to call her 'Treasure,' but he decided to take the liberty anyway. "Treasure," he paused, looking at his watch, "I need to head to a meeting. Listen, I was wondering if you were still interested in speaking to the boys this weekend. Perhaps, it will get your mind off things."

The abrupt shift in the conversation confused Treasure, but she went with it. "Of course, Mr. Newall," she said. At his raised brow, she quickly added, "I mean, Seth. Let me check my calendar." She slowly walked behind the counter and grabbed her phone. "What day? Time?"

"Friday," he said, cheerfully. "Let's say around six o'clock. The boys would have been there since four, so by six, they are good and hungry. We feed the boys a good meal before they leave so their mamas don't have to worry about it on a Friday night. So, they'll be a captive audience, and I know you'll make a perfect treat for them." Newall emphasized "treat," and Treasure had to stop herself from shivering from disgust.

"Alright, I'll see you then. At the BMU Center, right?" Treasure typed the details into her phone.

"Yes. See you then." Seth smiled broadly. He left the store more satisfied than he had been in a while. Getting Treasure alone on Friday would ease the pain of losing Ernest. He bopped to his Mercedes S-560 like he drunk from a fountain of youth. And, in some ways, that's how he felt knowing he had Treasure Jordan right where he wanted her. All he had to do now was get Treasure alone Friday night. Seth Newall would show her what a grown man did when his woman was in danger, not like that boy, Riley Taylor. He was still smiling when he slid on the leather seats and pushed the ignition button, Marvin Gaye's "Got to Give It Up" came blasting through his speakers. Seth grinned to himself as he pulled out of the parking lot, tapping the steering wheel in time to music. Things are definitely going my way, he thought, cruising down Lakeland Drive to meet his wife, Gail, for dinner at the grand opening of the Gulf Oyster Bar.

He might even let Gail make love to him tonight. He was feeling that good.

~

Treasure pulled her car slowly into the Black Men United parking lot at 5:45p.m. A few cars littered the lot, but that was to be expected. She saw Seth Newall's Mercedes parked by the front door, so she parked a few spaces down.

"Tell me what you see, baby," Riley said. Riley's voice sounded much calmer than it was. He, Kenzo, and Marcus were in another car behind her with Marcus driving. Treasure told him everything she saw. She saw a young man pass by the window who looks about twelve. She exhaled. Marcus had double-checked that the boys were going to be there, but she didn't feel safe to enter until she saw one. She wouldn't have put it past Seth Newall to cancel the boys' Friday night event and have her walking into an empty center, so he could have her alone. She shuddered sickened by the thought.

"I'm getting out now, Riley. Remember, you'll be able to hear everything, but please, don't talk to me. I can't focus with you in my ear."

Riley grunted a halfhearted "okay." He didn't like this at all. It was different with Grace. Grace could handle herself, and she still got kidnapped. "Baby, please be careful. If you get in any kind of trouble, I'll be right there. I love you."

Treasure closed her eyes and took a deep breath. "I love you too, Riley. I'll be fine. We have to end this. Tonight," she said with determined finality. She needed to get her mind ready to deal with Seth. "Grace, can you hear me?" Treasure asked. She wished that Grace could have come with her, but that would have aroused Seth's suspicion. Plus, Seth wanted Treasure alone. And the plan was to let him think she was alone.

"I hear you, Treasure," Grace said. "Remember, the cross pendant is capturing video and sound, so don't touch it or move it around too much."

"Okay," Treasure replied through clenched teeth. She was still a few feet from the building's entrance. "Newall is at the door."

She heard Grace issue the final order. "Alright, folks, she's going in. Everyone stay alert, and do not move until I say so."

Treasure got out of the car and walked toward the door. Seth Newall opened the door for her, and she felt a little like Little Red Riding Hood meeting the wolf. "Good evening, Treasure. The boys are getting their dinners now, so let's give them a few minutes before going inside. If they see you, all hell will break loose." He laughed at his joke. "We can stay here in the lobby. They'll be settled in a few moments."

"Alright, then. That's fine." Treasure rolled her bag behind her. She was going to talk to the boys about personal style. She brought each young man a bow tie and a necktie so they would practice on each other as they learned how to tie each one. There were about eighteen ways to tie a tie, but she thought the basic Windsor would be easy for them to learn. The bow ties were a bit easier.

"Let me get that, bag, Treasure," Seth said as he reached for the bag. Treasure almost jumped when he got close to her. She could smell his cologne. Lord, he's still wearing Obsession, she thought.

"Thank you. It's a little heavier than usual. I have some tabletop mirrors in there as well," she said, inching away from him.

A young man stepped into the hallway. "Mr. Newall, the boys are seated and ready."

Seth nodded, "Thank you, Ray." He turned toward Treasure. "Ready?"

"Indeed," Treasure replied, glad that he didn't know how ready she was and what exactly she was ready for.

~

After her presentation, Treasure hugged each little boy. She met their parents and spoke to them. Though most of the parents were mothers and grandmothers, she met some fathers and grandfathers too. She spoke to the young college students who served as mentors in the program. She had such a good time that she almost forgot why she was there. Treasure thought about Riley as a little boy and was smiling to herself when Newall invaded her space.

"I need to get some things from the office. It's down this hallway. I don't want to leave you in the front alone." Seth looked at her expectantly.

Treasure pretended to consider. "I really should get on home."

Riley listened with his fists balled up. Treasure made him promise not to say anything, but if that man tried to touch her, Riley would have Seth Newall's head. And he wouldn't feel bad about it. Hell, he had Amanda Alexander on speed dial. No way he would go to jail. Kenzo saw the rage building across Riley's face and touched his shoulder. Helplessness and rage were emotions Kenzo knew all too well.

"Won't take long, I promise." Seth Newall had already started walking down the hallway quite pleased with himself. He opened the door to the business office and walked to the desk. He pulled out a bottle of cognac and poured himself a glass. "Would you like a drink? It's been a long day for both of us."

Treasure's mind raced. They hadn't covered this possibility, but she politely declined. "No but thank you. Maybe next time." She watched him as he threw his head back and drank the shot.

"Suit yourself," he said. "I made a few calls, Treasure. You know the guy who attacked you? They released him today on bail?" He searched her face for her reaction. He wondered if her friend Grace had told her anything.

Treasure feigned shock, awe, and disbelief simultaneously. "No, he didn't. Grace definitely would have told me if they released him." Tears formed in her eyes, not because she was acting, but because all of it overwhelmed her --Seth Newall, his lies, and now, her own.

Seth placed his glass on the desk and handed her a tissue. "Maybe Grace doesn't know, but I found out this afternoon," he lied. I have a few contacts in city government. Seems as though his attorney made a pretty decent appeal since he'd been attacked in jail."

Treasure said nothing as she wiped her eyes. She and Seth stared at each other for a few seconds. Finally, she said, "I'm so tired of this foolishness. I do want to know why he chose me to harass and attack though. I don't know him from Adam's housecat." She paused. "But he did look familiar. I could never place him. Maybe if I had..." Treasure looked directly at Seth. She half hoped that he would admit his involvement, which meant she could simply leave and let the police do their jobs.

Seth paused. "Treasure, I promise, everything will be alright." He cocked his head as if he were thinking about something. "Let me show you something." He walked around her and headed to the door.

Treasure followed. Grace issued orders to her team. "Alright folks, on alert." Seth led Treasure down the back hallway and opened the door. She gasped at the sight of E-Money tied to a chair in the middle of the room, looking like he'd been beaten to every inch of his life. His head hung low, blood dripping from his mouth.

A woman's heel clicked on the floor. Unmistakably a stiletto. Treasure blinked her eyes as shadowy figures coming from the back wall appeared in the light.

Shotgun stood behind E-Money and tugged his head up. E-Money's tongue hung out of his head. "Satisfied?" she asked Seth. Treasure knew the physical scars were a mixture of Shotgun and Chief. Shotgun had to rough him up a bit to make the makeup look believable. Treasure was still amazed that he'd agreed to it all. But her heart still broke for him. She held her head in her hands.

Seth touched her shoulder. "Look at him. Is this the man who hurt you, Treasure?" He repeated the question. "Is he?"

Treasure looked at Seth's hand on her shoulder and stepped away from him. She moved closer to the door. "Yes, he's the one."

Seeing Ernest that way gave Seth no comfort, but it was necessary. He nodded at Shotgun and looked at Treasure, "See, I'm going to make sure that he never hurts you again. Me. Not that young buck Riley Taylor. And what you do see here tonight stays here. Got it." Treasure noted how easily he transformed from the upstanding citizen to crazed criminal. She nodded.

Shotgun dropped E-Money's head, and Treasure winced. She glanced at Treasure and narrowed her eyes, cocking her sawed-off double barrel shotgun. "You brought a civilian in here? Are you insane? I'm gonna have to kill two people tonight, or maybe three."

Treasure gasped. Shotgun looked at her hard and began walking toward her. Treasure moved slightly, realizing that Shotgun was repositioning her in the room. "This is why I don't do boutique contracts. I should have popped his ass on the courthouse steps." Shotgun shifted her attention to Seth. "But this was a professional courtesy, Zeus, and since you paid extra for this show, here we are. But I need the balance before we go forward with anything else. Do you have my money?"

Seth reached behind his back.

Shotgun aimed her gun directly at Seth. "Easy, Zeus. Anything other than twenty stacks comes from behind your back, you'll be dead before the bullet leaves the chamber." And Shotgun meant every word.

Seth pulled two sets of bills from his back waistband and threw them at Shotgun's feet. He walked to E-Money and lifted his head. "Ernest, this pains me. It really does, but I can't afford you anymore." E-Money lifted his head. He said nothing but spit at Seth. Blood splattered across Seth's face. Seth wiped his face with the back of his suit. Uncouth ass, Treasure mused, rolling her eyes. Riley would have used a handkerchief.

"Because you're about to die, I'm going to give you that, nephew." Seth looked at Shotgun. "Make it quick."

"What about her, Zeus?" Shotgun casually aimed her gun between Seth and Treasure. A flick of her wrist, and she would be able to hit either one of them in a second.

"Don't worry about her at all. Right, Treasure?" Seth didn't look in her direction as if her acceptance was a foregone conclusion.

"Nice doing business with you," Shotgun said.

Grace and her team burst through the door. Grace's voice rose above the commotion. "Police! Hands up!" The authority in Grace's voice frightened Treasure. Seeing Grace in action was a surreal experience. Treasure's hands shot up along with Seth's and Shotgun's.

Confusion flashed across Seth's face. Zeus's beady eyed look transformed into a docile, upstanding Seth Newall in a flash.

"Thank God you're here! I'm Seth Newall, President of Black Men United. Ms. Jordan and I found this woman torturing this poor boy! Please call an ambulance." He sounded frantic, turning his head back and forth, looking very much like the upstanding Jacksonian he had been pretending to be all these years. An officer placed him in handcuffs as another officer untied E-Money.

Another officer placed Shotgun in cuffs and ushered her out of the room immediately. When Shotgun stepped outside, she spied Marcus standing outside with some officers with tears in his eyes. As the police officer placed her in the back of a squad car, Shotgun took solace in the fact that she would be able to tell Marcus about herself soon. She hoped that he would listen when she did.

Treasure backed herself into the shadows of the corner. Grace almost forgot she was there.

Grace stood in front of Seth. "Oh, no, Mr. Newall, we have exactly who we're looking for. Or should I call you Zeus?"

Seth and Grace stared at each other a full minute before she called one of the officers forward. "Read him his rights. Don't skip one word."

Grace realized Treasure was cowering in the corner, no doubt, in shock. She walked over to her. "You don't need to be here. Let's go."

As Grace ushered Treasure toward the door, Seth yelled, "Bitch, do you know who I am?" He spit at her, "Your career is over, Grace Harrington. I will rain sulfur on this city before I do a day."

Grace stepped in front of Treasure, shielding her. She turned her head and said to the officer at Seth's side, "Throw him in the back of a squad car NOW!"

Grace didn't want Treasure to walk near Seth, so she shielded her so the officer could walk Seth out of the room.

Seth realized that the officer walking him out was young and significantly smaller than him. Seth knew he could take advantage of his size. The officer was so green that he hadn't noticed that Seth turned his wrists so the cuffs weren't tight. Seth turned his right hand and freed it from the cuff. He grabbed the younger officer's gun and shot him in the leg. The sound of the shot bounced off the walls, and the officer dropped to the ground writhing in pain. E-Money had only seconds to react, hurling his body in front of Seth as he pulled the trigger again--this time at Grace and Treasure.

"Noooo!" E-Money hollered as the sound of the gunshot filled the room a second time. Grace threw Treasure to the ground and covered her body. Grace whipped around her gun in her hand. In seconds, she saw E-Money on the ground, and the glint of a gun in Seth Newall's hand. She shot the gun out of his hand, taking two or three fingers in the process. She fired another shot that hit Seth in the shoulder.

Seth Newall cried out in pain as the other officers toppled him. Riley rushed into the room with Kenzo right behind him. Riley picked Treasure up off the floor and rushed out of the room. "Baby, you okay?" He planted kisses over her face and held her tightly against him. Treasure threw her arms around Riley's neck and lay her head on his shoulder. "Take me home, Riley." Without a word, Riley walked out of the room with Treasure in his arms. Nothing else mattered but getting Treasure home, safe and sound.

With Seth finally back in handcuffs, Grace knelt by E-Money. The bullet pierced his abdomen. "Get a bus!" She tried to apply pressure on the wound as his eyes fluttered closed. "I need you to stay with me, Ernest!" Grace applied pressure but the wound pooled with blood. "Kenzo, hold his head up." Kenzo did as instructed and placed E-Money's head in his lap. He and Grace locked eyes. They didn't have to say it aloud. E-Money didn't need an ambulance.

E-Money's eyes opened briefly. He struggled to talk. His voice became raspy and labored. "I wanted to do something good before I died." Blood gushed from his mouth. Grace wiped his mouth and whispered, You did good, Ernest. Real good. Don't talk now. The ambulance is coming." Kenzo whispered "Amen," and she looked up at him with tears in her eyes. Ernest was already gone by the time the EMTs arrived.

Grace rolled her shoulders and turned to Kenzo. Emotions had to wait, especially with her work unfinished. "Call and check on Treasure. I'm going to the hospital, and I'm not leaving until Seth Newall is printed and booked. I can add attempted murder and manslaughter to the charges."

~

"We're home. Alright, Ken. Thanks." Riley hung up the phone and placed it on the nightstand. Treasure looked at him, her eyes flashing with questions. "The District Attorney charged Seth Newall with about five felonies, including murder. Since it's the weekend, his arraignment isn't until Monday. Kenzo doesn't think he'll get bail, not with the evidence Grace took to both the District Attorney and the U.S. Attorney."

Riley shook his head and looked at Treasure. "I didn't know Grace had pull like that."

Treasure smiled proudly. "Me either. What about Ernest Walker?"

Riley took a deep breath. "He didn't make it. Kenzo said he died before the ambulance arrived."

"That poor child," Treasure said. She nestled herself deeper into Riley's side.

Riley loved Treasure's heart most of all. After all, Ernest Walker had done to terrorize her, she still mourned his death. "You are an amazing woman, Treasure, and I'm so glad all of this is over. Now we can focus on starting our lives together."

"Riley, I…" She stopped speaking, trying to find the right words.

Riley didn't like Treasure's tone. Quietly, he asked, "Changed your mind?"

Treasure rolled toward Riley to look directly into his eyes. She saw fear in his eyes despite his attempts at nonchalance. "Riley, I want nothing more in this world than to become your wife, but I…"

"Say it, sweetheart." Riley couldn't accept anything before the "but" until what came after. "You want to wait until after the baby's born?"

"No, sooner than that." She smiled shyly at him and rubbed her stomach. "Before I start showing."

Riley's brow raised in confusion. So, in about five months?"

Treasure laughed. "No, sir, a month. Next month by your tree." When Riley didn't say anything, she threw her head back. "I guess a month is too soon to try to put a wedding together."

Riley laughed and flipped her on her back. Love and joy accompanied the mirth in his eyes. He kissed her deeply and so passionately that Treasure almost lost her breath. Riley tugged at her earlobe with his teeth and whispered, "I think we can safely say my tree is our tree now."

He kissed her again. "Are you sure? Here, at the house?" Riley heart constricted in his chest. That Treasure wanted to marry sooner rather than later, and at the house, meant the world. He stopped. "Sweetheart, you can have whatever kind of wedding you want. We don't have to rush and have it at the house."

Treasure smiled. "I always dreamed about an outdoor wedding, and for some reason, having it here, in that spot, feels special and something that belongs to us. Does that make sense?"

Riley placed a kiss on her forehead. "Tell me what you need me to do, baby, and I promise, I'll make it happen." He looked down at Treasure, and his eyes darkened with desire. He kissed her so deeply Treasure felt it in the depths of her core. Every cell in her body come alive. Her skin heated as Riley's hands caressed and teased her flesh. She opened herself to him. "Make love to me, Riley."

Riley smiled, "Whatever my Treasure wants, my treasure gets."

CHAPTER 18

Eighteen Months Later

Riley hung the last banner and balloons up at the gazebo. He was sick of banners and balloons. Pinwheels and Princesses. Hell, the black princess had been a frog most of the movie, but Treasure had gone all out with the decorations. She glared at him and crossed her arms when he dared to suggest that the baby wouldn't remember a thing about this party.

Riley couldn't believe his baby girl was a year old. Olivia Grace Taylor had turned his entire world upside down. He shook his head. If someone told him a few years ago that he would be happily married with a wife and child, he would have laughed in their faces. He sat down on a bench inside the gazebo and downed a bottle of water. Riley finished the bottle and held it as he reflected on how much his life had changed in the last couple of years. A wife. A daughter. Lord, he thought, this is payback. She already had him wrapped around her little finger, and she could barely talk. But her babble game is strong, he thought, laughing at her "argument" with Treasure that morning. He could have sworn Olivia had rolled her eyes at her mother. He was definitely glad it was Treasure who was the object of Olivia's wrath and not him that morning.

He stood as Kenzo's car pulled into the driveway. Treasure and Grace were setting up in the inside of the house with food and games. Of course, their wives ordered them to work outside. Riley waved as he approached. Kenzo and Grace unloaded their car with bags and their most precious cargo, their 9-month old son, Kenzo Jr.

"Hey! How much do you have there, man? You know we have toys here, right?" Riley was laughing as Kenzo struggled with Little Kenzo's portable play pen.

Kenzo shook his head. "I told Grace that she didn't need to bring everything, but I'm just his father."

Riley laughed heartily. "And I bet she said, 'Just in case, right.'"

Before Kenzo could answer, Grace chimed in. "Whatever, Riley. Come take one of these bags." She held out a big bag full of little bags.

Riley took the bag and looked inside. "What in the world is all this?"

Grace looked at him as if he asked the most stupid question in the world. "Party favors for Olivia's guests." She and Little Kenzo walked in the house and didn't look back to see if they had followed.

Riley looked at Kenzo, who was watching his wife walking into the house. "Man, what do one-year-olds need with party favors?"

Kenzo, smiling, shifted a bag in his arms and shook his head. "Who knows? My boy's party is in three months, so maybe we will know the answer by then."

Riley laughed, "Yeah right.

~

The party was a resounding success, Riley thought, as far as kids' parties went. No crying fits. No injuries. And all the children and their parents left on time. Only Kenzo and Grace remained. The house was nearly quiet. Perfect.

Riley walked to the playpen in the corner of the room. Treasure and Grace were sitting at the table, laughing and drinking a glass of wine. Kenzo was watching television and on his phone. No doubt checking emails, Riley thought, shaking his head. He looked down at his daughter and Little Kenzo sleeping in Olivia's playpen. Little Kenzo's playpen leaned up against the wall. He smiled. Kenzo's playpen was never unpacked. But it was never unpacked. Olivia and Kenzo were already so close that they never wanted to be apart.

As Olivia and Kenzo lay on their backs, he noticed that they were holding hands. Riley frowned. As innocent as it was, Riley didn't like facing the fact that one day she would hold another man's hand. Another man would make her face light up when he walked in the room. Riley leaned over the playpen. Maybe he could move them without waking them. Before he could touch them, Kenzo walked over.

Quietly, Kenzo whispered. "Man, did you ever imagine the two of us here? Married with children? Birthday parties? Playdates?"

Riley straightened his back. "Not in a million years. Hell, man, not five years ago. But I wouldn't change it for anything."

~

He'd surprised Treasure with a cleaning crew to clean up during the party and right after, so it didn't look like there'd been a party at all except a few lingering decorations. Kenzo and Grace eased their sleeping baby home about an hour ago. The house was serenely quiet, almost too quiet for Riley, and he realized that he hadn't seen Treasure in about fifteen minutes. With a quick glance to make sure Olivia was still sleeping in her playpen, Riley climbed the stairs in search of his wife.

When he entered their bedroom, he found her sitting on the edge of the bed. Riley entered tentatively, "Baby, you okay? Why are you hiding up here?"

Treasure looked up at Riley. "Nothing's wrong. I needed a moment to myself."

Riley's brow furrowed. Something was wrong. He stood in front of her and pushed a lock of hair from her face. "Is there anything I can do for you?"

Treasure didn't answer at first. After a moment, she sighed. "Been quite the year, hasn't it, Riley?"

Riley chuckled. "To say the least."

"Everything moved so fast, first with us, then the stuff with Seth Newall, marriage, the baby." Tears welled in her eyes. "We never got a moment to breathe."

Riley cupped her face. She was beginning to scare him a bit. "Hey," he said softly, "I love you and Olivia more than anything in the world. I wouldn't change what we have or how we got here for anything." He planted soft kisses on her eyelids.

She said his name again on a sigh and shook her head. "Are you sure?"

"Positive."

"I'm going to hold you to it, Mr. Taylor," she smiled. Treasure handed him the object she held. "Because Round Two is starting now."

"Round two," he asked. He looked down at the pregnancy test. "You're? We're?"

"Yep." Treasure's heart thumped in her chest as she waited for his reaction. She wondered if her husband, this beautiful man who had given her so much love, would be overwhelmed with two babies so close together. She asked the same of herself but prayed that he would be as happy as she was.

Riley's face broke into a grin and scooped Treasure into his arms. He placed a kiss on her forehead. Against her skin, he struggled to whisper. "Treasure, my treasure, thank you."

Treasure laid her head against Riley's chest. She leaned into his embrace as he held her tightly. "What are you thanking me for, Riley," she asked softly.

Riley stepped back so he could look in her eyes. He held her chin and kissed her lips softly. "For loving me. For Olivia." He paused and placed his hand on her stomach. "For this baby."

Tears sprang to her eyes. Every day since they married Riley surprised her with the depths of his love. She closed her eyes and said a prayer of thanks.

Riley gently cupped her face and gazed into her eyes. "But most of all, Treasure, for you. You, my love, are my greatest treasure, and wherever you are is where my heart is." He kissed her again, more passionately than ever. "Always."

EPILOGUE

Marcus gripped the steering wheel. For weeks after Seth Newall's arrest, he refused Kenzo's or Riley's explanation about why they kept him left in the dark about Shotgun's involvement or that she was a government asset. Or should he call her Shay now? All those years he wasted being angry at her for being a criminal when not only was she not a criminal but a government agent. And then, when Kenzo and Riley found out, they said nothing. Nothing! Marcus's heart shattered the moment police officers led Shotgun out in handcuffs. Learning she was part of the sting was bittersweet.

The hour and a half long drive to Natchez had him in knots. No one knew where Shotgun fled to after Seth Newall's arrest or his trial six months later. It was as if she disappeared without a trace. But Marcus had eventually traced her to a farmhouse in Natchez. He smiled at the memory that came to him one day. The four of them were on a school trip to visit Vicksburg Civil War Memorial and the plantations of Natchez at the end of their eighth-grade year. By the time they headed to lunch in Natchez, Marcus had decided to ask Shay if he could buy her lunch.

He'd just worked up the nerve when he realized the bus pulled up to Mamie's, a soul food restaurant and Natchez landmark. Steeped in the images of the old South and slavery, Maime's was a soul food restaurant in the shape of a black woman in a huge skirt, which was how you entered the restaurant.

"I'm not going in there," Marcus announced. A stand-off with Mrs. Higgen, their history teacher, ensued. Usually the epitome of austere calm, Mrs. Higgen immediately became flustered by his refusal and the refusal of every black student on the bus. The bus driver even smirked as he looked out of his window. Mrs. Higgen explained that this was an important landmark, its historical value, and that she frequented Maime's many times on this very same trip. It was part of her Civil War lesson plans and until now, no one had ever complained.

He was glad his boys and Shay had backed him from the start. When the four of them refused, the other black kids refused as well. The bus driver whispered to Mrs. Higgen that he would take them somewhere and be back to pick up the group. She never said another word, but just exited the bus and walked into Maime's with her head hung down. The bus driver, Samuel, took them to another restaurant. He remembered trying to find time to speak to Shay alone, but everyone was so hyped about Marcus's coup that they took over.

Marcus did find her though during their visit to the Rosalie Plantation. He never forgot the way she looked walking through those gardens. When she stopped in a field of white flowers, gardenias, she later told him, he thought she looked pure and perfect. He didn't want to interrupt her, but she waved him over to her. They talked about everything and nothing all at once.

After months of searching, Marcus found her, hiding in plain sight, right there in Natchez.

Marcus's GPS led him down a long stretch of gravel road surrounded by trees draped in moss. Somehow, the trees met in the middle of the air, creating a natural arch overhead. Marcus was glad he came early in the day, because there was no way he could navigate these back roads at night. But, I guess, that's the point, Marcus mused. He sat up further in his seat, trying to see how much road lay ahead. He spotted an opening to the right. Of course, Shay would have a hidden driveway, he thought, rolling his eyes.

He turned toward the spot and immediately spied a quaint, two-story farmhouse that looked like something out of an old western. Horses grazed in a nearby field. Flowers lined the gravel road leading toward the house. Marcus recognized the white roses, but the gardenias let him know he was in the right place.

But nothing prepared Marcus for the woman sitting on the front porch.

Shay sat on the edge of the front porch at the top of the steps, dressed in a white cotton dress. The dress gathered at her knees, a small basket between her legs as she snapped beans for her dinner that evening. Her long black hair in a single braid slung around her right shoulder. A cool breeze wafted across the porch. Lost in the rhythm of snapping the beans, Shay intensely followed a bee flit from flower to flower. Snap. She wondered if this was the bee's joy, to dance and twirl as it suckled a new nectar and gathered food for the hive. Snap. She wondered if the flower felt special, being chosen as a vessel of life. Did flowers tingle at the contact? Snap. Did flowers feel used as the bee moved to another? Snap. Like she did.

So lost in her reverie, Shay barely registered the sound of the car approaching her. She reached under the porch step for the small pistol anchored there. She didn't have visitors here--by careful design. Within seconds, she recognized the driver. Marcus. Shay dropped the unsnapped bean in her hand, rapidly blinking, to make sure she hadn't conjured him up in her mind. Perhaps, being alone in Natchez affected her mind, because she was seeing things. Shay waited for the mirage to pass.

Marcus sat in the car for a moment. During the entire drive to Natchez, he practiced his speech, buoyed by his frustration, and smugly glad that he found her. But now, seeing her, his mind was blank. He took a deep breath and opened his car door. He stood by the car a moment before he started walking toward the house. Both of them needed a moment to adjust to the sight of the other. Shay blinked several times, realizing that the mirage before her was real. Too real. She stood slowly, her dress billowing in the breeze.

She waited.

Marcus walked.

"How did you find me?" Shay asked, taking a step back. Marcus was too close to her even though he was only standing on the bottom step of the porch. His manly scent entered her nostrils as soon as he exited the car.

Marcus smiled. "Mamie's. Eighth grade field trip."

Confusion, then recognition, flashed across her face. "But how did you find me? Here? Now?"

Marcus took another step forward. Shay took another step back.

He placed his hands in his pockets to keep from grabbing her. "Your sisters. You named the shell company that bought a parcel of land with a house on it, no phone number, no wi-fi, no electricity after your sisters, Amina and Nandi. The AmNani Corporation? Dead giveaway." He paused. "For those who know you." The words hung between them.

"And if you'd been wrong?" Shay shifted her feet nervously.

Marcus shrugged his shoulders. "I would have kept looking until I found you," he said, climbing the remaining steps until he came face to face with her. "And believe me, I would have found you eventually."

Shay couldn't move. Marcus's eyes searched hers. "Why didn't you tell me, Shay?" he said quietly.

Shay closed her eyes as tears welled behind her lids. She couldn't answer him. She couldn't tell him the truth, not with her skin heating and her pulse racing and his scent invading her nostrils.

Marcus balled his fist in his pockets to keep from touching her.

Shay took a deep breath and summoned all the control she had. With a hoarse whisper, she croaked, "You need to leave, Marcus, and forget me and don't come back." She moved toward the basket. She needed something to stand between them.

Marcus blinked. Everything went out of his head but the one thing he wanted to do since the eighth grade. He pulled her to him, taking the basket out of her hands and dropping it gently on the floor. She jumped at the dull thud of the basket hitting the floor. Her pulsed raced. Her skin heated as a chill went up her spine. Marcus cupped her face with his hands. "Shay, I'm not going anywhere. At least, not until I get some answers, and definitely not until I get what I came for."